MW00623481

FRONDS
AND
ENEMIES

THE ENGLISH COTTAGE GARDEN MYSTERIES
BOOK FIVE

H.Y. HANNA

Copyright © 2021 H.Y. HANNA
All rights reserved.
ISBN-13: 978-0-6486936-9-7

This book is a work of fiction. Names, characters, places and incidents are the product of the author's imagination or are used fictitiously. Any resemblance to actual events, locales, business establishments, persons or animals, living or dead, is entirely coincidental.

This book is licensed for your personal enjoyment only. No part of this publication may be reproduced, stored in a retrieval system or transmitted in any form or by any means, electronic or mechanical, including photocopying, recording or otherwise, without written permission from the author. Thank you for respecting the hard work of this author

CONTENTS

CHAPTER ONE

Poppy Lancaster held her breath as she watched the woman on the other side of the wooden trestle table. Her anxious gaze followed the woman's hands as they hovered indecisively over several pots of young primroses and she felt a surge of hope as the woman lifted one of the pots at last.

"It's very small, isn't it?" said the woman with a sniff as she eyed the plant critically.

Poppy flushed. She knew that her bedding plants were on the small side, with spindly stems and small leaves that flopped over the edges of the pots. Somehow, despite her determined efforts and her careful study of textbooks and websites through the long winter months, she hadn't managed to produce the trays bursting with vigorous, bushy plants that she'd hoped to offer for sale as spring bedding.

1

Still, she tried not to let her chagrin show. Instead, she plastered a bright smile to her face and said, "They... they've got a bit of catching up to do, but once you get them in the ground or in a container, they'll take off and grow very quickly."

"Hmm..." The woman didn't look convinced. "There isn't much choice either, is there? You've only got two colours." She dropped the pot back onto the bench and turned away.

Poppy's heart sank and she struggled to keep the smile on her face. "I do have other colours, but they're... um... still growing and not quite ready for sale yet."

The woman cast a disparaging eye across the rest of the trestle table. "Is this it? Do you have any other stock?"

"Not at the moment," said Poppy apologetically. "But I have more plants growing in the greenhouse and they should be ready for sale by next week or the week after—"

"What good is that to me now?" grumbled the woman. She glanced again at the pots laid out on the trestle table. "So... how much are these?"

Poppy named the price that she had finally decided on after weeks of deliberation and agonising over her business accounts.

The woman scowled. "That's practically daylight robbery!" she complained. "I can get plants double the size for half that price at the big garden centres."

Poppy flushed again. "Well, you see, it's harder for

2

small nurseries," she tried to explain. "We haven't got the economies of scale like the big garden centres and—"

"Spare me the sob story," the woman cut in. "I came here because I'd been told that it's one of the best local nurseries, with a top selection of plants and good value for money." She cast a contemptuous look around. "I don't know what they were talking about!"

She turned to leave. Poppy bit her lip, then called after the woman:

"I can give you a special deal: two for the price of one! Just to make up for the... um... slightly smaller size."

"No thanks," the woman said over her shoulder. "I'm going to one of the big garden centres, where I should have gone in the first place!"

Poppy stood and watched miserably as the woman marched towards the front gate. The path wound past flowerbeds which were just coming out of their winter slumber and beginning to show the lush growth and colourful blooms for which the cottage garden was famous. The roses might just be growing their first leaves, and the other perennials only beginning to produce new shoots, but swathes of flowering bulbs were already filling the beds with rich colour.

Vivid hyacinths in jewel tones, surrounded by plump crocus blooms... clumps of jonquils and daffodils, their creamy white and lemony yellow flowers highlighted by dainty dwarf irises... and intermingled amongst the bulbs were mounds of violas, their happy little "faces" turned towards the sun, as well as clusters of forget-me-nots providing a carpet of soft blue. For Poppy—who had no idea that all these bulbs had been lying dormant beneath the soil during the long, cold winter—seeing them emerge in the past couple of weeks and transform the bare garden had been like watching a magical spectacle unfold.

The wonder was lost on the woman, though, who walked past the flowerbeds without a single glance and pushed her way impatiently out of the wooden front gate, swinging it shut behind her with a rattle that made Poppy wince. Sighing, she turned back to the trestle table and rearranged the pots into neat rows once again. Her shoulders slumped as she felt a wave of doubt wash over her.

Was I crazy to think that I could do this? she wondered bleakly. *I could never keep anything green alive before—why did I think I could suddenly run a garden nursery, just because I'd inherited one?*

When that letter had arrived from a strange solicitor last year, telling Poppy that she had inherited Hollyhock Cottage Gardens and Nursery, it had seemed like a gift from a fairy godmother. Or— as it turned out—an estranged grandmother, in this case. Poppy had just lost her job and her place to live in London, and she'd been needing a fresh start: a new home and new life somewhere. The quaint old cottage with its romantic, overgrown garden, in the bustling village of Bunnington, situated in the heart of the Oxfordshire countryside, had been everything Poppy could have wished for.

And she had soon discovered that she'd inherited not just a property but a legacy too. Her grandmother, Mary Lancaster, had been a renowned plantswoman and Hollyhock Cottage had gained a reputation far and wide for not only being one of the best examples of a traditional English cottage garden, but also for selling some of the healthiest, most vigorous plants in the country.

Poppy had nurtured a dream that she, too, could live up to the Lancaster name and had thrown herself into reviving her grandmother's nursery business, which had been sadly neglected during the latter's long illness. And—despite her inexperience—for a while, it had looked like it wasn't an empty dream. The summer months had been glorious, with the cottage gardens at their most beautiful, and Poppy had plunged into the world of gardening with delight. She'd embraced the Latin names of all the plants she'd come across, eagerly learned gardening skills like planting and pruning, and discovered a talent for creating gorgeous arrangements of fresh flowers cut from the garden—which had turned into an unexpected source of additional income.

Even when autumn had arrived, with the prospect of little income over the cold months of winter, Poppy had been undaunted. She had thought—naively perhaps—that if she could just sow several batches of seeds and root ample cuttings, she could produce enough young plants to be ready for sale in spring. Somehow, she had clung to the belief that if she could just get through the winter, then things would magically fall into place when the days grew longer and warmer weather arrived.

Poppy sighed again as she looked down at the rows of spindly little plants in front of her. The reality hadn't quite matched up to her fantasies. Producing enough healthy plants, grown to a good size and of consistent quality, had been much harder than she'd expected. Even though she had followed all the instructions she'd found both online and in textbooks, it had still been a challenge keeping the seedlings alive and thriving in her grandmother's greenhouse over the winter. And horticultural expertise aside, the simple business skills of managing stock and inventory were something that she had no experience in.

But she was living on the last of her savings now and she would need the nursery to start earning a decent income soon, in order to pay her bills and basic living expenses, never mind keep the business going...

Her thoughts were interrupted by the sound of the front gate opening, and Poppy looked up hopefully. An elderly lady pulling a shopping trolley stepped in. She looked timidly around, then her face brightened as she spied the colourful bulbs in the flowerbeds.

Feeling her spirits lifting once more, Poppy hurried up the path to greet the old lady, saying in her best "customer service" voice:

"Welcome to Hollyhock Cottage Gardens and Nursery! Is there something in particular that I can help you with?"

"Oh yes, my dear. I was hoping to pick up some new flowers for my containers," said the old lady, smiling at her. "I live in the village, you see, and I don't have a car. Normally my nephew, Dennis, comes to take me to one of the big garden centres... such a good boy! Well, I say boy, but, of course, he's really a man now, and well into his fifties..." She wagged a finger at Poppy. "I can still remember the day he was born, you know, as clearly as if it were yesterday! We were all so excited as he was the first grandchild in the family and my sister had been trying for such a long time. And then Dennis arrived early, and my sister was horrified because he came out with his wee willy all bent on one side! Can you imagine that?"

"Er... no... not really," stammered Poppy.

"The doctors assured her that it wouldn't affect the function, so to speak, but my sister was still worried anyway. How was Dennis going to get a girl? After all, what woman would want a husband with a bent willy?"

"Er..." Poppy stared at the old lady, lost for words.

"Well, as it turned out, he's been happily married for over twenty years now and has four strapping sons, so I suppose the doctors were right after all and being a bit crooked doesn't really matter between the sheets—"

"Um... so what kind of flowers do you like?" interrupted Poppy, desperate not to hear any more about Dennis's misshapen member.

"Ooh, I do love anything pink, dear," the old lady declared. "Although mauve is wonderful too."

"I've got some lovely purple pansies that are all ready to go in the ground, or in a pot," said Poppy eagerly. "And some beautiful primroses too, in a bright fuchsia pink. Or if you'd like something in a more pastel shade, I've got some gorgeous little cyclamens. Here, let me show you..."

She led the old lady up the path to the stone cottage in the centre of the gardens. A long trestle table had been set up in front of the cottage, with various pots of bedding plants and early flowering annuals displayed in neat rows on it. Poppy watched anxiously as the old lady went up to the table and examined the selection with interest.

"Ooh, yes, these do look lovely," said the old lady, picking up two pots of dainty pink cyclamens. "The pale pink flowers look so pretty against the dark green leaves."

Poppy, who had been bracing herself for another barrage of criticism like she'd received from the last customer, relaxed and beamed at the old lady.

"Thank you! Yes, I love that shade of pink too."

"Ooh, and you have johnny-jump-ups... aren't

they lovely?" said the old lady, moving down the trestle table and admiring the punnets of trailing violas with their distinctive yellow and purple markings. "I always think they're so much nicer than the bigger pansies, even though their flowers aren't as large. They produce so many more blooms and they keep going, even when the weather gets warmer." She moved on a few steps and picked up the primula that the previous customer had rejected. "And look at these primroses! I don't think I've seen that shade of pink before... lovely!"

Watching her, Poppy felt her hopes rising. Encouraged by the old lady's enthusiastic attitude, she mentally added up all the plants the other had admired and calculated what she would make from the total sale. Smiling with delight, Poppy said eagerly:

"Would you like two of each colour? Then you could mix and match in the different containers—"

"Oh, bless you, child, I can't buy them all," said the old lady, giving her a regretful smile. "I would love to, but I'm afraid my pension doesn't leave me with very much spending money." She reached out. "I'll just take these two cyclamen first. Perhaps next week, I'll be able to pop back for some more."

"Yes... of course..." said Poppy, trying to hide her disappointment.

Still, she was delighted to have made a sale at last, even if it was a small one, and she carefully deposited the two potted cyclamen into a shallow cardboard box, then helped the old lady place them into her shopping trolley. Then she walked her to the front gate and stood watching as the old lady trundled away up the lane, pulling her shopping trolley behind her.

Poppy returned to the trestle table and spent a few moments fussing over the remaining pots on display, rearranging them in the most attractive fashion. Her efforts were for naught, though, as the minutes stretched slowly into hours and no new customers came through the gates. Finally, Poppy glanced at her watch and sighed. It was nearly four-thirty—still half an hour before the nursery's official closing time—but with the chance of anyone arriving looking slimmer by the minute, she wondered if she should call it a day.

She shivered as she stood up from the stool by the trestle table. The temperature seemed to be dropping rapidly too. Although spring was officially here, the weather was still unpredictable, and the nights could still be on the chilly side. Poppy checked over the pots one last time, then began packing up the small, portable cash till that she'd set up at one end of the trestle table. She was just scooping the paltry amount of notes and coins out of the cash drawer when a loud rustling behind her made her pause and look over her shoulder.

She saw nothing and, after a moment, returned to her task. But within seconds, the loud rustling came again, and this time Poppy felt the hairs rise on the back of her neck. She spun around and stared into the shadows of the garden. Goosebumps prickled across her arms and she felt her pulse quicken as a sudden unnerving feeling swept over her. Someone was out there, watching her...

CHAPTER TWO

Poppy strained her eyes as she scanned the area around her. A light breeze stirred the leaves in the trees and rustled through the bushes lining the back of the beds. Shadows loomed large between the shrubs, morphing and shifting into ominous shapes.

It's just your imagination, she told herself sharply. *There's nothing there, no one watching you.*

But still, she couldn't quite shake off the sense of unease. She had been by herself at the nursery all afternoon and hadn't minded the solitude, but now, suddenly, she felt very alone.

"He-hello?" she called, her voice coming out slightly squeaky. She cleared her throat and tried again. "Is anyone there?"

There was nothing but the soft murmur of the wind and the rustle of the leaves in the trees—

sounds which should have been soothing and yet now seemed to take on a menacing tone. Poppy swallowed and wondered if she could muster up the courage to walk deeper into the garden and check if anyone was out there. The loud rustling came again, and her heart began to race. She could see tall grasses moving, bushes shivering, stems bending... something was moving through the undergrowth towards her.

She tensed, her hands unconsciously groping on the trestle table next to her for a weapon. She came up with nothing but a miniature pink watering can. *Great,* she thought. *Someone's coming to attack me and all I can do is water him to death.*

Then the rustling ceased as suddenly as it had begun. Everything was silent for a moment. But Poppy knew that someone was still out there. She could feel eyes watching her every move.

"C-come out!" she called, sounding braver than she felt. "I know you're out there! Stop skulking like a... a cowardly weasel and show yourself!"

"*N-ow?*"

The bushes near her parted and an enormous ginger tomcat stepped out. Poppy felt the breath leave her body in a rush of relief.

"Oren!" she cried, sagging against the trestle table. "My God, you gave me a scare! It was you, wasn't it, hiding out there, watching me? You bloody cat—I thought you were some kind of creepy stalker!"

Oren gave her a disdainful look, then strolled over

to stand next to her. When Poppy didn't move, he butted his head against her knees and looked up at her expectantly.

"You cheeky monkey!" said Poppy with an exasperated laugh. "After all that, you expect me to give you a chin rub?"

"*N-ow*," said Oren complacently.

Poppy rolled her eyes, but somehow she found herself crouching down to stroke the ginger tom.

Why do cats always get their own way? she wondered with a resigned grin as she rubbed Oren's battle-scarred ears and tickled him under his chin. She heard him purr happily in response. In spite of her exasperation, she had to admit that the big orange tabby cat was a charmer, and had wormed his way into her heart since her arrival in Bunnington. Oren actually belonged to her neighbour—the crime author Nick Forrest—who lived in the beautiful Georgian house in the large grounds adjoining Hollyhock Cottage, but it seemed to Poppy that the ginger tom spent just as much time on her side of the wall. When he wasn't loudly demanding pats or bossily telling her how to do her gardening jobs, he was waiting in the kitchen for tasty titbits or making himself comfortable on the best armchair in the sitting room. She had even taken to leaving a window in the greenhouse attachment, at the back of the cottage, propped open, so that Oren could get in and out as he pleased.

Now, as Poppy rose to her feet once more and

turned towards the cottage, she expected Oren to trot ahead of her, ready to demand an early dinner. But to her surprise, the ginger tom slunk away instead, heading once more into the bushes from which he had emerged. It was so unlike him that she paused to watch, and she saw his head dip down as he pushed his way behind some tall grass. A minute later, he raised it again and she caught sight of something soft held in his mouth. It was light brown, almost flesh-coloured, and Poppy shuddered as she wondered if it was a rat that Oren had caught.

She knew that there were rats in the area—in fact, she'd had the misfortune of uncovering a rats' nest in a shed at the rear of the property, and she still had nightmares about the experience. *Maybe Oren got fed up with that bland prescription food from the vet and decided to start hunting for his own dinner,* she thought with a wry smile. Well, she was glad that the tomcat was heading for his own home, across the stone wall, with his rodent prize, and not to her cottage.

Turning back to the trestle table, Poppy collected her things and made her way around the side of the cottage towards the rear. She entered via the greenhouse built on to the back of the cottage and paused for a moment to look up and admire the gleaming new glass panes and solid wooden frame. When one of the trees in the garden had come down during a wild storm at the beginning of winter and had smashed through the greenhouse roof, Poppy had thought that she'd lost everything. Her grandmother's greenhouse might have been old and dilapidated, but it had still been fully functional and, without it, there was no way she could have got a head start on growing the seedlings and annuals necessary for sale in spring.

Thank goodness Hubert came to the rescue, she thought, feeling a surge of gratitude. She still didn't quite understand why her normally self-serving cousin had suddenly made the generous offer of funds to pay for a brand-new greenhouse, but she certainly wasn't about to look a gift horse in the mouth.

Still, if I don't manage to sell more plants, even the best greenhouse in the world isn't going to help me, Poppy reflected gloomily as she walked through the connecting door which led into the kitchen of the main cottage.

"My lordy Lord, Poppy... why the long face?" asked the middle-aged woman sitting at the kitchen table, busily mending an old apron.

She had a round, kindly face, with rosy cheeks and a mop of curly grey hair, and looked exactly like the picture of Mrs Claus often seen on Christmas cards. Like Santa's wife, too, she was the epitome of maternal caring, and now Poppy looked at Nell Hopkins with love and affection. Once her landlady when she had been living in London, Nell had since become one of her dearest friends and the only "family" Poppy had after her mother had passed away last year.

Now Poppy sank into one of the chairs opposite Nell and fell into the familiar and comforting ritual of telling the older woman all her worries and frustrations.

"...I don't know what I'm going to do," she concluded with a sigh. "Selling a couple of cyclamen plants a day is hardly going to keep the nursery going."

"Maybe you could offer some of the plants at a discount and advertise that?" suggested Nell.

Poppy shook her head. "I already need every penny I make from each sale to cover the costs. Although I did get desperate and offer one of the customers 'two-for-the-price-of-one'," she admitted. "Maybe if I knew how much I could afford to lower the prices to, I could run some sales."

"What you need is a good accountant," said Nell. "That's what every business needs, but especially when you're inexperienced and starting out."

"Yes, you're right, although I don't know anyone. I suppose I ought to just look in the local business directory."

"Best to get a recommendation," said Nell. "You should ask around the village. What about Martin?"

"Martin?"

"You know, the owner of the Lucky Ladybird. Very shrewd chap he is, and the village pub always does great business."

"That's a good idea. I'll pop in the next time I'm

passing by and ask Martin who does his accounts," said Poppy, absentmindedly scratching her arm.

Nell's gaze sharpened as she followed the motion and she said: "I noticed you scratching at your arm last night as well. Do you have a rash?"

"N-no... not a rash," said Poppy, rolling up her sleeve to expose a nasty red swelling on her forearm.

Nell gave a little cry of dismay. "Oh my lordy Lord, Poppy! What on earth happened?"

Poppy shrugged. "It's nothing, Nell—just a scratch I got in the garden. I think I might have brushed against one of the rose bushes and got caught on one of the thorns." She peered at her reddened skin. "I suppose the area around it has got a bit inflamed."

"How long has it been like that?"

"I don't know... a couple of days? I actually thought it would get better, but it seems to have got more swollen and it's starting to itch like mad too."

Nell tutted. "It looks like it's getting infected. You need to go to the doctor and get that looked at, dear."

"Oh Nell, it's just a scratch—"

"A scratch can turn into something serious if you're not careful! No, don't shake your head at me, young lady. I've heard dreadful stories of people losing their hands or ending up in hospital for weeks because of a small scratch while gardening." Nell nodded her head emphatically. "There are all sorts of horrible fungi and bacteria in the soil—"

"It's a garden, Nell," said Poppy, laughing. "Of course there're going to be bacteria and fungi in the soil! I thought that was the whole point—you're supposed to encourage that in the soil; it's good for your plants."

"But not for your skin," Nell declared. "I'm telling you, if you don't get that checked out, you might end up very sorry. I read about a poor man in the Sunday papers once: got necrotising fasciitis, he did. The flesh on his hand was all eaten away! And then he ended up in hospital with septicaemia and organ failure. They said he was lucky not to lose his life!"

Poppy shifted uneasily. She didn't want to admit it, but Nell's words were beginning to make her nervous. "I suppose I could go and see the village GP tomorrow, if I have time—"

"No, you're going to see him now. I know his clinic is open late today. It's only a short walk across the village—it won't take you more than ten or fifteen minutes. I'm sure Dr Seymour will squeeze you in if you just go down there and explain that it's an emergency."

"But it's not an emergency," protested Poppy.

"It will be if you don't do something about it," said Nell darkly.

Poppy sighed. There was no arguing with her friend when her mind was set like this.

"Fine, fine... I'll go," she said, rising from the table. Slipping on a cardigan to ward off the evening chill, she set off across the village for the GP's clinic.

CHAPTER THREE

Dr Ralph Seymour, the village doctor, had eschewed the more common practice of joining an established General Practice surgery when he completed his training. Instead, he'd converted an outbuilding in the grounds of his large property at the edge of the village and set up his own practice in the purpose-built surgery there. It had caused quite a stir in Bunnington and there had been several heads shaking at the idea of a doctor with a clinic practically in his own sitting room. But the villagers had soon begun to appreciate having medical advice on their own doorstep. In fact, the bright, modern surgery, with its tasteful décor, comfortable waiting room, and inner consulting office—not to mention Dr Seymour's sensitive and sympathetic bedside manner—soon had patients coming to see him from far and wide beyond the village.

As Poppy made her way slowly through the village lanes which meandered past beautiful country houses and old cottages with mellow limestone walls, she reflected that she was glad not to have to drive to one of the surrounding towns to see a doctor. And she found that she was enjoying the walk across the village in the gathering twilight. It was actually far lighter than she had thought; the garden at Hollyhock Cottage, encircled as it was by the high stone wall and rows of mature trees, had been filled with shadows, but now that she was walking more in the open, she found that there was still plenty of light. Certainly enough for her to admire the gardens that she passed, and she had to stop herself from pausing at each one to ogle and try to identify the plants growing in the beds.

Poppy had walked through the village looking at the gardens before, of course, but she was discovering that there were unexpected changes and delights that appeared with each passing season. She had never experienced spring as a "gardener" before and she found that she was looking at everything with fresh eyes. She was also new enough to gardening that even the most common plants were still fascinating to her. Most of all, she loved seeing the different styles of gardens—from the traditional cottage gardens like her own to the more minimalist, modern designs, with their geometric beds dominated by tall architectural grasses and foliage plants. There were even a few where the owners had opted for full courtyards, with neatly clipped shrubs and trees in half wine barrels, and large troughs of herbs by the door.

Poppy loved looking at the different garden ornaments on display too, and speculating about the personality of the residents based on their tastes. Surely the owner of the rambling garden filled with pretty flowering annuals planted in rustic wheelbarrows had to be an old-fashioned romantic at heart? And the owner of that carefully clipped lawn with the strange modern sculptures... perhaps a trendy professional or an art gallery owner? And she didn't even dare guess what kind of person lived in the house with the flock of pink inflatable flamingos positioned around a Buddha fountain!

The one ornament that seemed almost ubiquitous was the garden gnome. Everywhere she looked, Poppy could see little statues of bearded men in pointy red hats, wearing the traditional belted coat, dark trousers, and big black shoes. She was surprised, though, to notice several variations from the conventional type, with a variety of gnomes in modern costumes and poses: surfing, fishing, playing the guitar, doing yoga... even one bending over and "mooning" passers-by. Poppy giggled at the sight of the last one.

Well, one thing I know about the owner of that house, she thought as she walked past. *They've got a naughty sense of humour!*

She rounded the corner of the lane and came at

last to a large handsome house. It was modern, but with classic lines, and it was surrounded by large, elegantly landscaped gardens (although Poppy noted with amusement that here, too, there were a couple of garden gnomes tucked into the corners). She followed the signs and walked up the path leading around the side of the main house to the self-contained surgery surrounded by carefully clipped shrubs. Stepping inside, she found herself in a cheerfully decorated waiting room with a young woman sitting behind a desk on one side and a row of chairs on the other.

"Hello. I'm Yvonne, the practice manager. Can I help you?" the young woman said smoothly.

Poppy couldn't help staring. At a glance, she and the young woman shared similar colouring and features: they both had the same shoulder-length, dark brown hair, slim figure, and pert nose with a smattering of freckles. But whereas Poppy had always felt that her looks only ranked as "passably pretty" in a girl-next-door kind of way, she saw wistfully that in the other girl, the same combination had produced something quite exotic and alluring. And it was enhanced by the way the young woman dressed, in a ruffled silk blouse with a deep V that revealed more than a hint of generous cleavage, paired with a tight pencil skirt that hugged every inch of her shapely hips, and completed by a pair of shiny patent stilettos. In fact, she looked almost too glamorous to be a practice manager in a village GP's surgery!

Suddenly realising that the young woman was still waiting for her to respond, Poppy blinked and said hastily:

"Er... yes, I was hoping I could see Dr Seymour. I haven't got an appointment, but it's... it's something that might be serious. You see, I scratched myself in the garden and I'm worried it might have got infected or something." Poppy rolled up her sleeve for the young woman to inspect her forearm.

The other girl's eyes widened. "Yeah, Ralph—I mean, Dr Seymour—had better take a look at that." She glanced at the computer screen in front of her. "He's got a pretty full clinic this afternoon but if you don't mind waiting, I should be able to squeeze you in at the end. Is it your first time here?"

"Oh thanks! Yes, it is. I only moved to Oxfordshire last summer and I haven't actually registered with a GP yet."

"In that case, fill in these forms and then bring them back to me."

Poppy took the clipboard and pen that had been handed to her and turned toward the row of seats on the other side of the waiting room. She dropped into a seat next to a young mother wrestling with a baby in her arms and a toddler beside her chair. The latter—a little boy of about two or three—looked red and flushed, his hair clinging damply to his forehead and his eyes unusually bright. He had a runny nose as well and was wailing and struggling as the young mother tried to get him to blow into a tissue. Suddenly, he squirmed free and jerked back, crashing into Poppy's legs.

"Oh, Tommy!" cried the young mother, trying to grab him. She gave Poppy a flustered look of apology. "Sorry!"

"That's okay." Poppy smiled at her. Then, as she watched the young mother still struggling to get hold of the toddler while cradling the baby in her other arm, she added impulsively: "Here... would you like me to hold the baby?"

The young mother looked up in surprise, then gave Poppy a grateful smile. "Oh, that would be a big help. Ta!"

She held the baby out to Poppy, who took the warm little bundle in her arms and smiled at the cherubic face raised to hers. Wide, unblinking eyes stared at her, then the baby gurgled. Poppy tried to imitate the sound, which caused the baby to give her a gummy grin.

"You're a happy little chap, aren't you?" said Poppy, smiling.

"Yes, he's always happy, that one, whereas Tommy..." The young mother sighed and looked down at the toddler who was now trying to climb into her lap, obviously wanting a cuddle. His nose was running again, and he opened his mouth in a loud wail.

"Aww... poor thing. He's probably just feeling rotten," said Poppy sympathetically.

"Yes, I suppose you're right," said the young mother, smoothing the toddler's damp hair back from his forehead. "It's just that, sometimes, it feels like it's one thing after another. Last week it was an ear infection... the week before that, an allergy which led to conjunctivitis... and this week, he's had a cold and hasn't been able to sleep properly, which means that he's grumpy all the time." She heaved another sigh. "I thought he was getting better but, after lunch today, he started getting feverish so I thought I'd better bring him in. Yvonne—that's the practice manager—said Dr Seymour only had the last appointment free, but I thought if I came in early, maybe he could squeeze Tommy in between some of the earlier patients—"

"You can go in before me, if you like," a new voice spoke up.

They both turned to see a middle-aged woman sitting on Poppy's other side. She was dressed in an old-fashioned tweed skirt, fastened with a large safety pin on one side, and a white blouse buttoned to the neck. The slightly garish pink lipstick that she had applied to her thin lips clashed badly with her sallow skin, as did the powder-blue eyeshadow she had dabbed liberally across her eyelids. It was obvious that she had taken some pains with her appearance, but unfortunately her efforts only seemed to make her look even more frumpy.

Bloody hell, if anyone is ripe for a makeover, she is, thought Poppy, then immediately felt ashamed of her uncharitable thought when the woman was obviously a kind soul.

"I don't mind waiting a bit longer," she was saying to the young mother.

"Oh, really? That's really kind of you," said the young mother. "Are you sure you don't mind? If you've got something urgent—"

"No, no." The woman smiled at her. "I've only got a bit of a tummy ache. It's been bothering me for days now, which is why I thought I'd better come and get it checked out. But it's not terrible or anything."

"Well, if you're sure… ta very much!" said the young mother, beaming. "It means I can get home earlier. I'll be able to get tea ready before my husband gets home."

The other woman turned to Poppy and said, "You can go before me, too, if you like."

"Oh no, I'm happy to wait. But thanks for the offer."

The other woman eyed the red swelling on Poppy's exposed forearm. "That looks really nasty, if you don't mind me saying so. I heard you talking to the receptionist… get that gardening, did you?"

"Yes," Poppy admitted. "I think I scratched myself on a rose thorn. It's probably nothing but I thought I'd better get it checked out, just in case."

"Well, I'm sure Dr Seymour will be able to put you right," the woman declared. "He's wonderful. Always so patient and so kind—"

"And so dishy too," added the young mother with

a smirk.

The middle-aged woman looked slightly scandalised. "I'm not sure we should be discussing him that way," she said primly.

"Aww, come on," said the young mother. "Anyone with eyes can see that our good doctor is drop-dead gorgeous. I tell you, if I was single..." She trailed off with a suggestive giggle.

At that moment, the door to the inner consulting room opened and a tall man stepped out, ushering a heavily pregnant woman. He led her over to his practice manager, saying:

"Yvonne, make Mrs Seymour an appointment for two weeks' time, will you? And please make sure that her blood tests are sent off as soon as possible as well."

"Yes, Dr Seymour," said the practice manager, fluttering her eyelashes at him.

Poppy eyed the doctor covertly and she had to agree that the young mother was right: Ralph Seymour was extremely handsome, in a male-model kind of way. He must have been in his late forties to early fifties, but he had the kind of suave good looks which only seemed to improve with age. In fact, like Yvonne, he looked almost too glamorous to be in a small village GP clinic.

They would make a good couple for a fashion magazine spread, posing against a stormy sky, thought Poppy, watching the two of them together. *Or maybe even on the cover of one of those bodice-*

rippers that Nell loves to read...

The doctor straightened and swung around to face the room. His gaze passed over Poppy and she flushed guiltily, hoping that her runaway imagination wasn't showing on her face. She was relieved when he gave her a polite smile, then turned to the elderly gentleman sitting on the other side of the waiting room and said:

"Colonel Bradley? Would you like to come in now?"

The elderly gentleman stood up stiffly and, with the help of his cane, followed the doctor into the inner office. As soon as the door had shut behind them, the young mother leaned towards Poppy and the middle-aged woman, and said with a wink:

"Definitely a dish! And what's more—" She glanced towards the reception desk, where the pregnant woman was still talking to Yvonne, and lowered her voice: "—I'll bet there's something going on between him and the practice manager."

"No, surely not," said the middle-aged woman, looking even more scandalised.

"Ooh, yes," said the young mother, smiling with relish. "Just watch their body language... and the way they look at each other..."

"But she must be half his age!"

"So what?" said the young mother, shrugging. "A lot of women like older men." She glanced at Yvonne again, her eyes sliding over the other girl's revealing outfit. "No woman comes to work looking like that unless she's trying to entice a man."

"Dr Seymour would never... He's married and he's an honourable man," said the middle-aged woman stiffly.

The young mother gave a cynical laugh. "He's still a man, isn't he? Any man can be led astray, especially by a girl who knows how to tease and seduce him." She nodded, her eyes sparkling. "I'll bet they're having a passionate affair, right under his wife's nose!"

CHAPTER FOUR

The sound of a demanding voice—faint at first but growing steadily louder—interrupted their gossiping and, a minute later, the door to the surgery swung open and a large woman wearing a headscarf, mackintosh, and dark green wellington boots marched into the waiting room. She had tightly permed, iron-grey hair, and a pinched mouth with deep grooves of disapproval etched on either side. She was talking bossily on her phone and Poppy winced slightly as her booming voice filled the waiting room.

"...no, no, no! I told you—I've already applied for the Neighbourhood Watch scheme. That is why I need support from local businesses like you... well, when you've been robbed and attacked and are at the mercy of ruthless criminals, you'll be sorry you ignored me!"

She ended the call and loomed over Yvonne at the reception desk. "I'm Valerie Busselton," she said loudly. "I have an appointment with Dr Seymour this afternoon. I'm slightly late—but I'm sure that won't matter, since GP clinics *always* overrun and I'd just be sitting here, wasting my time, if I'd arrived on time."

Yvonne compressed her lips in annoyance and looked as if she was restraining herself from making a retort. Giving the woman a tight smile, she said: "Please take a seat, Mrs Busselton. Dr Seymour will see you straight after his current patient."

Mrs Busselton swung around and scanned the rest of the waiting room. "Ah! Miss Payne!" she said, addressing the middle-aged woman next to Poppy. "You here to see Seymour as well, eh? Didn't you just come in last week?"

"Yes... well, my stomach... it's still not quite right," mumbled Miss Payne.

"Hmm... yes, can't be too careful," said Mrs Busselton, plonking herself down next to them. "That's what I told my son Arthur on the phone. He didn't believe me when I told him about my toe; said I was probably imagining things." She rounded on Poppy and said indignantly, "Me? Imagining things? I've never imagined anything in my life!"

"Er... what's wrong with your toe?" asked Poppy politely.

"Fungus," said Mrs Busselton, thrusting out a

foot. "All over my big toenail. Quite revolting, really. I can show you if you like—"

"Oh no, no, that's fine," said Poppy, hastily shifting back in her chair.

"It would be good for you to see what it looks like," said Mrs Busselton, wagging a finger. "Toe fungus affects a lot of people, you know. You might have it too and not know it!"

The toddler, who had been staring at Mrs Busselton wide-eyed, suddenly let out a wail and clutched his mother's neck.

"It's all right, Tommy—there's nothing to be scared of," said his mother soothingly.

Poppy glanced at the baby in her arms and was relieved to see that the little cherubic face was still wreathed in smiles. The baby wasn't watching Mrs Busselton but was busily playing with Poppy's necklace, pulling up the gold locket and trying to put it in his mouth.

"No, no..." said Poppy gently, disentangling the chain from his chubby fingers.

The baby gurgled happily and yanked at the necklace again. Trying to distract him, Poppy jiggled her knee, bouncing him up and down, and made popping sounds with her tongue, which had the baby squealing with excitement.

"It looks like you're more than ready for one of your own," said Miss Payne with a smile.

"Oh, heavens, definitely not!" said Poppy with a laugh. "I'm only twenty-five, and I can barely get my own life in order, never mind look after anyone else. Plus, I've just taken on my family business. I've got to focus on work first before thinking about settling down and starting a family."

"That's what all the girls say these days. Career, career, career!" said Mrs Busselton, pursing her mouth disapprovingly. She gave Poppy a stern look. "You'd better be careful; otherwise, before you know it, you'll be a dried-up old spinster, living all alone, like Miss Payne here."

Poppy gasped at the woman's patronising rudeness, and the young mother looked shocked as well. Miss Payne flushed bright red and looked down, fiddling with the safety pin on her tweed skirt.

"I... I didn't put career before family," she stammered. "I just never... never met the right person."

"Anyway, there's nothing wrong with living alone," said the young mother staunchly, giving Miss Payne an encouraging smile. "Let me tell you, when you've just come through a week of sleepless nights like me, changing nappies and mopping up snot all day, the thought of living alone with no one to be responsible for sounds like heaven!"

"Yes," Poppy chimed in, keen to show her support as well. "I have to say, the best thing about playing with other peoples' babies is being able to hand them back at the end of the day and going home to my selfish single life, where I can go out late at night if I want—"

"I hope you're not walking around the village alone late at night," said Mrs Busselton, frowning at Poppy. "Have you ever thought about how dangerous that is?"

"Well, I..." Poppy paused.

In actual fact, she'd never given it much thought before. Bunnington—whilst not one of the smallest villages in Oxfordshire—was still compact enough to feel cosy and intimate. A walk across the village felt a little like crossing your own extended backyard, and although she didn't know *every* resident in the village, Poppy was able to greet many people she encountered.

"No, I haven't, actually," she answered honestly. "I've never felt threatened when I've been out walking at night."

"Ah then, you've been living in a fool's paradise," said Mrs Busselton with smug superiority. "There's danger lurking around every corner and this village is rife with evil and corruption!"

Poppy stifled a laugh. "Surely you're exaggerating," she said. "I mean, I used to live in London, and this is nothing compared to places like Soho. You're hardly going to get mugged or sexually molested here."

Mrs Busselton's chest swelled with indignation. "Oh no, that's where you're wrong!" she cried. "You might think this is a sleepy little Oxfordshire village, but there is a sexual predator here, stalking all of us!"

"What do you mean?" asked the young mother, putting a protective arm around Tommy. "What kind of sexual predator?"

Mrs Busselton leaned forwards, dropping her voice to a dramatic stage whisper: "A filthy, disgusting peeping Tom who goes around spying on people!"

"Oh my goodness!" squeaked Miss Payne, reeling back slightly in her chair. "Are you sure?"

"Of course I'm sure," snapped Mrs Busselton. "I make it my business to know these things. And even though we don't have an official Neighbourhood Watch scheme in Bunnington—an absolute travesty which I've been trying to rectify for years now!—I have enlisted a group of friends to help me patrol the village. We call ourselves the Bunnington Brigade and we keep a watch on the comings and goings of all the village residents, so we can do our bit to protect the community."

So you can snoop on people without compunction, you mean, thought Poppy cynically. Aloud, she said: "So do you have any evidence of this 'peeping Tom'? I mean, have you actually seen him?"

"Well, not exactly," Mrs Busselton admitted. "But I've heard him: rustling in the bushes, creeping around my garden in the dark."

"But that could have just been an animal or something," protested Poppy.

"Oh no... no animal would have sounded like that," declared Mrs Busselton. "Besides, I had a feeling that I was being... *watched.*"

"Maybe you were imagining it," said Poppy, although she shifted uncomfortably as she suddenly remembered her own experience in the cottage garden just earlier that day: that prickly sensation sliding across her skin as she had felt the weight of eyes watching her. At the time, she had told herself that it was just Oren watching her from behind the bushes... but what if it hadn't been?

"Have you spoken to the police?" asked Poppy. "Have you reported your concerns?"

"The police!" Mrs Busselton snorted. "The police are utter imbeciles! I have called the local station several times and made multiple reports, but have they taken notice? No! Not one bit."

"Well, if you have no evidence other than a 'feeling', you can hardly expect them to take you very seriously," the young mother pointed out.

"I have more than just a 'feeling'," said Mrs Busselton indignantly. "I know there is a sexual pervert creeping around because he has been stealing from me as well!"

"What's he stolen?" asked Miss Payne breathlessly.

Mrs Busselton drew herself up and said with great dignity: "When I was doing my laundry recently, I discovered that some of my... er... unmentionables were missing."

"Your what?" said Poppy, puzzled.

"She means her knickers," said the young mother

with a guffaw.

"I most certainly do not!" cried Mrs Busselton in an outraged voice. "I am talking about my brassieres."

"Your bras?"

"Yes, two of my best Marks and Spencer brassieres have gone missing. They were hanging there on the washing line when I went out that morning and, by the evening, they were gone!"

"Could they have been blown away by the wind?" suggested Miss Payne.

"Impossible! That's what I told the police when they made that ridiculous suggestion. I make sure that all my laundry is securely fastened with clothes pegs. There is no way the bras could have become detached—not unless someone yanked them off the line." Mrs Busselton glowered at them. "And that is obviously what happened. This pervert creeping through the village at night is not only spying on women but also stealing their lingerie and keeping them as trophies!"

"Oh... that would be terrible if it were true," cried the young mother with a shudder. "But surely the police would take it seriously if there was any real possibility of that?"

"Of course there's a possibility! The police just don't want to admit it. Well, 'just you wait and see', I told them," said Mrs Busselton, looking like she almost relished the prospect of a sexual predator rampaging through the streets of Bunnington.

"Anyway, I decided this morning that I will not let them fob me off. I have personally written to the Police Commissioner and demanded that he send a CID team to come and do a full investigation of my underwear!"

Poppy's lips twitched and she had to fight to keep a straight face. She was saved from having to respond, though, because the door to the inner room opened at that moment and Dr Seymour came out, followed by the colonel with his walking cane. The GP left his elderly patient with Yvonne and turned towards the rest of the waiting room, saying:

"Mrs Busselton?"

The woman rose majestically and preceded him into the inner office. Poppy could hear her already starting to tell Dr Seymour about her toe fungus before the door even shut behind them.

"Whew!" said the young mother, grinning at Poppy. "I thought she was never going to shut up!" Then she sobered. "Still, do you think she's right? Do you really think there's a sex maniac loose in the village?"

"I've noticed a couple of items missing from my laundry," said Miss Payne, looking concerned. "You know, the odd sock and things like that. I hadn't really thought about it... but now I'm wondering if I've been a victim too? The thought of someone spying on me and stealing my personal clothing is horrible!" She shuddered.

"I would think a sexual predator would be more

into lingerie than socks," said Poppy reassuringly. "I'm sure everyone's had the odd sock go missing and mismatched pairs in their drawers. That's just normal."

"I *have* had a bra disappear recently, though," said the young mother, frowning. "It was similar to what Mrs Busselton described: I hung it out to dry the night before and, in the morning, it wasn't on the line."

"Was anything else missing?" asked Poppy.

"No, just the bra." She cuddled the toddler closer to her and looked worriedly at Poppy. "Do you think there could be a sexual predator among us?"

CHAPTER FIVE

An hour later, Poppy finally followed Dr Seymour into his inner office and sat down opposite his desk.

"Now, what can I do for you, Miss Lancaster?" he asked with a perfunctory smile.

In answer, Poppy rolled up her sleeve and leaned forwards to show him her swollen forearm.

"Oh dear... that doesn't look very good," the GP commented. "But don't worry—nothing a bit of antibiotics won't fix." He made a careful examination of Poppy's arm, asked her a few questions, then wrote her a prescription. "Otherwise, is everything else all right? Any other concerns?" He looked at her curiously. "You're new to the village, aren't you? I don't believe I've seen you before."

"Yes, I moved up from London about nine months ago, in summer last year," Poppy explained. "I suppose I should really have come to register with the practice when I arrived but... well, things have been really busy, and anyway, I haven't been ill."

Dr Seymour gave a dry smile. "Ah yes, the benefits of youth. Well, that should stand you in good stead as well with this scratch. You should heal up very quickly. Chances are, your body would have cleared the infection on its own anyway, but I always think it's good to err on the side of caution. Here..." He handed her the printed prescription. "Take this to the village chemist—they've got a good dispensary there."

"Thanks," said Poppy. "How long do you think it'll take to clear up?"

"Oh, probably a few days. In the meantime, you might want to wear long sleeves when you're gardening. And make sure you clean and dry the area carefully each day. If the itching and swelling get worse or if you start running a fever or feeling nauseous, then don't hesitate to call Yvonne—that is, Miss Nash, my practice manager—to make another appointment. If it's urgent, you can call the surgery after-hours—it will switch through to my house and I'm always happy to take calls from patients."

"That's very nice of you," said Poppy, surprised. "Don't you get a lot of disturbed nights if you lay yourself open like that?"

He laughed. "Well, I've been fortunate so far. Most people are quite considerate and tend not to bother you unless they're really ill. Of course, there can be one or two individuals who can be a bit tiresome, but

I don't really mind. Sometimes, all people really want is a sympathetic ear, you know? Besides, it's really a very cushy life, compared to some of my colleagues. Some of the chaps I used to be with at med school are now working as specialists in large hospitals. They have much more prestigious jobs and titles, of course, but their lives are very hectic, and they work incredibly hard. My life is a country idyll in comparison," he said, chuckling. "I have plenty of time after seeing my patients to potter around and spend hours gardening."

"Oh, are you a keen gardener?" asked Poppy, her ears perking up.

"Well, we have a man come to do the main garden maintenance. Clip the hedges and so forth," Dr Seymour admitted. "My real love is auriculas and I spend hours daily tending my collection."

"Auriculas?" Poppy frowned. "Are they a kind of flower? I haven't heard of them."

"You *have* heard of primulas, haven't you?"

"Oh yes—primroses and polyanthus and similar."

"Well, the Primula genus is actually a large family of plants with over 425 species. The primroses and polyanthus that you see in garden centres just happen to be the most common types found in people's gardens, but there are countless other types and thousands of hybrids within the group. The auriculas are a small branch of the family: they look a bit like primroses—the same rosette of leaves at the base—but their flowers are just superb! They're held up high on long, straight stalks and come in the most beautiful jewel-like colours, with different patterns on the petals and a wonderful dusting of powdery farina—"

Ralph Seymour broke off suddenly and gave Poppy a sheepish smile. "Sorry. My wife says I'm always boring everyone to death with my passion for auriculas. I forget that not everyone is as interested in plants and gardening—"

"Oh no, I'm very interested! In fact, you could say that I'm 'in the club'," said Poppy with a chuckle. "You see, I run Hollyhock Gardens and Nursery— well, I inherited it from my grandmother, actually— and I'm relatively new to the world of plants, so I'm still learning everything I can. So please, bore me all you like!"

Dr Seymour's eyes lit up. "Ah, so you are Mary Lancaster's granddaughter! I'd heard about her death and the transfer of her property, of course, and I'd been meaning to pop down for a visit but just hadn't got around to it yet. So you've taken over the business? That's brilliant!" he said eagerly. "You must consider stocking some auriculas in the nursery. They really are the most wonderful plants, you know, and more people ought to be introduced to them! It would be great to show people that not all auriculas are fussy and difficult to care for—the alpine group, for instance, would be ideal for beginners. They may not be as 'fancy' as the show types, but they still have the most beautiful flowers.

My favourite is the 'Gold-Laced Group': it has petals that are so dark, they are almost black, and they're edged with a border of yellow, which looks just like 'gold lace'—absolutely exquisite!"

"They do sound lovely," said Poppy, slightly overwhelmed by his enthusiasm.

Something must have shown in her expression because Dr Seymour sat back again in his chair and gave her another sheepish grin. "Sorry, I do tend to get carried away. It isn't just a personal hobby, you see; I'm also the president of the OAC—the Oxfordshire Auricula Club—and we're always looking to raise awareness about the plants, so that more people can learn to enjoy them." His grin widened. "I don't suppose you'd like to join? Membership is free and we hold a show once a year. It's in a couple of weeks, actually. You can come and see the most wonderful plants displayed in auricula theatres—"

"In theatres?" said Poppy, startled. "You mean... in a play?"

The GP chuckled. "No, no, an auricula theatre is what we call the wooden shelving unit created to display the show plants. It keeps the flowers from being spoilt by wet and windy weather, and helps shade them from the sun—and it's really the best way to show them off. I'll tell you what," he said suddenly. "I'll make up a theatre for you and fill it with some suitable auriculas and bring it down to the nursery! That way you can display it for customers to see, and hopefully they'll be inspired to have their own!"

"Oh, that's very kind of you, but—"

"No, no, it'll be a pleasure! It'll give me even more excuse to spend time with my auriculas," he said, laughing.

Poppy laughed too and was about to reply when the door to the consulting room opened and a woman carrying a supermarket plastic bag came in. She paused and narrowed her eyes as she saw them laughing together, and Poppy was surprised by the hostility in that cold gaze. It was as if the woman had taken an instant dislike to her, which seemed ridiculous when they had only just met. The laughter in the room died abruptly as Ralph Seymour quickly sobered and sprang up from his chair.

"Darling!" He turned to Poppy and added, "This is my wife, Emma."

Emma Seymour was a handsome woman in her late forties, with high, arched eyebrows, piercing grey eyes, and a patrician nose. She was elegantly dressed—almost *too* elegantly dressed—in a wool dress with a pearl brooch at the lapel that seemed more suitable for afternoon tea at The Ritz than a country village. Poppy gave her a tentative smile and was rewarded by a slight twitch of the woman's thin lips.

"Ralph—" Emma gave it the traditional British pronunciation of "Rafe", often favoured by the upper class. "—I thought the clinic would be finished by now," she said, her voice peevish.

"I'm sorry, darling," said Dr Seymour. "Things have overrun slightly—"

"It's more than slightly," said his wife, compressing her lips. "You should have been finished an hour ago! And this isn't the first time it's happened. You're always finishing late."

"You know GP clinics often don't run to schedule," he said mildly.

"Yes, well, perhaps if you didn't spend so much time laughing and chatting with your patients, it would go a lot quicker," said Emma, looking pointedly at Poppy.

Bloody hell, surely she's not jealous? thought Poppy. It seemed like such a ludicrous idea, and yet there was no denying the possessive glint in the woman's eyes.

"Sorry," said Poppy, standing up quickly, feeling embarrassed and also annoyed that the woman was making her feel that way.

"No, no, it was my fault," said Dr Seymour quickly. He gave his wife a sheepish smile. "We were talking about gardening and got sidetracked. And as for the clinic, I *would* have finished with Miss Payne, but Miss Lancaster came in as an emergency."

"Oh for God's sake, that Payne woman hasn't been *again*?" complained Emma. "She's here practically every week! And half the time, there's nothing wrong with her. It's all just an excuse to come in and sit here talking your ear off—"

"Emma, I think the poor lady is lonely and she appreciates having someone to talk to about her concerns," said Dr Seymour with a sigh. "You know, as GPs, our job isn't just to diagnose medical illnesses. We also play an important role of providing mental health support in the community. Sometimes people just need a listening ear and to feel like someone cares about them. It can be more important than any medicine—"

"Oh rubbish!" said Emma rudely. "You didn't go to medical school to become some bloody Good Samaritan! If she wants a gossip and a shoulder to cry on, she can go to the local tearoom and find one of the village cronies. There's no need for her to sit here, cluttering up the clinic waiting room. I mean, she often gets here at lunchtime when her appointment isn't until four in the afternoon! It's obvious she has a sad, empty life with no friends, so she uses the appointments as an excuse to hang around our waiting room, hoping she can latch on to the other patients and oblige them to talk to her out of politeness!"

Poppy shifted uncomfortably. She was shocked at Emma's cruel words and heartless attitude. It was probably true that Miss Payne was a lonely spinster using the visits to the GP clinic to bolster her meagre social life, but that seemed more like something to be pitied than mocked. Poppy glanced at the door, wondering if she could just leave. It seemed rude to just suddenly rush out, but at the same time, she didn't want to keep standing there, caught between the Seymours as they argued—especially as she didn't think she should have been hearing half of what Emma was saying.

Ralph Seymour obviously shared her thoughts because he gave her an embarrassed look and said, clearing his throat: "Yes... well... thanks for coming to see me, Miss Lancaster. Don't hesitate to call back if you have any further issues with your arm."

Poppy followed him gratefully out of the inner consulting room, conscious of Emma's brooding presence behind them. She felt like a child escaping the headmaster's office. Back in the waiting room, she looked around. It was empty now, but Yvonne was not alone at her desk. A middle-aged man with a goatee was perched on the edge of her desk, talking earnestly to her. He jumped up when the inner door opened and the three of them came out.

"Tim!" exclaimed Ralph Seymour. "What are you doing here, old chap?"

"Oh... I had some OAC business to discuss with Yvonne. I wanted to go over some of the items we mentioned at the last committee meeting, since she's now helping—"

"What's this?" asked Emma sharply. "I didn't realise Yvonne was getting involved in the Oxfordshire Auricula Club business."

"Yvonne has very kindly offered to help with some of the administrative duties, like typing up the minutes and sorting our accounts," said Dr

Seymour, smiling at his practice manager. "It'll be great to have someone with more organisational ability manage things." He elbowed the other man, saying in a teasing voice: "Tim's the official Treasurer, but he's been hopeless! We seem to have got ourselves into a complete muddle with the club funds." He turned back to his wife. "And you know things need to be shipshape now, darling, since we received that research grant."

"You could have asked me to help," said Emma.

The GP looked surprised. "But darling, you've never shown any interest in the club. Whereas Yvonne says she'd love to get involved and she's got time free in the evenings. She could just stay late a couple of nights a week for us to go over things together. But don't worry, we can use my office here in the surgery, so it won't disturb you in the house."

Emma compressed her lips and shot Yvonne a dagger look. "Well, I'd like to help," she said. "I go over the surgery accounts at the moment, so I can easily look after the accounts for the club as well. There's no need for Yvonne to get involved." She gave the practice manager a contemptuous look. "Miss Nash hasn't got any accountancy training, anyway. She can just do the typing and other mundane secretarial work, for which she's suited."

Yvonne flushed angrily and looked as if she might retort, but Dr Seymour hastily stepped in and said:

"Ah... that would be wonderful, darling... marvellous if you took a greater interest in auriculas." He turned towards the goateed man and took the other's elbow. "I'm glad you popped in, Tim. I wanted to ask you what you thought about changing the judging for the alpine category. Maybe have the 'Matched Pair' and 'Fancy' classes before the 'Seedling Light-Centre', eh? And do you think we should scrap the 'Named Variety raised by the Exhibitor' altogether...?"

The two men moved away, talking earnestly. Emma Seymour walked up to the reception desk and pulled a bunch of lilies out of the plastic bag she was carrying. Poppy stared in surprise at the flowers: they were absolutely gorgeous—enormous trumpets of pure white, with contrasting orange stamens and a gentle fragrance. She knew that lilies didn't bloom in England until the summer months, so she guessed that Emma must have purchased expensive imported blooms.

"Here. Put these in a vase. I want them displayed here on the desk," the GP's wife told Yvonne.

The girl pulled a face, obviously not impressed by the lilies. "Are you sure? The pollen gets everywhere and leaves a nasty stain."

"Lilies provide the perfect balance of sophistication, beauty, and understated elegance. They are one of the few blooms that complement any interior design style," Emma said, looking down her nose at the practice manager. "But then, I don't suppose someone with your level of education would know that."

Yvonne's eyes flashed. "I don't need to be Einstein to know that lilies are a pain," she retorted.

Emma coloured angrily. She cast around for a moment, as if trying to think of a comeback, then suddenly said: "What kind of outfit is that?" She looked pointedly at Yvonne's sheer blouse with its plunging neckline showing ample cleavage.

Yvonne raised her eyebrows. "This? It's what everyone's wearing now—but then, I don't suppose someone of your age would know that," she added, giving Emma an insolent smile.

The doctor's wife flushed, furious at having her own words thrown back at her. But she managed to keep her voice cool and controlled as she said: "Nevertheless, it's hardly appropriate for a doctor's surgery."

"As long as I can type up the letters and make the appointments and answer the phones, what does it matter what I wear?" said Yvonne.

"It's crucial to project an image of respectability, and having the practice manager looking like a street trollop is hardly going to help that," snapped Emma. "Kindly make sure you do not turn up to work dressed like this again."

"If *Ralph* doesn't have any objection, I don't see what your problem is," said Yvonne, subtly stressing the use of the doctor's first name. "In fact, he told me this morning that he thought I looked very nice." She paused, then added in a provocative voice: "It's a nice change for him to have someone enjoyable to look at."

Emma's face went an unpleasant shade of red. She made an incoherent noise at the back of her throat and glared at Yvonne. Poppy nearly drew back at the fury and hatred burning in the older woman's eyes. For the first time in her life, she truly understood the expression: "*If looks could kill...*"

The next moment, Emma Seymour whirled and stormed out of the surgery, slamming the door behind her.

CHAPTER SIX

When Poppy arrived back in the cul-de-sac where Hollyhock Cottage was situated, she was surprised to see a crowd of people filling the lane and milling around outside the stone walls of the cottage garden. As she got closer, she realised that they were not, in fact, outside her property, but the house on the lane just before it—Nick Forrest's house. She stopped in front of the large wrought iron gates which barred the entrance to Nick's property and looked curiously at the crowd of people next to her. It was composed of men and women brandishing microphones and cameras, all jostling for a view through the gate.

They look like... paparazzi! thought Poppy with surprise.

Then the sound of a purring engine behind her made her turn around and she saw the crime author's car approaching down the lane. She wondered what Nick was going to do; normally, he would drive in through the gates to park his car in the garage but if he did that now, no doubt the paparazzi would surge through the gates with him. Nick had obviously had the same thought because he brought the car to a stop in the lane outside his house and quickly got out. Instantly, he was engulfed by excited shouting and exploding flashbulbs as a hubbub of questions rose in the air:

"Mr Forrest! Mr Forrest, what do you say to the allegations that your book has inspired a ruthless killing spree?"

"Mr Forrest, do you agree that life imitates art?"

"Nick! Did you steal details from reports during your time in the CID to come up with the gory descriptions of the murders?"

"Mr Forrest, as an ex-detective, do you feel guilty that your books are now encouraging criminals to act out their sick fantasies?"

"Let me through!" snarled Nick Forrest, trying to ignore the microphones thrust at him from either side.

His lean, six-foot frame gave him an advantage as he forced his way through the cluster of reporters and photographers, and he glanced impatiently at Poppy as he came past her. She was standing by his gate, gaping in surprise, and started to ask:

"What on earth—?"

But before she could finish, Nick grabbed her arm

and hauled her after him as he pushed his way through the crowd. He shoved one of the gates open, hustled her through, and clanged it shut behind him in one fluid movement, before any of the paparazzi could follow. Then he bundled her up the path and the steps to the front door. It wasn't until they were safely in the house that Nick spoke.

"Bloody journalists! I'm sick and tired of the lot of them! I'd like to kill them all!"

"Why are they here?" asked Poppy.

"Because some stupid tabloid newspaper decided that the recent spate of serial killer murders in London bore some resemblance to those in my last book," Nick growled. "So they found some attention-seeking pop psychologist who gave an interview, warbling on about how the murderer probably used my book as inspiration—"

"But that's ridiculous!" cried Poppy.

Nick's dark eyes flashed, and he gave a grim nod. "Since that interview was published, all hell has broken loose. Now one of the morning TV shows has gone so far as to suggest that there is excessive 'inspirational violence' in all my books and that, given their popularity, I could be responsible for any number of crimes up and down the country." He threw his hands up in exasperation. "I'm a crime writer! I write about the worst aspects of humanity! People don't buy my books to read about pretty rainbows and fuzzy puppies—they buy them to read about the depraved members of society. Crime novels are a way for us to overcome our fear of the bogeyman by trying to understand what motivates him, and to have the satisfaction of seeing justice done—in fiction, at least, if not in real life. But just because I write about something doesn't mean that I condone it!"

"Maybe things will blow over soon," said Poppy soothingly.

"Not likely," Nick muttered. "Now that the vultures on social media have got wind of things, the whole scandal will probably go viral and morph into something even worse." He heaved an angry sigh. "And I'm just about to sign a new deal with my publisher for two more books... I wouldn't be surprised if they got cold feet after this."

"Well, it's not going to help your case if you go around saying you'd like to kill all the journalists," Poppy said in a dry voice.

Nick gave her a reluctant grin. "At least I didn't say it out *there*. Anyway, the papers have already had a field day with my reputation and image—they said I have the worst temper in publishing!"

They're probably not far wrong, thought Poppy with an inward smile. When she had first met her mercurial neighbour, she had been taken aback by Nick's brusque manner and short temper. But since getting to know him better, she'd realised that while Nick might have the typical artist's moody temperament, there was also a noble and compassionate core beneath that prickly exterior. He could be incredibly charming too when it suited him. In fact, with his brooding good looks, Nick had quickly gained legions of female fans who were probably as captured by his sexual magnetism as by the writing in his best-selling crime thrillers. Even Poppy had to admit that Nick was very attractive... *In a purely theoretical way, of course,* she hastened to remind herself as she followed the crime author into his sitting room. *Not that I am, in any way,* personally *attracted to him...*

Nick stopped suddenly as he stumbled on something in his path. "What the—?" He bent and picked up what looked like a sock, grumbling: "That new cleaning lady is completely useless! What the hell is this doing here? It doesn't even look like it's mine."

"You have a new cleaning lady?" said Poppy, surprised.

Nick made a face. "Dorothy, who normally comes, has had to return to Poole to look after her mother, who's had a stroke. So in the meantime, I've got a temporary lady coming to clean the house—on the recommendation of one of the villagers, actually." He shook his head in disgust. "That'll teach me to go to the pub for lunch when I'm in the middle of writing."

"What do you mean?"

"I was stuck on a plot hole the other day and decided I needed a break—you know, a change of scene to help clear my brain. So I decided to go to the Lucky Ladybird for lunch. Well, I'd barely sat down before this damned woman latched on to me and wouldn't leave me alone!" Nick scowled. "Never met anyone so bossy and interfering—kept telling me how to write my books! That is, when she wasn't telling me about her bloody toe fungus."

"Oh." Poppy chuckled. "I think I know who you're talking about."

Nick gave an irritable sigh. "Anyway, when I mentioned what had happened to my cleaning lady, she immediately recommended her friend 'Theresa'. Kept badgering me to hire her. In the end, I was so desperate for her to shut up and leave me alone that I agreed. And now I'm saddled with this infernal busybody. I mean, Theresa does a fair job on the house, but I wish she wasn't so bloody nosy!"

"Nosy?"

"Yes, the blasted woman is always rifling through my desk, going through my research notes, and poking around in all my files and folders. I told her from the start not to touch anything in my study, but the minute my back's turned, I catch her going in there. Keeps telling me that the place is a mess and she wants to tidy it up."

Poppy felt a momentary flash of sympathy for the woman. Having seen the utter chaos of Nick's study, with its leaning piles of books, scraps of loose paper, Post-it notes stuck on random surfaces, and half-drunk mugs of coffee everywhere, she wasn't surprised that any self-respecting cleaning lady would want to tidy it.

"Your study *is* a bit of a mess," she said, giving Nick a sideways look. "Maybe it wouldn't hurt to let her tidy it up a bit. Then you might be able to find things easier, you know—"

"I don't need to have it tidied. I know where everything is," snapped Nick. "I have a system."

Poppy resisted the urge to snort. Personally, she thought that it was a miracle Nick managed to write a coherent paragraph, never mind a full novel, in his study, but she wisely kept her mouth shut.

"Anyway, she wasn't just tidying—she was snooping," Nick continued. "She keeps asking me personal questions too."

"Like what?"

"You know—whether I have a girlfriend, where my parents live, that sort of thing. I'm sure she's been going through the drawers and cupboards in my bedroom, poking around for personal items like cards or photographs or a diary."

"Well, as long as she doesn't dig up something to sell to that crowd of paparazzi camped outside," said Poppy dryly.

"Oh God, that would be all I needed now," groaned Nick. "I'm already having to plan every trip I make out of the house to try and avoid them. Still, at least I'm not on a book tour at the moment, so I can hole up in here and just hope they lose interest and go away eventually. The only place I need to go to in the next few days is the vet in Oxford: Oren has his follow-up appointment the day after tomorrow."

"Oh, that's come around quickly. Do you think the vet will say that Oren can come off the special diet food?" asked Poppy hopefully.

"Probably. It's been nearly six months since he was put on it and he's lost most of his extra weight. But that still doesn't mean you can start giving him all sorts of treats again," warned Nick, looking at Poppy sternly.

She gave him a guilty grin. "Oh... all right. Hey, least the paparazzi can hardly spin a story out of something as innocuous as you taking your cat to the vet, can they?"

Nick gave her a sour look. "I wouldn't count on it. Those vultures can spin a story out of anything. Any innocent activity can end up as salacious front-page news these days!"

"In that case, they're going to be having a field day with you grabbing me outside just now and dragging me in here without so much as a by-your-leave!"

Nick looked sheepish and said with a rueful smile, "Ah... sorry. I wasn't really thinking. You're right. They're probably concocting all sorts of sordid stories about us now. They'll ferret out your identity and find out that you live next door, and then start making all sorts of insinuations."

Poppy laughed. "Don't they say any publicity is good publicity? To be honest, if it will bring some business to the nursery, they can write whatever they like!"

CHAPTER SEVEN

Poppy sighed with weariness as she undressed for bed later that evening. It felt like it had been a very long day, although she hadn't really done anything beyond the usual—other than her trip to the village GP that evening. Still, she felt mentally drained and she was looking forward to snuggling under the covers in bed. As she stepped up to the bathroom sink to brush her teeth, however, she paused and looked in the mirror, frowning. Something didn't look right... Suddenly, she gasped and clutched her throat.

Her locket! She had been wearing it earlier that day, but it wasn't around her neck now. Where could it be? Poppy thought back over her movements during the day: she was sure she had been wearing it when she went to the GP clinic, but after that...

had she still been wearing it when she had gone into Nick's house?

On an impulse, she picked up her phone and called Nick, hoping that he hadn't gone to bed yet. She knew that the crime writer tended to be a night owl—in fact, one of the first times she'd met Nick was when she'd found him wandering around the gardens of Hollyhock Cottage in the middle of the night. It had given her a fright until Nick had explained that her grandmother had invited him to visit the cottage gardens whenever he liked, because the wild, untamed style of the flowerbeds seemed to help hugely in creative thinking. Poppy had decided to continue to honour her grandmother's invitation and, since then, she had occasionally seen Nick meandering through the garden paths late at night or sitting on one of the stone benches in the early hours of the morning as he wrestled with writers' block.

Now, she was delighted when he answered on the first ring, although her heart sank slightly as he sounded even more bad-tempered than usual.

"What?" he snapped. "I'm in the middle of a scene and I've already had to rewrite it twice, so this better be good!"

"I'm sorry, I wouldn't disturb you except that... I can't find my locket," she said in a rush. "It was my mother's and it's the only thing I've got of hers—"

Her voice wobbled and a sudden lump came to her throat as she thought of losing the necklace. It had been the only piece of valuable jewellery that Holly Lancaster had possessed, and it had been given to Poppy just a few days before her mother had passed away. While it wasn't worth very much in itself—being nothing more than a simple gold locket on a chain—Poppy had treasured it as one of the few mementos she had from her mother.

Nick's voice softened. "Can you remember when you were last wearing it?"

"I... I think it was at the doctor's surgery. I went to see the village GP this evening," she explained. "That was just before I got back and we went into your place. I know I had the locket at the GP's but I can't remember if I had it when I met you... I know you won't remember what I looked like, but I was wondering if you could have a search—"

"Of course I remember what you looked like. You were wearing jeans and a rose-pink jumper, and you had your hair pulled back in a ponytail, like you often do when you're working in the garden," said Nick. "You were wearing a watch, but your neck was bare. You were also wearing a slight fragrance—orange blossom, I think."

"I... I didn't realise you noticed so much about me," said Poppy, surprised.

"I notice everything about you," said Nick, sounding amused. "Call it my writer's habit of observation. Anyway, since you weren't wearing your locket when you met me, it looks like you might have dropped it at the GP. Maybe it got caught on something while you were—"

"Oh! I just remembered," cried Poppy. "The baby!"

"What baby?"

"I was helping one of the other patients hold her baby. He kept trying to play with my locket—he was grabbing the chain and putting the locket in his mouth. I wonder if he yanked it off my neck when I wasn't looking and then maybe dropped it... yes, that must be what happened."

"Well, I wouldn't worry then," said Nick. "Just pop over tomorrow morning. It'll probably still be there, on the floor between the chairs in the waiting room."

Poppy hung up a minute later feeling a lot better. Somehow, despite Nick's grouchy demeanour, he had a way of always cheering her up and making her feel safe and reassured. She climbed into bed and was asleep within minutes, and awoke naturally the next morning just before sunrise. Moving quietly so as not disturb Nell, who worked as a cleaning lady and had had a late job the night before, Poppy washed and dressed, then let herself out of the cottage.

She retraced her steps through the village to the GP clinic, barely noticing the gardens around her this time, and arrived flushed and warm after her brisk walk. She slowed as she arrived in front of the Seymours' property, hesitant about calling on them so early in the morning. Then, as she glanced across at the surgery building, she was pleased to see that the front door seemed to be ajar. Obviously, the good doctor or his practice manager had arrived at work early, perhaps to catch up on some things before the rush of the day began.

Poppy turned and started up the path towards the surgery building, relieved that she wouldn't have to knock on the front door and meet Emma Seymour again. That woman's vitriolic manner was a bit too much to take, especially first thing in the morning! Poppy paused outside the surgery doorway and knocked on the half-open door, calling out:

"Hello?"

There was no answer.

"Hello? Good morning?" Poppy tried again. Then she pushed the door fully open and stepped inside.

For a moment, she thought that the place was empty. The waiting room looked almost identical to when she had left it yesterday evening, except that some of the chairs had been rearranged and magazines, which had been scattered around, had been tidied into neat piles. As she walked further into the room, Poppy was surprised to see a smashed vase on the floor, with the bunch of white lilies that Emma had brought yesterday strewn across a large puddle of water. But she had barely had time to register the mess before she saw something else that made her heart give a sharp kick in her chest.

The back of a shapely leg was protruding from the other side of the reception desk. Trying to ignore the ominous feeling closing in on her, Poppy walked slowly around the desk, stepping carefully to avoid the broken vase and the puddle. Then she stopped short as she saw the crumpled figure on the floor behind the desk.

It was Yvonne the practice manager and she was dead.

CHAPTER EIGHT

Poppy stared down at the body, not quite believing her eyes. Yvonne was lying face down on the floor, with her arms extended and her legs tangled in the folds of her dress. Her face was turned away, but Poppy knew that she had to be dead: no one could have survived the horrible bloody wound at the back of the girl's head. Still, Poppy felt that she had to check—just in case. So she took a deep breath, swallowed back the nausea, and forced herself to step closer and bend over the body.

"Y...Yvonne?" she said in a trembling voice, reaching a hesitant hand out to touch the girl's arm.

Her skin was cold to the touch and Poppy jerked her hand back, fighting the urge to turn and run screaming from the room. Instead, she straightened and stepped slowly back from the body, her heart thudding uncomfortably in her chest.

I've got to go and get help... she thought numbly. *I've got to call the police—*

"Why... Miss Lancaster!" said a male voice behind her.

Poppy whirled around to see Ralph Seymour standing in the surgery doorway. He stepped in, smiling at her.

"Are you having more trouble with your arm? Not to worry, I'm sure I can have a quick look again before the first appoint—"

He broke off suddenly as he walked over to join her and Yvonne's body came into view. Poppy saw his eyes bulge and he clutched the side of the desk for support. With a broken cry, he rushed towards the girl, saying:

"*Yvonne!*"

"You'd better not touch anything," said Poppy quickly. "It looks like she's been attacked, which means that this is a crime scene. We don't want to disturb any forensic evidence."

The doctor choked back a sob. He reached out, as if to caress the dead girl's cheek, then stopped himself and rose slowly to his feet. He stood looking down at the body, tears coursing down his face. Poppy couldn't help staring. She knew that employers could grow very fond of their employees, especially if they'd had a loyal secretary or assistant look after them for years, but this seemed a very emotional reaction, even taking that into account! If she hadn't known better, she would have thought that Ralph Seymour was mourning a dead lover, and she couldn't help remembering the gossip she'd heard the day before in this very waiting room.

Before she could think further, there was the sound of brisk steps approaching outside and, the next moment, Emma Seymour stepped into the surgery. She paused at the sight of them, then came forwards, frowning.

"Ralph? What's going on?" Then she stopped short as she, in turn, saw Yvonne's body. Unlike her husband, though, her reaction was tightly controlled, almost cold. She stared silently at the dead girl for a moment, then said:

"We need to call the police. And the patients. You'll need to cancel the morning's clinic."

Without a word to Poppy, she grabbed her husband's arm and propelled him out of the building. He went quietly, moving like a man in a daze, although Poppy saw him throw an agonised look over his shoulder at Yvonne's body as he left. She hesitated, then followed them outside. Emma Seymour had made no effort to acknowledge her and she wasn't sure if she would be welcome to follow the couple back into their home. On the other hand, she knew enough about crime scenes to know that she couldn't just leave either—she had to remain to give a statement, even if it meant hovering alone outside the surgery building.

As it turned out, when she stepped outside, she

found that Emma had abandoned her husband in the garden and had returned to the house alone. Poppy joined Dr Seymour and stood awkwardly next to him as he attempted to compose himself.

"Um… was Yvonne working late last night?" asked Poppy at last, feeling compelled to fill the silence with some kind of conversation.

The GP said in a strained voice: "Not really. I mean, the clinic overran, of course, but once you'd left, I told Yvonne that she could go first while I closed up. I think she had a date with her boyfriend last night."

"Yvonne had a boyfriend?" Poppy looked at him in surprise. After all the gossip, not to mention the flirtatious behaviour she'd observed, she had been convinced that if Yvonne had had a romantic relationship with anyone, it would have been with the doctor himself.

Dr Seymour nodded. "Yes, one of the lads in the village, I believe. I've seen him outside in the lane sometimes, waiting for Yvonne to finish."

"Had they been together for long?"

"Well, I think they knew each other as children, and had been dating on and off for a while. I don't think it was very serious on Yvonne's part, but he seemed to be much more earnest."

"Was he waiting for her last night?" asked Poppy.

Dr Seymour shrugged. "If he was, I didn't see him."

"So what makes you think they had a date—did

Yvonne tell you?"

"No, but in there, just now..." He swallowed and pointed at the surgery building. "Yvonne's wearing a different dress to what she was wearing during the day yesterday. She looks like she'd dressed up to go out."

"Oh, yes, of course..." said Poppy, berating herself for not noticing that earlier. Yes, Yvonne had been wearing a slinky satin dress, and had obviously spent time on her hair and make-up. Somehow, the thought of her pretty dress and glamorous appearance made the death of the girl seem even more tragic.

Dr Seymour seemed to share her thoughts, because he said suddenly in a choked voice: "She was so lovely, Yvonne... so full of life... I can't believe that she's gone!" His face crumpled and he broke down in tears again.

Poppy looked at him in dismay, not sure what to do or say. She was almost relieved when Emma came out of the house and rejoined them.

"The police will be here any minute. It just so happens that there was already an officer dispatched to the village this morning—that old dragon Mrs Busselton had insisted on a visit—so they're already on the scene, so to speak," Emma said. Then she glanced at her husband, who was still crying, and hissed: "For God's sake, Ralph—pull yourself together!" She yanked a crisp white handkerchief out of her pocket and thrust it at him. "You disgust me!"

Poppy was slightly shocked by the woman's cold attitude towards her husband, although she had to admit that it worked. By the time the police car pulled up in front of the house, Ralph Seymour had dried his tears and only someone looking closely would have noticed his red-rimmed eyes. The couple presented a united front as they faced the police constable—a young officer who was clearly out of his depth being the first responder on a murder.

"Um... er... so when did you discover the body?" he asked, clearing his throat in an important manner.

"It was this young lady here who discovered Yvonne," said Ralph, pointing to Poppy.

"Ah..." The constable turned to her and said nervously, "I'll... I'll need to ask you some questions, madam. I'm not CID—the detective inspector is on her way—but I've been told to start proceedings—"

"You might want to seal the crime scene," said Poppy kindly, pointing to the surgery building. "You know, make sure no one can go in to disturb any forensic evidence. I'm afraid both I and Dr Seymour handled the doorknob when we arrived, so we've probably smeared any prints that were left there, but there might still be other prints inside—unless the murderer wore gloves, of course."

"Oh... er... right," said the young constable, looking both grateful and slightly overwhelmed. "I suppose—" He broke off and turned as another car pulled up in front of the Seymours' property with a screech of the brakes. A slim brunette woman stepped out, followed by a middle-aged man in plainclothes.

"Ah! The DI and her sergeant are here," said the constable with a look of immense relief.

The sergeant hurried off towards the surgery building, but the woman walked purposefully towards them. She was wearing a smart trouser suit, with her sleek dark hair styled in an elegant bob, and she looked more like a fashion magazine editor than a police detective, but Poppy knew that Suzanne Whittaker's elegant looks belied the sharp mind of a shrewd investigator. As a woman in a male-dominated field, Suzanne had had to work hard to prove herself, and Poppy had always admired how the other woman could project cool authority and compassionate warmth at the same time. Now, she looked up eagerly as Suzanne approached them. They might have first met on a murder investigation, but they had quickly become friends, and Poppy sometimes felt like Suzanne was the older sister she'd never had.

"Poppy!" said Suzanne. "I didn't realise that you were here."

"This young lady here discovered the body, ma'am," said the police constable.

"Ah..." Suzanne gave Poppy an ironic look. "Why am I not surprised that if there's a dead body in Bunnington, you'd be near it?"

"Trust me, it's not by design!" said Poppy with a

wry smile.

She waited with the Seymours while Suzanne went into the surgery building to have a look at the crime scene, then—when the detective inspector returned—she recounted how she'd found Yvonne's body.

"And you, Dr Seymour—when was the last time you saw your practice manager?" asked Suzanne, swinging around to face the GP.

"Last night... just... just after we closed for the day," stammered Dr Seymour.

"The clinic closes at five, doesn't it?" asked Suzanne.

"Yes, officially, but it often overruns, so it's not uncommon for us to finish later. Last night, we didn't finish until nearly seven. I told Yvonne I'd lock up, so she could leave first."

"Do you know if she was going out anywhere?"

Ralph Seymour repeated what he'd told Poppy about Yvonne's boyfriend, adding: "I didn't see him waiting for her last night, though, so I'm just guessing that she was meeting him. She didn't actually say."

"And you? Where were you, sir, for the rest of the evening?"

"Well, I was in the surgery for a bit longer after Yvonne left, dictating some patient notes, and then I locked up and went back to the house for dinner. I was quite late and Emma was a bit put out about that." He glanced at his wife.

"And after dinner?"

"Er... well, I—"

"He was at home with me all evening," said Emma quickly. She gave her husband an exaggerated loving smile. "We were watching a film together... weren't we, darling?"

"Oh? What was the film, Dr Seymour?" asked Suzanne.

Ralph Seymour squirmed under her keen gaze. "It was... uh... I'm afraid I don't remember the title." He gave a nervous laugh. "I'm terrible with things like that. I can never recall the names of half the things I watch."

"What kind of film was it?" asked Suzanne. "Surely you can remember that?"

"Oh... er... it was... er—"

"A science-fiction thriller," said Emma smoothly. "You know, one of those about robots taking over the world. They've made so many similar films, it's hard to remember their names now." She gave a trill of laughter. "We weren't really watching it very closely anyway—it was just something to pass the evening."

"I see," said Suzanne, eyeing her thoughtfully.

Poppy thought that she was going to prod further, but instead she changed tack and said to the GP:

"Are you sure you locked the surgery door last night?"

Dr Seymour nodded. "Definitely. I always double check that."

"So how did Yvonne get in? The lock wasn't

forced."

"She had a key," said Dr Seymour. "She sometimes arrived before me in the mornings, just to air the place and give it a tidy-up before the patients started arriving." He hesitated, then asked, "Was she... was she killed last night?"

Suzanne inclined her head. "I believe so. Of course, I'll have to wait for the autopsy to confirm things and the forensic pathologist will probably give me an estimate once he arrives, but based on the condition of the body, I would guess that she's been dead for several hours." She paused for a moment, then mused: "I wonder if she came here last night after her date. She seems to be dressed for a night out. That isn't what she would normally wear to work, is it?"

"It's not far off," muttered Emma, which caused Suzanne to raise an eyebrow.

"I'm sorry?"

Ralph cleared his throat. "What my wife means is that Yvonne was always... er... fashionably dressed. But no, that wasn't what she was wearing at work yesterday. She... er... would wear more conservative outfits for the surgery hours."

Emma snorted, which caused Suzanne to raise her eyebrows even further. Before she could comment, however, they were interrupted by the sergeant who had arrived in the car with her. Poppy felt a familiar prickle of dislike as she watched Detective Sergeant Amos Lee join them. She'd never liked the man, finding him arrogant, patronising, and inclined to jump to conclusions just so he could have the satisfaction of a quick arrest. Now, he turned to Suzanne, triumphantly brandishing a plastic evidence bag.

"Look what we found in her handbag, guv," he said with a smug smile.

Suzanne took it from him and frowned at the piece of crumpled paper that was contained in the evidence bag. Poppy craned her neck to see and thought she could make out a few squiggles of writing on the paper.

Suzanne raised her head and narrowed her eyes at the GP. "Dr Seymour, you said the last time you saw Yvonne was when she left the clinic yesterday evening."

"Yes, that's right," said the GP nervously.

"In that case, why is there a note in Yvonne's handbag asking her to meet you here in the surgery late last night?"

CHAPTER NINE

Poppy walked slowly back to Hollyhock Cottage, her mind buzzing with all that had happened that morning. She had been slightly shocked when Suzanne had produced the note with Ralph Seymour's handwriting, and it seemed that his wife had been too, because Poppy had seen Emma draw a sharp breath and her eyes fly to her husband accusingly.

But Dr Seymour had been vehement in his denial, insisting that the note was a fake: "I didn't write that! That's someone pretending to be me!"

"Are you saying that this isn't your handwriting?" Suzanne had asked, holding up the crumpled piece of paper showing the typical, barely legible doctor's scrawl.

"It looks like my writing," he admitted. "But I'm

telling you, I didn't write that note. Someone must have faked my writing to lure Yvonne to the clinic under false pretences!"

"Well, we can confirm that easily enough, if you give a sample to our handwriting experts to compare," said Suzanne.

"Yes, yes, of course," said the GP quickly. "Whatever you need."

Suzanne eyed him speculatively. "It *is* interesting, though, that Yvonne responded to the note without question. I imagine most employees would have rung to ask their boss why they needed to come in so late... was she in the habit of meeting you at the surgery building after work?"

Emma stiffened and turned to glare at her husband.

Ralph Seymour cleared his throat and said, "Er... well, I *have* asked Yvonne to put in extra hours on occasion... so... um... she *has* come in on the odd weekend or... er... stayed late after the clinic at times. Perhaps... perhaps she thought it was something similar."

It had sounded lame and it was obvious that Suzanne had thought so too, although she was too shrewd an investigator to show her hand early. She had surprised the Seymours by not pursing that line of questioning. Instead, she had asked her sergeant to get a handwriting sample from the GP and then, with a brief parting smile to Poppy, she had gone off to speak to the forensic pathologist.

Could Ralph Seymour be the murderer? wondered Poppy as she turned into the lane which led down to the cul-de-sac where Hollyhock Cottage was situated. The man's shock and distress at seeing his dead practice manager had seemed all too genuine. Of course, he could have been putting on an act for her benefit. *If he was, it was bloody good acting*, thought Poppy.

She sighed as she arrived at her own front gate. *Anyway, I haven't got time to ponder the mystery of Yvonne's murder—I've got a garden nursery to run,* she reminded herself. A glance at her watch told her that it was nearly the nursery's official opening time—she had lost the extra hours gained from her early rising with the long delay at the Seymours'—and she would barely have time to wolf down some breakfast before she had to open the nursery to customers.

Poppy hurried up the path to the cottage, and around the side, to let herself in through the greenhouse attached at the rear. She walked into the kitchen to find Nell standing by the sink, watching an old man who was wearing what looked like giant moonboots with sponges attached to their soles. A scruffy little black terrier, who had been hovering around the old man, turned as soon as Poppy came in and ran over to her. He jumped up on his hind legs and danced around, waving his front paws and barking excitedly.

"Hello Einstein," said Poppy, smiling as she bent

over to pat the dog. Then she glanced back at the old man who was shuffling around the kitchen and talking earnestly to Nell:

"...as you walk around, your shoes will clean the floors at the same time, neutralising all dirt, dust, and bacteria via the rotary engines—"

"Well, I don't know," said Nell sceptically. "What's wrong with doing it the old-fashioned way using a mop?"

"This enables you to multi-task, dear lady! You just go about your daily chores in the house and the floors will be getting a top-notch clean at the same time. In fact, one could even turn this into an exercise routine, by increasing the speed of one's movements..."

The old man demonstrated by pushing a button on the side of one moonboot. Instantly, the shoes began shuffling faster and faster, scissoring his legs back and forth at double speed. Suddenly, there was a spark as the moonboots struck each other and, the next moment, there was a hiss and the wooden floorboards erupted in flames.

"Oh my God!" cried Poppy, staggering back just as Nell grabbed the fire extinguisher she kept by the kitchen sink and aimed the nozzle at the flames.

When the fire had been put out, leaving a mess of dried powder and scorch marks, Nell glared at the old man and pointed accusingly at the wooden floor.

"You've just given me even more cleaning to do!"

"Bertie! Are you all right?" asked Poppy, going up

to the old man, whose grey hair was slightly singed.

"Never better, never better, my dear," Dr Bertram Noble said, beaming at her. "It must be the floor polish that was used to coat your floorboards. Highly flammable in certain circumstances. But never mind! I will include a miniature fire extinguisher jet in the heels in the next prototype."

Poppy looked at the old man with affection. It was hard to believe that this slightly unkempt old man with his mop of wild grey hair, owlish eyes behind thick spectacles, threadbare tweed jacket, and mismatched socks was one of the most brilliant minds in the United Kingdom. Once an eminent professor at Oxford University, Bertie was now semi-retired and, when he wasn't providing top-secret consulting for government security agencies, he filled his time coming up with ever-wackier inventions.

Now, he turned eagerly to Poppy and said: "Ah! I'm so pleased to see you, as I've got something for you too, my dear."

"For me?" said Poppy nervously. Gifts from Bertie had to be treated cautiously.

"Yes, Nell was telling me about your troubles with your seedlings not growing vigorously enough, so that your stock isn't quite large enough to sell well. Well, I have the perfect solution for that! Now... where did I put it...?" He groped around the various pockets in his tweed jacket, waistcoat, and ancient corduroy trousers before finally producing a small glass vial and handing it to Poppy.

"What is it?" she asked, holding it up warily. The vial was filled with a thick amber liquid and seemed innocent enough, but she had learned the hard way that you could never tell with Bertie's inventions.

"It's a plant growth serum!" said Bertie excitedly. "It's an experimental mix of plant DNA, activated growth hormones, cytokines extracted from tumour cells, and regenerative tissue from *Hydra*—with a dose of bioactive gibberellin for good measure. A few drops of this on your seedlings and they'll be growing like weeds!"

"Wow, really?" said Poppy, intrigued in spite of herself. Then she remembered her past experiences with Bertie's inventions and reined in her excitement. In fact, she could see from Nell's expression that her friend thought the best thing to do was to chuck the vial in the bin. Still, the old man was looking at her so eagerly—like a puppy waiting for a word of praise—that she didn't have the heart to refuse his offering.

"Thanks, Bertie, this sounds great," she said, smiling at him. "It's so sweet of you to think of me. I'll... um... definitely try this on my seedlings."

She tucked the vial into her jeans pocket and soon forgot about it, however, as the nursery was opened and the day got going. Poppy had expected another slow day like yesterday but, to her surprise, she had barely flipped the sign on the gate to "OPEN" before a steady stream of customers began arriving.

They were mostly residents from the village and

she quickly realised that they had come more to pick up some juicy gossip than to buy a cyclamen or potted primrose. News had travelled quickly along the local grapevine; everyone seemed to know that she was the one who had discovered Yvonne's body, and they were now keen to get more gory details straight from the horse's mouth. Poppy was glad for the chance of extra business but, by the late afternoon, she was thoroughly sick of answering the same questions over and over again.

"What did she look like when you found her?"

"Was there a lot of blood?"

"Do they think it's murder?"

"I heard that her head was smashed in—just like a squashed melon! Is that true?"

Poppy shuddered and looked with some alarm at the speaker: a white-haired septuagenarian in a floral dress, with tissues stuffed into her cardigan sleeves. *Since when did sweet old ladies become so bloodthirsty?*

"I didn't really take a good look," she replied honestly. "Yvonne did look like she had been hit on the back of the head."

"Do you know what with?" asked the old lady eagerly.

Poppy shook her head. "No, I'm sorry, I—"

"It was a heavy, blunt instrument," declared a new voice behind her. "That's what the police are looking for as the murder weapon."

Poppy turned to see Mrs Peabody coming up the

path, followed by a group of her cronies. Her heart sank slightly at the thought of facing one of the worst busybodies in the village, but her feelings for the woman were also tempered by affection and gratitude. Over the course of the last few months in Bunnington, she'd found that Mrs Peabody was unexpectedly kind and wise, especially when it came to helpful advice about gardening and growing plants for the nursery.

The woman also seemed unrivalled in being able to pick up all sorts of unofficial information. Poppy gave her an impressed look and asked:

"How do you know that? The murder was only discovered this morning! Surely the autopsy report can't be complete yet?"

"Ah... but my neighbour's niece knows a lad whose aunt works at the coroner's office and she... *ahem...* happened to overhear the pathologist talking to the coroner about the preliminary findings," said Mrs Peabody, looking smug. "They are sure that Yvonne was hit on the head by something blunt and heavy."

"And the police haven't found anything at the crime scene which could be the murder weapon?" asked Poppy.

"No, no," said one of Mrs Peabody's friends breathlessly. "Which means that it's still out there!"

"Probably hidden in one of the houses in *this* village!" added another woman from the group, looking delighted at the prospect.

"Of course, we all know which house it's most likely to be in," said Mrs Peabody, waggling her eyebrows.

Her friends seemed to know what she meant, and they exchanged nods and meaningful glances, but Poppy looked at her blankly.

"Whose?" she asked.

Mrs Peabody leaned closer and said in a dramatic undertone: "Bryan Murray's. Yvonne's boyfriend."

"What makes you say that?"

"Violent tendencies," said Mrs Peabody succinctly.

Poppy frowned. "You mean... Bryan has a history of assault?"

"Well, he hasn't actually been arrested by the police," Mrs Peabody admitted.

"But he's come close," said one of her friends quickly. "He's been in a dozen fights at the pub and Martin the publican has had to chuck him off the premises several times."

"Yes, the last time it happened, I heard Martin tell Bryan that if he did it again, he would be banned for good!" said another woman.

"It's the drink—he gets really shirty when he gets drunk," another woman piped up.

"Yes, almost 'literally' once!" said another woman, giggling. "Do you remember the time Margaret's younger brother Ron came for a visit and he started flirting with Yvonne at the pub, and you could see steam coming out of Bryan's ears... then all of a sudden, he grabbed Ron by the front of his shirt?"

"Ooh yes, I was there that night," the first woman said. "I thought Bryan was going to smack him against the wall!"

"He told Ron that if he didn't keep his hands off his girl, he would make him sorry," her friend added.

"He does sound very possessive," said Poppy. "But from what you're saying, all his aggression is directed towards other men. I don't see how that leads to him murdering Yvonne."

"Well, she probably pushed him too far," said the first woman.

"Yes, Yvonne was a terrible tease," agreed her friend.

"She also shared her favours around," a third woman added. "She was always one of those girls who liked to have a good time and didn't really care who she had it with."

"I think she enjoyed being fought over by men, so she encouraged other men to flirt with her, just to wind Bryan up," the first woman said.

"And the silly lad played right into her hands," declared Mrs Peabody. "But you know what they say about playing with fire. You can only taunt a man like Bryan for so long before he snaps."

"Do you really think that he killed Yvonne in a jealous rage?" asked Poppy doubtfully.

"Well, he certainly sounded jealous enough when they were rowing in the pub last night," said Mrs Peabody.

"Last night? They were at the pub? Fighting?" said

Poppy, surprised.

"Oh, didn't you know? Yes, we were all there and we saw them," said Mrs Peabody. "They were having the most awful row. Yvonne was all dolled up, so they must have gone somewhere for dinner first before stopping there for a drink, but they didn't look like they were having a good time. Faces like thunder, the pair of 'em!"

"Bryan accused Yvonne of cheating on him," said one of the other women with relish. "Said she was seeing another man behind his back."

"Yes, and we all know who *that* might be," said Mrs Peabody, exchanging more meaningful looks with her friends.

Poppy had a good idea too, but she feigned ignorance: "Oh? Who?"

Mrs Peabody gave a sniff. "Well, I'm not one to gossip," she said virtuously. "Let's just say that I don't think doctors should be too handsome. It's not good for their reputation."

Poppy tried another tack. "Did Bryan look as if he would hurt Yvonne? Did she seem scared when you saw her at the pub?"

"Oh, no, she just laughed in Bryan's face," said one of the other women.

"Yes, she said he was just jealous because he couldn't match up to her other lover," said another in the group.

"That really got Bryan's back up," said another woman, her eyes lighting up at the memory. "He started calling Yvonne all sorts of dreadful names. So she slapped him across the mouth and stormed out."

"And that," added Mrs Peabody in an ominous voice, "was the last time anyone saw Yvonne alive."

CHAPTER TEN

Poppy glanced up as the gossiping session was suddenly interrupted by a loud commotion outside the garden walls. She hurried out of the cottage gardens and into the lane, with Mrs Peabody and her cronies hard at her heels. Poppy's eyes widened as she saw Mrs Busselton, accompanied by another middle-aged woman and the young police constable she'd met that morning, coming up the lane. They were marching towards Nick Forrest's house and were surrounded by a crowd of paparazzi who were following them with the eagerness of foxhounds who had scented blood.

Mrs Busselton arrived at the iron gates and turned to the woman with her, who fumbled with the lock. Poppy was surprised to see that the woman had a key. A minute later, they were through and marching up the front steps to the door. Poppy ran after them, pushing her way through the crowd of paparazzi to slip through the gates in her turn and conscious of Mrs Peabody and her friends trying to follow her example. She arrived at the front door just in time to see Mrs Busselton banging the knocker loudly.

A silence fell over the assembled crowd as the front door swung open and Nick Forrest stepped out.

"Yes?" he snapped.

His dark hair was tousled, his jaw unshaven, and his eyes slightly bloodshot. He was still wearing the same clothes Poppy had seen him in the night before and she wondered if he had been up all night, working on his manuscript. It certainly wouldn't have been the first time. From the scowl on his face, it didn't look like the writing had gone well either, and she pitied his visitors who were going to bear the brunt of his inevitably foul mood.

Mrs Busselton didn't seem daunted, however. She stepped forwards before the police constable could speak and said in a loud, carrying voice:

"We're here to expose you, you filthy man!"

Nick's brows drew together. "What?"

The constable cleared his throat and said, looking very embarrassed, "Er... Mr Forrest? I'm terribly sorry to disturb you, sir, but we were wondering if you wouldn't mind answering a few questions?"

"About what?" demanded Nick. "I've been up all night stuck on a scene and I've *just* finally got things flowing again. What's so important that I need to stop?"

"Er..." The constable shifted uncomfortably. "Well, you see, Mrs Busselton here insisted on coming and... er...she claims that you... er..."

"We are here to reveal your dirty secret!" said Mrs Busselton with glee.

"What the hell are you talking about?" asked Nick impatiently.

Mrs Busselton drew herself up. "I'm talking about the proof of your sexual crimes!"

There were gasps of delight from the paparazzi and Poppy heard several cameras clicking rapidly, snapping shots of Nick's flabbergasted expression.

"My *what?*" he said.

"Oh yes, don't try to deny it," said Mrs Busselton. "You are just like those evil men you write about—you're a nasty, sleazy degenerate yourself!"

"Is this more of that nonsense from the tabloid papers?" Nick glared at them. "I haven't got time for this bollocks! I have a book to write!" He turned and would have gone back into the house, but Mrs Busselton grabbed his arm and cried:

"Not so fast! I'm not going to let you go and destroy the evidence!"

Nick swung back to stare at her. "What evidence? What are you rabbiting on about, woman?"

"Evidence of your disgusting perverted tendencies!" said Mrs Busselton. "Yes, that's right—you didn't think anyone had discovered your filthy secret, did you? But I'm onto you. I know you've been creeping through the village, peeping at women through their windows and stealing their underwear—"

"What? You're out of your mind!" said Nick, starting to laugh.

"This is no laughing matter!" cried Mrs Busselton, outraged. "And you're not going to wriggle out of it by pretending that you don't know what I'm talking about. I have proof! Theresa helped me obtain it!"

She turned to indicate the other middle-aged woman who had been skulking behind her. Nick's face darkened as he saw her and she squirmed, looking abashed and guilty. But at a prod from Mrs Busselton, she raised her chin and said in a sharp, nasal voice:

"Yeah, I've been cleanin' Mister Forrest's house, an' yesterday I discovered what he's been hidin'!"

There was a ripple of excitement through the crowd and several cameras flashed again. Their eagerness seemed to give Theresa confidence, for she turned towards the crowd and began addressing them. Her cheeks were flushed and she was obviously loving her moment in the spotlight.

"I was hooverin' under his bed, right, an' the machine caught on somethin' an' I thought: wot's this? An' I pulled it out an' blow me, it were a black lace bra!"

"That's it? A black bra?" said Nick incredulously. "That's proof that I'm a sexual deviant?" He gave an exaggerated sigh. "At the risk of stating the obvious, I *am* a bachelor. I might have had a lady friend spend the night, who could have left that item of clothing."

"Well, of course I know about gentlemen an' their... their *lady friends*," said Theresa with a fastidious sniff. "But I tell you, I recognised this bra, all right."

"You *recognised* it? What—you mean, you knew its name and family tree?" said Nick sarcastically.

Theresa ignored him and addressed the crowd. "See, I do cleanin' for Mrs Fuller on the other side of the village an' I remembered her tellin' me one o' her bras had gone missin' from her washing line. A black lace bra, she said. From M & S. With a red bow between the cups an' detachable straps... and this were it!"

"For the love of God..." groaned Nick, clutching his head in one hand. "Did it not occur to you that Marks and Spencer might have sold more than one black lace bra?"

"It were Mrs Fuller's," Theresa insisted. "I took it an' showed it to her, an' she said it were hers. She wrote her name on the label, see," she added with a triumphant look at Nick. "It's a habit from when she were at school an' used to lose stuff all the time, an' her mum made her write her name on everythin'. So she still does it. It were there, in black marker on the label: her initials 'LF' for Louise Fuller."

"And there is no way that Louise Fuller could be one of your *'lady friends'*," added Mrs Busselton, leaning towards Nick and eyeballing him. "She's a decent, respectable housewife with two small boys and another on the way. She would never take up with the likes of you!"

Before Nick could respond, Mrs Busselton turned to the police constable and said, pointing at the house: "We need to get in there and search the place before he has a chance to destroy the evidence of his crimes."

"We can't do that," protested the young officer. "For one thing, you'd need a search warrant, and for another, you can't just accuse an innocent man and—"

"He is not innocent!" Mrs Busselton thundered, shaking a fist. "He's a criminal, a sexual deviant, and he must not be allowed to cover up—"

"Aaaahh, for God's sake...!" Nick made a sound of exasperation. He threw open the front door. "Come in! Search wherever you like! Just hurry up so I can get back to the book!"

Mrs Busselton swept past him and into the house with her head held high. Theresa scuttled after her, and, after a sheepish look at Nick, the constable followed too. Poppy slipped over to Nick's side but, before she could say anything, there was a crow of triumph from within the house.

"Bloody hell... what now?" muttered Nick, heading indoors.

Poppy hurried after him and a few minutes later found herself in what was obviously the master bedroom. It was a very masculine room, decorated in muted tones of forest-green and dark mahogany—which made the little pile of lacy lingerie on the floor next to the king-size bed all the more startling.

"Aha!" said Mrs Busselton, her face flushed with glee as she pointed at the pile. "What do you call that?"

Nick said nothing, just stared in bewilderment. Poppy's heart sank as she saw that the tangled pile contained bras in a myriad of fabrics and colours. There were red lace scraps and silky satin balconettes, embroidered padded cups and comfortable cotton bralettes.

The young constable cleared his throat and said diffidently, "Sir, can you explain why you have this collection of bras underneath your bed?"

Slowly, Nick shook his head. "I have no idea. I've never seen them before in my life."

"Liar!" cried Mrs Busselton. "You stole these from women around the village! Don't deny it!"

Then she gave an indignant squeak and bent suddenly to snatch something out of the pile. She straightened, brandishing an enormous beige nylon bra with enough fabric and underwire to support a WWI Zeppelin.

"This… this is mine!" she spluttered. She glared at Nick, clutching the baggy garment to her chest. "How dare you! You disgusting man! You've been titillating yourself with my Endless Comfort Lift and Support!"

Nick stared at her, looking as if he didn't know whether he wanted to throttle her or burst out laughing.

Hurriedly, Poppy spoke up: "Look, isn't it possible that these bras somehow got here without Nick's knowledge?"

"Yes, yes," said the constable eagerly, seizing on a possible way out. He turned to Nick and asked: "Do you always lock your door when you leave the house, sir?"

"Well, of course. What d'you take me for?" said Nick impatiently.

"I noticed that you have an alarm system—do you always make sure that's set?"

"No, I don't use it, actually," Nick admitted. "I have a cat and the bloody animal is always coming and going at all hours. Oren's got his own cat flap. So I can't set the alarm, otherwise he'd trigger the motion sensors."

"Don't listen to anything he says!" cried Mrs Busselton. "He's a writer! He's good at making up stories. It's not as if the bras were found outside in the garden or even tossed in through a window. They were *hidden* under his bed! Who else could have been responsible but him?" She narrowed her eyes at Nick. "In fact... now that I think about it, he could be responsible for the murder of that poor girl too!"

"Now, hang on a minute—" said Nick, starting to look really annoyed.

"Yes!" cried Mrs Busselton, filled with new fervour

at her idea. "Everyone knows that stealing women's underwear is considered a 'gateway' crime—the first sign of a sexual predator." She whirled towards the police constable. "Officer, if you don't arrest this man, you will be guilty of letting a murderer escape!"

The constable looked incredibly uncomfortable. He glanced sideways at Nick's scowling face and it was obvious that he was weighing up the relative evils of getting into trouble for potentially letting a murder suspect slip versus angering a famous crime author. The former won. He turned to Nick and said:

"I'm sorry, sir, but I think it would be best if you came down to the police station with me—just to answer some questions," he added hastily.

Nick threw up his hands. "Fine! I can see that I'm not going to get any writing done anyway. The faster we clear up this nonsense, the sooner I can get back to my manuscript!"

He turned and stalked back out of the house. Poppy followed him silently, with the others bringing up the rear. As soon as they stepped out the front door, they were greeted by exploding camera flashes and a barrage of questions:

"Mr Forrest! Mr Forrest, is it true that you've been spying on women in the village?"

"Nick! Are you a voyeur?"

"Mr Forrest, do you deny the allegations that you're a sexual pervert?"

"No comment," growled Nick, just as the constable stepped out of the door behind him, awkwardly clutching the collection of bras.

Instantly, the camera lenses swung towards the hapless young officer, who stopped for a moment, blinded by all the flashes. The questions rose to a fever pitch as everyone jostled for a better view and microphones were thrust in Nick's direction with yells of: "Are those your sex trophies?"

Then the din was broken by a shrill yowl. The crowd of paparazzi parted in surprise as an enormous ginger tomcat shot in from the lane, through the iron gates, and up the steps to the front door, followed by a scruffy black terrier barking manically. Oren leapt for one of the Doric columns flanking either side of Nick's front door and somehow managed to swarm up the smooth stone until he reached one of the ledges in the pediment above the door. Balancing perfectly, the ginger tom turned around, sat down, and looked down at the dog with a smirk on his whiskered face. Einstein let out a howl of outrage and bounced around the base of the column, barking and shouting canine insults at his nemesis. Oren watched him for a moment, then calmly began to wash his face.

Everyone had watched the dog and cat with bemusement and now they turned in unison back towards the iron gates as they heard a voice shouting:

"Einstein! Come back here, boy!"

A minute later, Bertie trotted in from the lane, brandishing a dog leash in one hand and—for some reason—a frying pan in the other. He faltered to a stop as he took in the mob of villagers, reporters, and camera crew. Then his face brightened as he spotted Nick and he hurried up the front steps.

"Son! I have had the most wonderful breakthrough," he said, beaming. "You remember you were wondering if it would be possible to create a device which could see through people's clothes? Well, I have been tinkering with a prototype and I think I may have found a way to do it!"

Mrs Busselton made a horrified noise in her throat and clutched both hands protectively to her ample bosom, while there was a collective gasp of unholy delight from the crowd.

Nick groaned. "That was a theoretical question, Dad. I was wondering about a fictional situation, in a *book*—not in real life!"

"Oh, but fiction is often a precursor to reality. It's well known that science-fiction novels are the best predictors of the future. If man can imagine it, then he can make it happen—and you have a marvellous imagination, son," said Bertie proudly.

Mrs Busselton made a triumphant sound and a hubbub of excited speculation rose from the crowd.

Nick gritted his teeth. "Thanks, Dad. You're really helping."

The constable stepped forwards. "*Ahem... yes...* uh... well... I think we'd better just get down to the police station as fast as possible," he said, looking like he wished he'd never got up that morning. He made a polite gesture at Nick. "If you don't mind coming with me, sir—"

"I'd like to drive my own car, if I can," said Nick grimly.

"Oh, where are you off to?" asked Bertie brightly. "Can Einstein and I come too?"

CHAPTER ELEVEN

When Poppy finally returned to Hollyhock Cottage, she was glad to see that it was well past the nursery's official closing time and she could shut up for the evening. In any case, there were no customers to be seen since everyone seemed to have joined the crowd of paparazzi following Nick and the police out of the village.

Poppy tidied up the garden, checked her young plants growing in the greenhouse, then retreated into the cottage and sank gratefully onto the sofa. It was late and she should really have been thinking of dinner, but she had missed her tea that afternoon and she couldn't resist enjoying a cup now, along with some chocolate digestives. She was still sprawled on the sofa an hour later when Nell arrived home from her cleaning jobs.

"My goodness, Poppy—what are you doing eating chocolate biscuits now?" Nell admonished. "You should be having supper!"

Poppy followed her friend into the kitchen and watched as Nell began bustling around, getting food ready.

"Everyone's talking about the murder, even at the office in Oxford where I was cleaning this afternoon. I'll bet it's all over the news," said Nell, moving over to the small TV perched at the end of the kitchen counter and flicking it on.

The monitor blinked into life and Poppy froze in surprise as she saw herself on the screen. She was with Nick and she was being hustled up the front steps of his house. The cameraman had somehow managed to make them look very furtive and zoomed in on Nick's handsome scowling face as he shoved her through the front door of the house, then disappeared inside behind her.

A disembodied voice said:

"...while bestselling author Nick Forrest has been detained for questioning and remains in police custody, disturbing footage has emerged of the crime author with an unidentified young woman. This was taken yesterday outside his house, where Forrest was seen grabbing the young woman and forcing her into his house. There were concerns over whether she was being held hostage, but she later claimed that she was his neighbour."

The screen cut to a woman being interviewed on

the street.

"Well, that's what she says, but how do we know it's true, eh? She could be his lover or an accomplice in his crimes... or what about an abuse victim who's been forced to lie—"

"That's ridiculous!" burst out Poppy angrily. "Where do people get their crazy ideas from?"

"It did look like Nick was manhandling you in that footage," said Nell.

"That's just because he wanted me to get into the house quickly because we were being harassed by all these paparazzi. You know how impatient Nick gets!"

"Well, he'd better start learning to hold on to his temper, otherwise he's going to be featured on national television a lot more—and not in a good way," said Nell tartly.

A loud yowl sounded outside the back door of the cottage, followed by several plaintive wails of "*N-ow? N-ow? N-ooow?*"

"Oh, that's Oren," cried Poppy. "He must want his dinner. I suppose I'd better pop next door and feed him since I don't know how long they're going to keep Nick at the police station. He might not be back until very late, in which case Oren will be starving."

"And making sure that we know it," said Nell, chuckling.

Poppy took the ginger tom back to Nick's place, using the spare key that the crime author had given her for convenience, since she often helped to feed Oren when he was away on his book tours and other author commitments. She measured out the obligatory amount of special diet biscuits into Oren's bowl, ignoring his grumbles of displeasure, and watched him sulkily begin to eat his dinner.

Didn't Nick say that Oren has a follow-up visit at the vet the day after tomorrow? I really hope they'll let him return to his normal food, she thought as she did a quick check of the house, switched on the appropriate lights, then locked the door and returned to Hollyhock Cottage.

She was surprised the next morning to find the tomcat outside the kitchen door once more, loudly demanding his breakfast. Poppy looked over at Nick's house, frowning. Hadn't he come back last night? With Oren accompanying her, she retraced her steps from the night before and found the large Georgian house still and empty. After she'd fed the ginger tom, she wandered through the rooms, noting the half-drunk mugs of coffee in Nick's study and the used plates in the kitchen sink—all obviously from the day before. She realised that Nick must still be detained at the police station.

Poppy felt a prickle of worry. Surely they should have released him by now? As she walked slowly back to Hollyhock Cottage, she pulled out her phone and called Suzanne Whittaker. As the lead investigator on the case—not to mention Nick's ex-girlfriend—Suzanne would surely know what was happening.

"Oh hi, Poppy," said Suzanne, sounding slightly

harassed. "Sorry, I can't talk long. I'm just about to go into a briefing."

"Sorry to bother you. I was just wondering about Nick. I thought he'd be back last night, but I went over to his place to feed Oren this morning and it seems that he's still at the station?"

Suzanne sighed. "Yes, I'm afraid he's still being held in custody."

"But why? Surely they don't believe Mrs Busselton's ridiculous accusations?"

"No, it's not just that. It turns out that one of the bras in the collection found under Nick's bed belonged to Yvonne. In fact, it's from a set, and she was wearing the matching knickers when she was found. But no bra."

"Oh."

"I'm sure I don't need to tell you the significance of that," said Suzanne grimly. "There are questions now around whether Yvonne had intentionally gone out without a bra that night or whether she was wearing the matching bra and the murderer had removed it…"

"They think Nick attacked her and took her bra?" said Poppy, aghast.

"It's a fair assumption," said Suzanne. "He has an item of clothing which matches what the murder victim was wearing, and he doesn't have a good explanation for why it was in his possession. Not just in his possession, but deliberately hidden under his bed. Then there's his alibi—or lack of one, rather.

Nick says that he was at home all night working on his book but there's no one there to corroborate that."

"I saw Nick that night," said Poppy quickly. "I mean, earlier in the evening, after I got back from the GP clinic. Nick had just got home, and the paparazzi were camped outside his house—"

"Ah yes, I saw that on TV," said Suzanne, a hint of humour entering her voice. "A lot of interesting speculation accompanied that reporting."

"It's all a load of rubbish!" said Poppy hotly. "The outrageous suggestion that Nick might be holding me hostage or the... the stuff about us being lovers—it's not true! You know what the village gossips are like... just because Nick is single and happens to live next door, but there's nothing between us! Nothing at all!"

She stopped, suddenly aware of the puzzled silence on the other end of the line in reaction to her vehement denial. Clearing her throat, Poppy hurriedly continued: "Anyway, surely you don't believe that Nick could be guilty?"

"No, of course not—"

"Well, then, can't you vouch for him? After all, you're respected at the station and you know Nick personally."

"That's part of the problem," said Suzanne wearily. "In fact, I have a feeling I'm going to be taken off the case soon."

"What? Why?"

"Conflict of interest," said Suzanne. "As someone

who knew Nick as a colleague when he was still a detective in CID, never mind being his ex-girlfriend, I cannot be considered an impartial investigator, which means I probably shouldn't be working on a case involving him as a potential suspect."

"But... but that's ridiculous!" protested Poppy.

"Don't worry, until I'm officially taken off the investigation, I will continue as normal, but I have to be careful, Poppy. If I want to stay on the case, I can't be seen to be giving Nick any special treatment—which means I can't really plead his case."

There was nothing else to say and Poppy knew that she had to be satisfied with that. She sighed and prepared to hang up, then suddenly remembered something:

"Oh, wait—Suzanne! Do you know if the forensic team happened to find a gold locket at the surgery?"

"A locket?"

"Yes, on a gold chain. It's the reason I was at the GP so early yesterday morning. I think I dropped it in the waiting room the day before and I went back to look for it. It belonged to my mother, you see, and it's quite precious to me. When I found Yvonne's body, I totally forgot about it, so I never had a chance to search the waiting room. And of course, the whole place is roped off as a crime scene now."

"No, I don't recall seeing any mention of a gold locket in the reports. But I'll check again, as soon as I have a free moment, and speak to the head of the SOCO team as well," Suzanne promised.

Poppy hung up feeling deflated and spent most of the day brooding on the situation, in between serving the customers that arrived at the nursery. Business was even busier that day as the notoriety from the murder attracted more people to Bunnington. Poppy found that in addition to the villagers, she was now having to deal with residents from the neighbouring towns and even visiting tourists, all keen to satisfy their vulgar curiosity. She was frustrated to find, though, that—like the day before—while most people were keen for the chance to pick up more gossip, they were not so keen to put their hands in their pockets when it came to buying an actual plant. It didn't help that her stock didn't look particularly appealing, Poppy admitted to herself as she cast an eye over the rows of pots on display. Most of the bigger, better-grown plants had been sold, which meant that only the spindliest and sparsest specimens were left.

I wish there was some way I could make them grow faster! she thought wistfully. Then Poppy remembered Bertie's gift and her hand slid involuntarily into her pocket, where she found the little glass vial still safely tucked in its folds. She fingered the vial for a moment, then hastily withdrew her hand. *No, no way,* she chided herself. *You should know better than to try any more of Bertie's inventions!*

Finally, the day drew to a close and Poppy flipped the sign on the gate to "CLOSED" with a sigh of relief. She walked slowly back into the cottage. Nell had gone out for a night of bingo with some new friends and Poppy was left to her own devices for dinner. But although there was a home-made casserole in the fridge, she didn't fancy an evening alone with just her thoughts for company.

I know, I'll go to the Lucky Ladybird for dinner, she decided suddenly. *It'll be a nice treat for a change. Maybe I'll have a roast beef dinner or some fish and chips, with a plate of their famous apple crumble to finish. Mmm...*

Her mouth was starting to salivate at the thought, and she hurried to wash her hands and face, and change out of her grubby gardening clothes. She wriggled into an oversized sweater and dark leggings—items inherited from her mother and which carried a certain bohemian flair—and then loosened her hair from its ponytail and gave it a good brush. Finally, Poppy dabbed some gloss onto her lips and, feeling almost glamorous, grabbed her coat and stepped out of the cottage.

The temperature had dropped sharply, even in the short time since she'd come in from the garden, and she was surprised by the nip in the air. *But it's perfect for a brisk walk to the pub*, Poppy told herself with a smile as she started up the lane and headed towards the centre of the village.

CHAPTER TWELVE

The village green—the large, triangular, grassy field in the centre of Bunnington—was the unofficial social heart of the village. It was where the locals gathered to exchange gossip on Sunday mornings after church, where the annual village fair was held, and where the tourist coaches and other visitors paused to peruse the poster map showing the various village attractions: from the quaint high street with its antique shops and local boutiques to the village pub, housed in a large limestone building overlooking the green.

Poppy headed towards the latter now, admiring the mellow stone façade which was lit up with glowing lights and looked wonderfully cosy in the gathering dark. Inside, the cosy ambience continued, with ceiling beams, dark wood furniture, and an enormous fireplace against one wall. Poppy paused just inside the door and inhaled the wonderful aroma of home-cooked food. The place was filled with the noisy hubbub of conversation, laughter, and the cheerful clink of glasses, and she could feel her spirits lifting already. Eagerly, she made her way through the throngs of people standing around, clutching pints of ale and lager, until she reached the bar.

The large, beefy man standing behind the counter smiled as he saw her. "Hullo, hullo—haven't seen you in here in a long time," said Martin the publican. "I hear that you're the heroine of the hour."

Poppy blushed slightly. "Oh no, not really. I just happened to be the person who discovered that poor girl's body."

"That's enough for celebrity status in a place like this," said Martin, chuckling. "I reckon all the local old biddies have been up at your nursery, pumping you for the gory details, eh?"

"Tell me about it! Not that I mind. I mean, it's great to have people coming in at all." Then, suddenly realising how that sounded and remembering the PR maxim of always projecting a positive image, Poppy added hastily, "But business is going well."

Martin gave her a shrewd look but all he said was: "Well, I think it's great you decided to stay and make a go of it. Everyone thought you'd just cash in on your inheritance and bugger off. Can't have been easy, stepping into your grandmother's shoes, especially when you didn't know much about plants, did you?"

Poppy hesitated, then seeing the genuine kindness in his eyes, decided to come clean. "Yes, I was hopeless," she said with a laugh. "I couldn't even keep a plastic plant from IKEA alive. But I've been learning really fast since I arrived in Bunnington and I'm getting much better."

"It's just trial and error, luv—just like with cooking," said Martin's wife, a homely woman with a blunt manner that was belied by her warm smile. She had come out of the kitchen and now joined them at the counter. "Experience is the best teacher. But you'll pick things up quickly—you'll see. I think it's wonderful what you've achieved already."

"Oh, thanks," said Poppy, flushing with delight. "Thanks, that's really nice of you to say so."

"It's no more than the truth," she replied briskly. "There's many who wouldn't even have attempted to take on what you did. Not just the plant side of things but resurrecting a failing business. In the last six months of your grandmother's illness, the place really went into a decline."

"Yes, that's been scaring me more than the horticultural challenges," Poppy confessed. "I mean, learning how to grow plants is one thing, but learning how to run a business is something else entirely! I'm even struggling to get on top of things like stock management and cash flow and keeping track of expenses—"

"Ah, what you need is a good accountant," said Martin.

Poppy looked at him hopefully. "Actually, that was something I wanted to ask you about. I don't suppose you could recommend anyone?"

"I could give you the name of my bloke," said Martin. "He's not exactly a barrel of laughs, but he's good at his job. Saves us a pretty packet in taxes each year, actually, and even offered us some investment advice, though we didn't have the spare cash just then to take advantage of the scheme he recommended. Shame, as it sounded really good too: a chance to buy a share in a foreign holiday home, guaranteed time in the sun each year... now wouldn't that be nice? Anyway, he lives in the village, but his office is up in Oxford. Albrecht & Son, just off St Giles. Reasonable fees too."

"He sounds perfect," said Poppy, quickly making a note on her phone. "I'll look him up."

"Now that's sorted, let's get down to the important stuff," said Martin, his eyes twinkling. "What can I get you, luv? Pint of cider? Vodka and Coke?"

"Actually, I was hoping for some dinner," said Poppy. She smiled at the publican's wife. "After the day I've had, I decided that I needed a treat—so I came straight down here to spoil myself with some of your delicious cooking."

The other woman beamed. "Aww... ta, miss. Well, you're in for a real treat tonight. There's crispy battered haddock with chunky chips, minted peas, and tartare sauce... or a really nice steak-and-ale pudding, with buttered greens and cauliflower mash... or the special tonight is roast pork chops with black pudding and beer gravy."

"It all sounds delicious. I don't know what to pick!" said Poppy with a laugh. "I think I'll go with the special and then a serving of your scrumptious apple crumble to finish?"

"And where will you be sitting, luv?" asked Martin after she had paid for her order.

"Hmm... I don't know. It all looks quite full, doesn't it?" said Poppy, turning to scan the room. She couldn't see a single empty table.

"Spot over there... if the gentleman doesn't mind sharing," said the publican, pointing to the far side of the room.

Poppy followed his finger and, at first, she thought that Martin was pointing to an empty booth in the corner. Then her eyes widened as she saw the man hunched over a glass at the deep end of the booth.

"Oh, that's Dr Seymour," she blurted.

"Yes, he's been here all afternoon," said Martin, frowning. "I'm surprised he hasn't gone home by now."

"Knowing who's waiting for him back at the house, I'm not surprised he's dawdling here," said his wife. "That sourpuss would put any man off going home."

Poppy glanced at her, surprised at the acerbic comment. "You mean Emma?"

Martin made a tutting sound. "Now, now, Abby,

you know it's not right to gossip—"

"It's not gossip; it's a fact," said his wife tartly. "That woman orders him about like a dog. 'Course, she practically bought him, so maybe she feels entitled—"

"Abby!" said Martin, looking slightly shocked.

"You know it's true," she said, giving him a look.

"What do you mean—she 'bought him'?" asked Poppy, avid with curiosity now.

Abby turned to her, eyes bright at the prospect of a new audience. "Emma Seymour comes from 'old money'. Her family is real posh—not quite Lord or Lady, but fairly close, if you know what I mean. They own a big estate in the Cotswolds and Emma's always grown up with the best. She's used to getting what she wants and the minute she laid eyes on our Ralph, that was it. Poor bugger never stood a chance."

"She's been good to him, though," protested Martin. "She was the one who put up the money for him to do the conversion and establish the GP surgery here in the village."

"She didn't do that out of the generosity of her heart," scoffed his wife. "It was just another way for her to keep control. Having him join a partnership and work at another practice where he might be away all day, mingling with pretty nurses and female doctors and other women... oh no, Emma wasn't going to have that! No, she wanted 'Rafe, darling' close so she could keep her beady eye on him and check up any time she wanted." Abby paused, then added with a smirk: "Not that it did her any good. The good doctor was having an affair right under her nose!"

Martin groaned. "Not that thing about him and Yvonne again! You can't accuse every poor sod with a pretty secretary of having an affair with her."

"There's no smoke without fire," his wife insisted. "And if you'd seen the way Yvonne behaved with him, not to mention the way Emma looked at her…! You could have cut the air with a butter knife when those two women were together."

Poppy had to agree as she thought back to the day before and the nasty little scene she had witnessed between Yvonne and Emma Seymour at the surgery. The two women had been fighting over something more than just the appropriate kind of outfit to wear to work.

"If you ask me," Abby continued, leaning confidentially towards Poppy, "the person the police should be looking at is the doctor's wife. I wouldn't be surprised if she had something to do with the murder."

"You think Emma could have killed Yvonne?" said Poppy.

"It's well known that she's a sore loser—ask anyone in the village. At our annual village fair last year, we had a Victoria sponge cake competition and Emma's submission was tipped to win, until Kate Doherty produced a cake she'd baked at the last minute. Kate's one of the girls at the chemist. Works in the dispensary," she explained to Poppy. "Well, anyway, you'd never seen such a hullabaloo when they announced the winner! Emma was screaming and shouting and insisting that the judges had deliberately side-lined her. She just couldn't accept that another woman was better than her. Well, after the contest, poor Kate got badly scalded in the tea tent when a kettle was knocked over and sloshed boiling water over her."

"That could have been an accident," said Martin.

"No, it couldn't," retorted his wife. "I was there, Martin. The kettle was sitting securely on a stand, well away from the edge of the bench. There was no way it could have been knocked over Kate—not unless someone had shoved it on purpose." She gave Poppy a meaningful look. "Several people said they were sure they saw Emma Seymour hovering near the bench just before the accident. No one wanted to come out and say it, but we all knew that she had done it to get back at Kate for winning the cake contest."

"Well, even if that's true—there's a big difference between a spiteful accident and murder," argued Martin.

"The only difference is how badly someone is hurt," said his wife sharply. "Kate was lucky she didn't end up in hospital, but she could have! Which shows that Emma wasn't afraid to be ruthless to get revenge." She turned back to Poppy. "So if she thought that Yvonne was getting her claws into her husband and there was a chance the girl might win... well, I wouldn't put it past her to do something drastic."

Poppy stared at the other woman, her mind whirling. *But would Emma Seymour have done something as drastic as murder?*

CHAPTER THIRTEEN

"Enough with the gossiping, Abby," said Martin, shooing his wife towards the kitchen door. "I'm sure Poppy didn't come in here to have her ear talked off by you."

"Oh no, I don't mind—" Poppy said quickly, but the publican's wife gave her a cheerful wave and retreated into the kitchen.

"Now, you take this number, luv, and I'll bring the food out shortly," Martin said, handing her a metal number stand and gesturing in the direction of the booth.

"Oh, but... I don't really want to disturb Dr Seymour," Poppy said.

Martin shook his head. "I'm sure he won't mind you sharing his table. In any case, he's been monopolising it long enough."

Before Poppy could protest any further, she found herself being propelled across the pub and presented to the village GP. Ralph Seymour looked up in surprise but made no objection when she was settled at the other end of the booth. When Martin had gone and left them alone, Poppy looked hesitantly at the doctor. He looked very different to when she'd last seen him. He was unshaven, with his shirt undone and his hair dishevelled. His shoulders drooped and his entire being seemed to give off an air of dejection.

Poppy felt the need to say something but wasn't sure what to say. Having been there when they found Yvonne and been with him during the police questioning, she felt that she couldn't just come out with the usual "I'm sorry for your loss" platitudes that most of the village were no doubt greeting him with. On the other hand, she didn't feel like she could say nothing and pretend that nothing had happened either.

Finally, she offered him a weak smile and said: "I hope it hasn't been too disruptive with your clinics. I mean, with cancelling the patients and stuff."

Dr Seymour shrugged. "I'm shut for the rest of the week. The whole surgery is a crime scene now. I suppose I'm lucky they haven't kicked me out of the house—not that Emma would ever allow it," he said with a humourless laugh.

They lapsed into an awkward silence again, which was only broken when the GP asked: "You're not drinking anything?"

"Oh, I'm waiting for my dinner to arrive," Poppy explained.

"The food here is very good," Dr Seymour said politely.

"Yes, it is," said Poppy, feeling slightly ridiculous to be having this inane conversation. "I'm really looking forward to it—I'm absolutely starving! It's been a long day in the nursery and I never realised how physically demanding gardening work is. My previous jobs have always been office-based—"

"Ah yes, sedentary office jobs are the evils of our modern society," said Dr Seymour, sounding more like his usual GP self. "It's something I tell all my patients. Sitting at your desk for long periods causes more health problems than anything else. I'm always encouraging people to take more breaks and find ways to include more physical activity in their day. Yvonne was marvellous at chatting to them and thinking up activities they could do. She would look up local gyms and suggest hobbies they could try or clubs they could join. I don't know what I'm going to do without her..." He sighed. "And the OAC club... I was depending on her to help. Especially now that we've got this research grant, you know?"

"Er... no, not really," said Poppy, struggling to follow him. "I'm sorry, I don't know what research grant you're talking about, Dr Seymour."

"I beg your pardon—I thought I told you about it the other day in the clinic. You see, throughout history, *Primula auriculas* have been used in many folk remedies and, among herbalists, they are renowned for their medicinal benefits. Their leaves are used in treating coughs and also as a cure for headaches, and they're also believed to have astringent, antispasmodic, and pain-relieving properties," Dr Seymour said, some colour coming back into his face and animation into his voice. "As a doctor with an interest in herbal remedies and a passion for the plants, I have long wanted to study their potential in more detail. So last year I got in touch with some of my old Oxford University contacts and managed to apply for a research grant... and I was delighted when the Oxfordshire Auricula Club was granted several hundred thousand pounds to research the plants' medicinal value!"

"Oh, congratulations," said Poppy.

"Thank you. Of course, with such a responsibility and so much funds in the club accounts, we have an obligation now to ensure that all financial records are meticulously kept. Yvonne was going to help with all that, but now she's gone—Oh God!" he said suddenly, clutching his head in his hands. "What am I going to do without her? The thought of walking into that surgery and not seeing her sitting at that desk, waiting for me..."

Poppy watched him uneasily and couldn't help thinking once more about the circulating rumours and what Abby the publican's wife had said about an affair. The arrival of the barmaid with the food was a welcome relief and she quickly tucked into her dinner, glad to have something to occupy her. She was just finishing the last delicious mouthful of apple crumble when Dr Seymour spoke again:

"Do you know if the police have picked up any new leads?"

Poppy shook her head. "It's early days yet, though," she said. "The murder was only discovered yesterday, and the investigation will have only just got going. I'm not even sure if they'll have the results of the full post-mortem yet."

Dr Seymour heaved a frustrated sigh. "That CID sergeant came to see me again this morning. They just keep asking me the same questions over and over. I've *told* the police that the note wasn't from me and I never asked Yvonne to meet me at the clinic that night, but they just don't seem to believe me! They won't listen to me either when I tell them I know what really happened—which is ridiculous because it's so obvious!"

"It is?" said Poppy in surprise.

"Of course! That sexual pervert that everyone's talking about; the peeping Tom who's been scaring women in the village—that's the real culprit! Yvonne must have fallen foul of him."

Poppy frowned. "But the door to the clinic wasn't forced, so either Yvonne opened the door to her attacker, or he arrived and went in with her. Either way, it implies that she knew him. Are you suggesting that the... er... 'sexual pervert' is someone she knew?"

Dr Seymour nodded eagerly. "Yes, it could be her boyfriend. I mean, lots of people have hidden secret sexual fetishes. Maybe Yvonne found out that her boyfriend is the one creeping around and she confronted him, and he killed her to stop her exposing him."

As if on cue, the door to the pub burst open and a young man rushed in. He looked around, a belligerent expression on his face, and his eyes narrowed as he spotted Ralph Seymour sitting with Poppy in their corner booth. Shoving people out of his way, the young man stormed across the room and loomed over them.

"What did you tell 'em, you bloody wanker?"

"I beg your pardon?" said Dr Seymour.

"Don't 'beg your pardon' me!" snarled the young man. "I'm not impressed by your fancy crap, even if Yvonne was." He leaned forwards and jabbed a finger in the doctor's face. "You killed her, didn't you? And now you're trying to put the blame on me! Yeah, that's right! You sicced the police on me! You told 'em I killed her. That's why they've been hounding me all evening, asking questions—"

"I never told the police anything about you!" cried Dr Seymour. "I mean, other than mentioning that you were Yvonne's boyfriend—"

"Bollocks to that! You told 'em I tried to hurt her!"

"Well, that's true," said Dr Seymour, showing a bit of spirit for the first time. "I saw the bruises, Bryan. I know you hit Yvonne once."

"That was an accident!" said the young man impatiently. "We were arguing, and things got out o' hand. Yvonne hit me too, you know. Gave me a right black eye, she did. But we kissed and made up later, and everything was fine." He scowled at Dr Seymour. "We wouldn't even have been fighting if it wasn't for you. So don't try to act all cool—you're nothing but a dirty old man!"

"How dare you!" cried the GP, jumping up from his seat. He swayed slightly and it was obvious that he'd been drinking more than he should have. Perhaps all the alcohol had lent him Dutch courage, because he stepped out from the booth now and faced Bryan, demanding: "Who are you calling a dirty old man?"

"You!" said Bryan nastily, shoving his face up to the doctor's. "You're old enough to be her father— yeah, that's right—and you were drooling over Yvonne like some sad dog over a juicy bone."

"How... how dare you!" spluttered Dr Seymour. "My... my feelings for Yvonne were pure and true! We had a special relationship. We... Don't you dare besmirch her memory with these filthy lies! You're the one who's the animal. You know what they say about men who have to resort to hitting women. They're inadequate little squirts who are trying to make up for something, because they lack what it takes to be a real man—"

"AAAAAAGGGHH!" Bryan let out a roar and lunged forwards, punching the doctor in the jaw.

Ralph Seymour reeled back and, for a moment, Poppy thought that he was going to collapse back into the booth; but to her surprise, the GP rallied and returned with his own swing, landing a vicious punch against the side of Bryan's head, which caused the younger man to stagger back.

"YOU BASTARD!" yelled Bryan, his face suffused with fury. "I'M GONNA KILL YOU FOR THAT!"

He rushed at the GP and, in a second, the two men were locked in a vicious tussle, kicking and punching and shouting and cursing. Poppy shrank back against the booth as their wrestling bodies slammed against the table next to her and she narrowly missed being hit by a swinging fist.

"Oy! Stop that! Stop that this minute!" shouted Martin, barrelling out from behind the bar counter.

The rest of the pub had frozen in shock for a moment, but now people sprang forwards and attempted to get between the fighting men. Finally, they managed to prise Bryan and Dr Seymour apart and hold them back as they glared at each other. The GP was bleeding from a cut lip and was sporting a black eye, and Bryan didn't look much better with a swelling on his head and what looked like a broken nose.

"That's enough from both of you!" snapped Martin, looking thoroughly fed up. "There's to be no fighting in this pub." He turned to the doctor. "You, sir, have had too much to drink. It's time you went home to sleep it off. And you—" He turned savagely towards Bryan. "I've warned you already that I'll not put up with any more of your fighting. This is the last time you're setting foot in this pub. You're banned from coming in here again."

Bryan's face turned ugly. "What? But he was the one who—"

"NOT ANOTHER WORD!" thundered Martin, raising an arm with biceps that bulged like a Christmas ham joint.

Bryan eyed him warily, then threw a sullen look at the other people around the pub. "Ah, piss off!" he said. Jerking himself free, he stumbled out of the pub.

As the door slammed shut after him, Dr Seymour swayed on his feet. Now that the adrenaline was seeping from him, his face looked grey and drawn, and he sagged against the side of the booth. Poppy sprang up in alarm and caught his arm.

"Are you all right?" she asked.

"Fine... fine... just a bit shaken," he said in a faint voice. He made a move to stand up. "I suppose I ought to be getting back home and seeing to these injuries..."

"Are you sure you're up to walking back alone?" asked Martin, eyeing the doctor worriedly. Then he glanced around the room, obviously wondering who he could ask to accompany the GP back to his house.

"I'll go with him," Poppy volunteered. "I've finished eating anyway and I don't mind."

"Well, if you're sure..." Martin gave Poppy a

grateful smile. "Thanks, luv."

Poppy turned back to Dr Seymour, who was protesting weakly: "I'm fine... fine..." and said in her best imitation of Nell's no-nonsense, maternal manner:

"Come on, Dr Seymour... let's get you home."

CHAPTER FOURTEEN

Poppy helped Dr Seymour as he limped down the lanes which wound through the village until they arrived at his house. It was well lit on the outside and she could clearly see the surgery building, with its door barred by crime-scene tape. She saw the doctor grimace as he saw it too, and he turned swiftly away from the reminder of Yvonne's murder. He led the way to his front door and Poppy waited as he fumbled in his pocket for the keys.

"I'm sorry to have spoilt your evening. The least I could do is offer you a cup of tea," Dr Seymour said with a shamefaced look at Poppy.

"Oh no, there's no need," she said. She really just wanted to bid him goodnight and leave, but it was obvious that the GP was still very drunk and she felt uncertain about abandoning him in his present condition. "Er... is your wife home? I just want to make sure that you won't be left alone."

"She should be," said Dr Seymour vaguely as he opened the door and stepped inside the house. "In fact, I'm surprised she hasn't come to the door..."

It was soon apparent why: the house was empty. Emma Seymour was nowhere to be seen.

"That's odd," said Dr Seymour, looking around, frowning. "She never said she was going out this evening."

Poppy said reluctantly, "Um... I might stay a bit, just to make sure that you're okay. Have you got a first-aid box? Oh, sorry—stupid question to ask a doctor." She laughed.

Dr Seymour gave her a glimmer of a smile. "As it happens, I do have a box of supplies..."

He led the way to the spacious modern kitchen, where he pulled a large first-aid box out of one of the cupboards. After washing his hands, he began the laborious process of dealing with his wounds. Poppy stood beside him and watched uncertainly, wincing as she saw how his hands shook when he tried to cut some gauze with a pair of scissors.

"Here—let me do that," she said impulsively, reaching out to grab the scissors before he accidentally stabbed himself. "I don't think you should be handling any sharp objects at the moment."

Hastily, she cleaned her hands with an alcohol wipe, then began attending to his wounds. Ralph

Seymour sat, meek and silent, as she cleaned away the dried blood, disinfected the cuts, and applied plasters and dressings. Despite his tall figure and silver-templed good looks, he reminded her of a young boy, happily submitting to be cared for. Poppy couldn't help thinking that the doctor was one of those men who seemed to need and want a woman to mother him all the time. *Maybe everyone's being unfair on Emma; maybe her bossy, domineering ways actually make her the perfect wife for him,* she mused.

As she turned to put everything back in the first-aid box, Poppy was dismayed to see that Ralph Seymour was crying again. The silent tears rolled down his cheeks and dripped off his chin.

"Hey..." She touched his arm gently. "It's all right—"

"No, it's not all right!" he burst out. "Yvonne is gone! Gone! I'm never going to see her again!" Then he put his face in his hands and dissolved into sobs.

Poppy shifted from foot to foot, not knowing what to do. There was something awful about watching a grown man cry, and she wasn't sure whether to soothe him with words of comfort or to offer a bit of "tough love"—or even whether she should pretend not to notice his distress at all? Finally, in desperation, she turned to the great British panacea for every problem in life.

"Er... how about a nice cup of tea?"

To her surprise, the GP responded. His sobs lessened and he raised his head from his hands.

"The... the mugs are in the cupboard over there," he said, sniffing. "The tea and sugar are in those jars on the counter, milk's in the fridge..."

Poppy busied herself making the tea and, by the time she returned to Dr Seymour with two steaming mugs of hot, milky tea, she was relieved to see that he had regained some control of himself. He sat back, his face slack and exhausted, and sipped his tea quietly for a few minutes. Then, to Poppy's astonishment, he suddenly said:

"I loved her, you know."

Poppy stared at him, not sure how to respond. There were a dozen questions on the tip of her tongue, and it was obvious that Ralph Seymour wanted to talk, but a part of her felt slightly guilty about taking advantage of his emotionally vulnerable state. On the other hand, *he* was the one who had brought the subject up...

"You mean Yvonne?" She hesitated, then asked: "Were you having an affair with her?"

Dr Seymour made a face. "An affair! That sounds so sordid. We were more than just illicit lovers. We... we were soulmates."

Poppy resisted the urge to roll her eyes. "So, did you lie to the police when you said you never sent Yvonne that note?"

"Oh no, I didn't write *that* note. I stand by that. But I did lie to the police about never meeting Yvonne after hours in the surgery," he admitted. "We did often meet there. It was the easiest place, although we had to be careful, of course, since Emma could walk in at any moment. But... er... that was part of the excitement." He flushed. "But it wasn't just about the sex. What I felt for Yvonne—what we felt for each other—it was special. She said we were meant to be; she wanted us to start a new life together."

Poppy raised her eyebrows. "You were going to leave your wife for her?"

"Yes... no..." stammered Dr Seymour. "I mean... nothing had been decided yet. Yvonne... she was pushing me to do it but I... well... I mean, I didn't want to hurt Emma either... and besides, there was the practice... all my patients... not to mention my position as the president of the OAC and..." He trailed off and made a vague gesture which took in the house around them.

Poppy hid a cynical smile, wondering if it was really consideration for his wife's feelings which had held Dr Seymour back. It might have seemed romantic to talk about running away with his young lover, but to really have done it would have meant abandoning the comfortable life he had. Without his wife's financial backing, Seymour would simply be an out-of-work GP with a demanding mistress in tow and a scandal blackening his professional reputation. No wonder he hadn't been keen to give it all up!

"Do you think Emma knew that you were planning to leave her?"

"I'm certain she didn't," said Dr Seymour, looking

horrified. "I don't think she even knew about the affair. I was always very careful around Yvonne when she was there. Besides, I begged Yvonne not to say anything to Emma before I was ready—"

"What do you mean? Surely you weren't planning to let Yvonne do your dirty work and be the one to tell your wife you wanted to leave her?" said Poppy, disgusted.

Dr Seymour flushed. "No, no, of course not! I would have told Emma myself. But Yvonne... well, she was getting impatient with me. She kept pushing and pushing... and then that morning—on the day of the murder—she said that if I didn't confess everything to Emma soon, she would tell the whole village." He clutched his head in his hands. "I didn't know what to do! It was on my mind all day and, after dinner, I went for a walk to try and sort things out—"

"Wait, didn't you tell the police that you were home all evening?"

"Oh... yes... that's right," said Dr Seymour, looking sheepish. "I... er... I suppose I told a fib."

"It wasn't just a fib. You lied about your alibi," said Poppy.

"Well, it wasn't really me," said Dr Seymour quickly. "I *was* going to tell them, then Emma cut in with that story about us watching a film on TV. I couldn't really say anything after that, could I, without contradicting her?"

Poppy flashed back to the day before, when she'd

stood listening to Suzanne Whittaker question the doctor and his wife. It was true that Emma had jumped in before her husband could answer the detective inspector's question about what he had done after dinner the night before:

"He was at home with me all evening," said Emma quickly. She gave her husband an exaggerated loving smile. "We were watching a film together... weren't we, darling?"

"Oh? What was the film, Dr Seymour?" asked Suzanne.

Ralph Seymour squirmed under her keen gaze. "It was... uh... I'm afraid I don't remember the title." He gave a nervous laugh. "I'm terrible with things like that. I can never recall the names of half the things I watch."

"What kind of film was it?" asked Suzanne. "Surely you can remember that?"

"Oh... er... it was... er—"

"A science-fiction thriller," said Emma smoothly. "You know, one of those about robots taking over the world. They've made so many similar films, it's hard to remember their names now." She gave a trill of laughter. "We weren't really watching it very closely anyway—it was just something to pass the evening."

Now Poppy looked thoughtfully at the man in front of her and wondered why his wife had been so keen to hide the fact that he had been out that night from the police. Was it to protect him? Or was it something else?

"When did you get back from your walk?" asked Poppy.

"Uh… I'm not sure. Ten-thirty… maybe eleven? To be honest with you, I lost track of the time. I was just wandering around in circles, deep in my thoughts."

"In the dark?" said Poppy sceptically.

"Oh, I know the woods behind the house very well. There are several well-worn tracks. Besides, there was a moon that night."

"It must have been freezing."

Dr Seymour shrugged. "I suppose. I was wrapped up warmly and didn't really notice."

"And you didn't notice anything odd over in the surgery building when you went past?"

"Well, the path into the woods is on the other side of the house, so I didn't really walk past the surgery. But no, there weren't any unusual lights or noises or things like that."

"What happened when you got back home? Was Emma waiting up for you?"

"No, actually. We… we'd had a bit of a row during dinner," he said, looking embarrassed. "She'd already gone to bed and I went to sleep in one of the guest bedrooms. I saw Emma at breakfast the next morning, though, and she seemed fine by then."

"Were you fighting about Yvonne?" asked Poppy delicately.

"Well, not just about Yvonne… there were… there

were other things... to do with money..." He hesitated, then burst out: "Emma treats me like a child all the time! She never thinks I can do anything on my own; she's always laughing at me and mocking me... I'm not stupid, you know! I might not be born into money like she was but I'm not completely ignorant when it comes to financial matters," he said sulkily. "I can speculate and invest too; I'd recently bought into an overseas scheme which stands to deliver great returns in the future, and in the meantime it will give us a holiday home for free—"

He broke off suddenly, looking chagrined and embarrassed. Poppy got the impression that the alcohol had loosened the doctor's tongue and now he wished that he hadn't revealed so much. She was about to say something to smooth over the awkward moment when she heard the front door opening. A minute later, Emma Seymour walked into the kitchen. She stopped short when she saw Poppy sitting with her husband at the breakfast bar and her eyes narrowed.

"Darling!" Dr Seymour sprang up. "We were wondering where you were."

"I went into town," said Emma shortly.

"Oh? You didn't say that you were meeting friends tonight."

"I wasn't. I noticed a sign for a professional restorer who specialises in garden statuary the last time I was in town, so since I had the afternoon free, I decided to take our garden gnomes down to be cleaned."

Ralph looked puzzled. "Our garden gnomes?"

"Yes, they were filthy," said Emma quickly. "Absolutely disgusting. Covered with bird poo and grime and heaven knows what. I'd been wanting to get them cleaned for ages, so this seemed as good a time as any." She paused, then continued airily, "I managed to get there just before the restorer closed at five-thirty and by the time I'd finished, I was famished. I hadn't had any tea, so I decided to have an early supper in town. There was no point rushing back anyway—I knew you were ensconced at the pub and hardly likely to be home for dinner," she added peevishly. She looked pointedly at Poppy and added: "I didn't realise that *you* were having company this evening, darling?"

"Oh! Miss Lancaster is here because she helped me home from the pub," said Dr Seymour quickly.

Emma looked at his black eye and the various plasters and swellings on his face and person. Her lips curled in disgust. "You've been in a fight."

"Just a... a disagreement with one of the village lads."

"What about?" asked Emma sharply.

"I... he... there was some misunderstanding about Yvonne—"

'You were fighting over Yvonne?" said his wife shrilly.

"No, well... I..."

Poppy stood up suddenly. She didn't want to get

caught in the middle of an ugly domestic quarrel, and besides, she was very tired and really longing for her bed now.

"Well, I'd better be off," she said brightly. She turned towards the kitchen door but found Emma barring her way.

"So you helped Ralph home from the pub? That was nice of you," said Emma. It should have been a expression of thanks, but instead, it came across as a sneer.

Poppy felt her temper prickle. She'd had enough of Emma Seymour's attitude. The woman had been incredibly rude so far, making no effort to greet Poppy when she'd arrived home, and was now even eyeing her with jealous suspicion.

"Yes, I happened to be sitting near Dr Seymour at the pub," said Poppy evenly. "He'd suffered quite a few injuries in the fight, and Martin the pub owner was looking for someone to help him home, so I volunteered. Dr Seymour had had a bit too much to drink and, since you weren't home, I didn't think it was a good idea for him to be alone in his condition. But now that you're here, I can leave him to your tender loving care," she said sarcastically.

Then, with her head held high, Poppy swept past the woman and stalked out of the house.

CHAPTER FIFTEEN

Poppy fumed as she walked down the lanes, heading back across the village to Hollyhock Cottage. *The gossips are right,* she thought. *Emma Seymour is an absolute cow! I've never met such a jealous, mean-spirited, rude woman in my life!*

Then another thought made her pause. *Are the village gossips right about something else? Could Emma Seymour be a murderous cow as well?* The GP's wife certainly had motive. Jealousy of a romantic rival might have been a cliché, but things became clichés for a reason. Emma wouldn't have been the first woman—nor the last—who resorted to murder to hang on to her man. What if Ralph Seymour had been wrong and Emma did know about Yvonne's attempts to force a divorce? Or maybe Yvonne had ignored the doctor's pleas and told

Emma about their affair, plus the plan to leave, just out of spite? Poppy thought of the scene she had witnessed at the GP surgery two days ago: it had been obvious that Yvonne enjoyed taunting Emma and showing off her hold over the doctor.

In either case, the thought of losing her husband to the other woman might have been enough to tip Emma over the edge. After all, according to the village gossips, she was already no stranger to using violence to exact revenge on a rival. And maybe the murder hadn't even been intentional. Maybe the two women had got into a heated argument and Emma had lashed out, hitting Yvonne on the head with whatever had come to hand...

The vase that had been holding the lilies! thought Poppy suddenly. Could that have been the murder weapon? It made sense: Emma herself had brought the lilies into the waiting room—so the vase would have probably been one of the first things she thought of when she was reaching for something to hit Yvonne with. It would explain why the vase had been smashed to pieces: not because it had been knocked off the desk and fallen to the floor, but because it had been deliberately whacked against the back of the girl's head.

Poppy frowned. But surely the police would have tested the vase fragments found at the crime scene? In which case, they should have found forensic evidence tying it to the killing. The fact that they were still searching for the murder weapon suggested that the vase hadn't been involved in the crime...

Poppy was interrupted in her musings by the sight of something further down the lane in front of her. She frowned, straining her eyes to see. There were few streetlights in the village, so the lane was mostly in shadow, but the moon was bright enough for her to make out the figure of an old man, hunched over and moving furtively, as if he were following something or someone.

It's Bertie! Poppy realised with some surprise. She quickened her steps until she had caught up with him and tapped him on the shoulder.

"Bertie! What are you doing?" she asked, keeping her voice low.

The old inventor swung around, and his face lit up as he saw her. "Poppy, my dear—fancy meeting you here!" he said, as if they were meeting at a local tearoom and not skulking down a village lane in the middle of the night.

"What are you doing, Bertie?"

"Ah... I am on the trail of a thief," said the old man with a smile. He pointed further down the lane and Poppy followed his finger just in time to see the end of an orange-striped tail disappear around a corner. Realisation dawned on her.

"You're following Oren?"

Bertie nodded eagerly. "Yes. You see, I believe that he is the one responsible for stealing those bras."

"Oren?" Poppy said incredulously. "But... why on earth would a cat want to steal bras?"

"Cats are known for stealing all sorts of things. It's a phenomenon known as 'feline kleptomania'," Bertie explained. "There have been news stories about it: cats roaming all over the neighbourhood and stealing shoes and stuffed toys and socks and even things like kitchen sponges. So, why not lingerie too?"

"But..."

"So I've fitted Oren's collar with a tracker," Bertie continued eagerly. "This enables me to monitor his movements. If I can catch Oren in the act, then I will have proof that will help Nick. The police will have to release him because I will have found the real culprit!"

"But how are you going to catch Oren in the act?" Poppy asked.

"By following him," said Bertie. He beckoned urgently. "Come on! We're going to lose him if we don't hurry!"

"Wait, Bertie—"

Poppy found herself speaking to empty air as the old inventor trotted off and disappeared around the corner. She hurried after him and, a few minutes later, found herself crawling through a hedge, wondering if she had gone completely mad.

"Bertie... wait..." she gasped, trying to keep up as the old inventor pushed through a thick clump of leaves and stems and disappeared.

She couldn't believe how fast Bertie could move for an elderly man. It took her another few moments to fight free of the hedge and, as she stood up on the other side, she brushed herself off while looking around. She was standing in a large garden with carefully tended herbaceous borders running down either side of a lawn that had been clipped with ruler-like precision. Even the plants in the beds looked like they had been positioned to all face the same way.

"Wow," muttered Poppy. Despite the neat perfection, she found this garden off-putting after being used to the wild, rambling profusion of the garden beds at Hollyhock Cottage.

She took a few hesitant steps forwards, peering around, trying to see where Bertie had gone. Then she spotted him: he was just darting around one corner of the house on the far side of the garden. Poppy took a deep breath, then scurried across the darkened lawn, feeling horribly exposed. When she finally reached the other side and made her way around the house, Poppy found herself in a small courtyard where a large rotary clothesline had been erected. She nearly careened into Bertie—the old inventor had stopped abruptly just beside the wall of the house.

"Bertie! We shouldn't be here," Poppy hissed. "We're trespassing and if we get caught—"

"Shhh!" Bertie admonished her, putting a finger to his lips. "We don't want to put him off."

Poppy looked over his shoulder to see Oren sitting underneath the rotary clothesline, with its spider's web of washing lines stretched across the umbrella-shaped frame. He was gazing up at several garments pegged to the lines, the tip of his tail flicking and twitching on the ground. Then, suddenly, the ginger tom leapt up with astonishing athleticism and pulled himself onto the central pole of the rotary clothesline. Balancing gracefully, he walked down one of the radial arms until he reached the section where a flimsy cotton bra was pegged to the line and fluttering in the breeze.

As Poppy watched in disbelief, Oren reached down with one paw and caught the peg with his claws, then jerked upwards with expert timing. The peg popped free and the bra fell to the ground. Instantly, Oren followed, landing nimbly next to the fallen undergarment. With a chirp of satisfaction, he picked up the bra between his teeth and turned away, stumbling slightly over the long straps and walking almost bowlegged as he dragged it across the stone tiles of the courtyard.

Poppy made a convulsive movement. "We've got to stop him! We can't let him steal another bra—"

"No, no, my dear," said Bertie, grabbing hold of her arm and restraining her. "We need to let Oren complete his theft so we can get the proof."

"Proof?"

"Yes, I've fitted a micro-camera to his collar as well as the tracker," Bertie explained. "It should get some excellent footage and, if we can show Oren stealing the bra from the clothesline, then carrying it back to Nick's house and hiding it under his bed... well, then we'd have enough evidence to show the police and prove that Nick isn't the bra thief."

"Yes, but what if Oren doesn't go straight home? We can't—"

Poppy broke off as a voice could suddenly be heard, coming from within the house. She glanced urgently at the windows nearest to them. They had been dark but now they transformed suddenly into rectangular oblongs of light. She hunched instinctively, before realising with relief that the windows were frosted and unlikely to give a clear view of the outside area. Someone was definitely moving around in there, though, and as the voice drifted out again, clearer this time, Poppy froze. She recognised that booming tone:

"... yes, we must discuss that at the next meeting but—look, can I ring you back, Edna? I just realised that I'd forgotten to bring my washing in, and I must go out to fetch it... certainly not! I never leave anything hanging outside overnight and neither should you... what if it rains?... Well, all right, in summer perhaps, but at this time of the year... no, no, don't call him yet—I told you we have to discuss it at the next meeting first—"

Poppy turned urgently to Bertie and tugged his sleeve. "We need to get out of here!" she hissed. "That sounds like—"

"Oh dear, he's dropped it," said Bertie, obviously not listening to a word she'd said.

His eyes were glued on Oren, who had indeed dropped the bra. The orange tomcat circled the undergarment, eyeing it speculatively, as if trying to decide how to pick up and carry a particularly difficult prey. Poppy had to resist the urge to run over, snatch up the bra, and return it to the clothesline. Instead, she glanced warily at the house again and gave Bertie's sleeve another tug.

"Bertie, come on," she pleaded. "We need to go. It's fine if Oren is seen—he's just a cat—but if we're found skulking around—"

A sudden metallic banging sound made her jerk her head around. Oren had somehow managed to pick up the bra again and had scrambled up the wall around one side of the courtyard. One of the bra straps, however, had looped around the handle of a large, galvanised metal dustbin sitting alongside the wall. Now, as the ginger tom yanked on the strap with his teeth, trying to tug the bra free, the entire metal bin was jerked repeatedly against the wall, thudding against it with rhythmic metallic bangs.

"Shhh! Oren, stop that!" hissed Poppy, jumping up in a panic and running over to the cat.

The ginger tom paused for a moment and looked innocently at her. "N-ow?" he said.

"Yes, now!" said Poppy in exasperation. "You're making too much noise!"

Oren ignored her and started tugging on the bra once more. Poppy reached up to seize the bra strap and pull the garment out of the cat's reach. Oren batted her hands with his paws, trying to grab the bra strap back from her, then suddenly he gathered himself and lunged, pouncing on her hand and rolling into a ball, kicking frenziedly with his back feet.

"Ow! Oren!" cried Poppy involuntarily as his claws raked across her skin.

She jerked her hand back in a reflex action, then gasped as the movement caused her to reel backwards and lose her balance. With a squeak of dismay, she tumbled over and crashed into the dustbin, which was empty and fell onto its side with a resounding metallic BOOM that seemed to echo through the whole village.

Oh no... Poppy groaned.

Bertie hurried over to her side and bent over her with concern. "My dear! Are you all right?"

Poppy sat up shakily. "Yes, I think so..." She saw the bra on the ground next to her and snatched it up, shoving it at Bertie. "Quick! Put this back on the line and let's get out of here!"

To her relief, Bertie didn't argue but took the bra and trotted off to the rotary clothesline. Poppy got painfully to her feet, then she froze as she heard the sound of hurrying footsteps, of locks and bolts turning. The next moment, the back door of the house was flung open, spilling light into the courtyard.

"Who's there?" demanded the familiar booming voice.

Poppy nearly groaned out loud as Mrs Busselton marched out of the house, her hair arranged in rollers around her head and her body wrapped to the neck in a pink flannel housecoat. She gave a screech of outrage and stopped in her tracks, her eyes bulging as she stared at the rotary clothesline. Poppy, following the direction of her gaze, felt her heart sink.

Bertie was standing underneath the web of clotheslines, holding the huge white cotton bra. She knew that he must have been trying to peg the item back up, but unfortunately it also looked like he had been caught in the act of taking the bra off the line.

"What are you doing to my brassiere?" screeched Mrs Busselton, advancing on him like a pink flannel battleship.

Bertie blinked at her. "Me? I'm simply hanging it back up—"

"How dare you!" shrieked Mrs Busselton. "You're just like your son—a filthy, thieving sex pervert!"

"My dear lady, I must correct you there. Perversion is defined as a type of behaviour that deviates from the normal—but it all depends on your definition of 'normal', you know," said Bertie, sounding like he was back in Oxford University, giving one of his tutorials. "What we consider to be perversion may be perfectly acceptable in other countries or other times in history. For example, Cleopatra married her own brother—something that was perfectly acceptable at the time. In fact, the subjective nature of this definition is the topic of one of Freud's essays on the theory of sexuality. He

believed that perversion in childhood was the norm—
"

"What?" cried Mrs Busselton. "Are you trying to tell me that perverts are normal?"

"Well, as I explained, it all depends on the time and place. You yourself might be doing some things which other people would consider perverted," Bertie explained.

Mrs Busselton's face went beetroot red and her bosom swelled in outrage. "ME? HOW DARE YOU!"

"Oh, there was no criticism implied, dear lady," Bertie assured her. "We academics don't judge. We simply study. And there is so much to learn in this field, such a fascinating diversification of inclinations in the human experience! Things like foot fetishism, exhibitionism, hermaphroditism, necrophilia—"

"I'm... I'm going to call the police!" Mrs Busselton spluttered, her chest heaving.

"No, wait!" cried Poppy, rushing out from where she had been watching, horrified, in the shadows.

Mrs Busselton faltered, looking incredulously at Poppy. "Where did you come from?"

"I was standing over there; you didn't see me when you came out... I came with Bertie—I mean, Dr Noble. We were following the cat, you see. The big ginger tom who belongs to Nick Forrest. He's the one who took your bra off the clothesline. Dr Noble was telling the truth. He was just putting it back."

Mrs Busselton looked suspiciously around, then gave Poppy a hard look. "I don't see any cat."

Poppy glanced around and saw with a sinking heart that the wall which Oren had been sitting on was now empty. The ginger tom had obviously taken advantage of the distraction from Mrs Busselton's arrival to jump over the wall and disappear, leaving her and Bertie to face the music.

Grrr. Typical cat, thought Poppy, grinding her teeth.

She turned back to Mrs Busselton and took a deep breath. "He must have run off. But it's true, Mrs Busselton, I swear. Oren was the one who removed the bra from your washing line." She gave the woman her most ingratiating smile. "The whole thing has been a dreadful misunderstanding. But it's all cleared up now and no harm done..."

Reaching out, Poppy grabbed Bertie's arm and started edging away, still talking manically: "You must be freezing, Mrs Busselton! Why don't you head back into the warmth of the house, and Dr Noble and I will be off as well... Have a lovely evening. Good night!"

CHAPTER SIXTEEN

Poppy awoke the next morning to find Oren sitting at the foot of her bed, watching her with an unblinking yellow stare.

"I don't believe it!" she said, sitting up in bed and glowering at the orange tomcat. "Do you know how much trouble you caused last night? Bertie and I nearly ended up in a police cell because of you. Stop looking so smug or I'll wipe that smirk off your whiskers!"

Oren gave her a cheeky look. "*N-ow?*"

Poppy grinned reluctantly. It was hard to stay cross with the orange tomcat for long. "So where did you go for the rest of the night?" she asked him. "I hope you didn't steal any more bras from another house!"

Oren gave a disdainful twitch of his whiskers.

Then he jumped off the bed and trotted to the bedroom door, where he paused and looked over his shoulder. *"N-ow? N-ow?"* he said.

Poppy frowned as she realised that the cat was hungry and wanted his breakfast. Which meant that Nick hadn't come back yet; he was still being held at the police station.

I need to speak to the police and tell them my suspicions about Emma, she thought. *They can't just keep focusing on Nick when there's someone else with a much better motive!*

She got up and hurried to wash and dress, then went across to Nick's house with Oren trotting beside her, complaining loudly about his late breakfast. As she went to get his special diet food out of the cupboard, Poppy's gaze fell on the calendar hanging on the kitchen wall. In the empty space under the day's date, she could see "VET VISIT" scrawled in Nick's bold handwriting and she suddenly recalled the crime author telling her that Oren was due for his veterinary follow-up that morning.

"I suppose I'd better take you," she said to the ginger tom, who was circling his food bowl.

"N-ow!" Oren said, eyeing the empty bowl pointedly. *"N-OW!"*

"All right, all right, Your Majesty!" said Poppy, rolling her eyes.

A couple of hours later, Poppy set off for the vet with Oren in tow. She was worried that they would be late for their appointment, as it had taken her longer than she'd expected to catch Oren and wrestle him into his cage. While the ginger tom had been too much of a gentleman to use his teeth or claws on her, he had still struggled and resisted with all his might, leaving her out of breath and more than a little dishevelled by the time she finally bundled him into her car and started on the road for Oxford.

Thank goodness Nell's cleaning jobs are in the evening today and she has most of the day off, Poppy thought as she negotiated the roads leading to the university city. Her friend had offered to look after the nursery until she returned and Poppy had gratefully accepted. Aside from enabling her to take Oren to the vet, she was secretly glad of the chance to have a break from answering the incessant questions about Yvonne's murder.

But it seemed that she wasn't going to get away from reminders of the murder that easily. After she'd staggered into the vet's reception, lugging Oren in his cat carrier, and was directed to a seat in the waiting room, she found a familiar face in the chair next to her.

"Oh... hello," said the dowdy middle-aged woman, looking up and recognising Poppy as well. She beamed and said chattily, "We met at Dr Seymour's surgery, didn't we? You're the girl who runs the garden nursery."

Poppy returned her smile. "Yes, that's right. I'm Poppy Lancaster. And you are... Miss Payne?"

The woman's smile widened. "Yes, I'm Adeline

Payne. How nice of you to remember!"

"It was a pretty memorable day," Poppy said with a grimace. "I don't think I'm going to forget it in a hurry, especially as I've had to go over and over it for the police."

Miss Payne's face clouded. "Yes, I keep thinking how awful it was that we were all sitting there, chatting, with that poor girl at her desk nearby... and then a few hours later, she was dead!"

"Have the police questioned you?" asked Poppy.

"Oh yes. I tried to tell them everything I could remember, but I don't know how much help I was. Well, you don't think of noticing things, do you, when you're just out and about normally? If you knew there was going to be a murder later, then you'd pay extra attention so you could pick up a clue to give to the police," said the other woman ingenuously. She gave a sigh. "Poor Dr Seymour. I wonder what he's going to do now?"

"Well, I suppose, eventually, he'll have to find a new practice manager," said Poppy. "And in the meantime, his wife could probably help him out at the surgery."

Miss Payne's lips curled. "His wife? She never thinks of anyone but herself. She's always out gallivanting about at all sorts of hours."

"What do you mean?"

"The night the murder happened—I saw her driving out of the village. My cottage is at the end of the lane, just at the edge of the village, and the road that leads in and out of Bunnington runs past my back garden. I can see the cars going past beyond the hedge if I look out of my kitchen windows," Miss Payne explained.

Poppy wondered how much time the woman spent peering out, spying on other residents of the village.

As if she'd read Poppy's thoughts, Miss Payne said, slightly defensively, "I happened to be at the sink that night, filling my kettle, when I looked out and saw a car going past: Emma Seymour was at the wheel." She pursed her lips. "She was driving too fast, if you ask me. People really need to slow down when they're driving in the village."

"But Emma told the police that she was home all evening," said Poppy. "She said she was watching a film with Dr Seymour..." She trailed off as she suddenly remembered that the doctor himself hadn't been at home. He had gone out after dinner for a walk and hadn't returned until around midnight. And he had said that he'd slept in the guest bedroom and hadn't seen his wife until breakfast the next morning. All of which meant that he was in no position to confirm if his wife had really been home all evening...

Poppy realised that Miss Payne was speaking to her and she snapped out of her reverie. "Sorry," she said, giving the other woman an apologetic smile. "My mind wandered for a moment."

"I was just asking what your cat's name was," said the other woman, looking curiously at Oren in his cat carrier. "He's very well behaved."

After protesting loudly during the entire drive, Oren had gone curiously quiet since they'd arrived at the veterinary clinic. Poppy leaned over to peer into the carrier. The ginger tom had settled down with his front paws tucked under his chest and was now occupying himself making nasty faces at an unfortunate golden retriever on the other side of the room.

"Oren's not actually my cat, and he's not usually so docile either," said Poppy with a chuckle. "He's a real troublemaker; he's probably just biding his time while he thinks up some new mischief. He belongs to Nick Forrest the crime author," she explained. "Nick lives in the property next to Hollyhock Cottage and he's... er... busy this morning, so I'm just helping out by bringing Oren in for his check-up."

She glanced at the small cardboard box the other woman was holding on her lap. It was very still and silent, and she couldn't imagine what sort of animal would fit in there. It looked too small even for a mouse. "Um... is that your...?"

"It's my slug," said Miss Payne.

Poppy blinked. "Your... your slug?"

"Yes, I found him in a head of cabbage I'd bought at the market and decided to keep him as a pet."

"Oh... right." Poppy was slightly at a loss for words. "Er... do they... do slugs make good pets?"

"Well, they might not be as sweet or beautiful as more conventional pets, but I think they're very underrated," said Miss Payne defensively. "Slugs have a lot of love to give, you know."

Poppy fought down the urge to laugh and asked politely, "Have you given him a name?"

"Yes, I call him Solly—short for Solomon," said the woman. "Would you like to see him?" Proudly, she lifted the lid of the box and Poppy peered in to see a slimy brown slug stretched across a soggy lettuce leaf.

"Er... he's... um... lovely," said Poppy.

Miss Payne beamed. "I think so too. But I thought he looked slightly unwell this morning, so I wanted the vet to have a look at him and advise me on his diet. I mean, I've been supplying Solly with lettuce leaves and some cucumber, but I wonder if he needs a more varied diet?" She looked keenly at Poppy. "You must have seen slugs in that cottage garden of yours. What do they eat?"

Poppy gave a snort of laughter. "Everything! Including all my new seedlings. Maybe you should try growing some seedlings just for Solly to munch on," she said jokingly.

Miss Payne's face brightened. "That's not a bad idea! I will ask the vet what he thinks. He's so lovely, Dr Russell—he's always so patient and he doesn't mind if I have lots of things to ask him."

Poppy wished she could see the vet's face when Solly the slug went in for his consultation. She also couldn't help remembering Emma Seymour's cruel words about Miss Payne attempts to bolster her meagre social life. Perhaps the woman—having been denied access to Ralph Seymour's kindly attention since the GP clinic was closed until further notice—was now looking for others to take his place? Rather cynically, Poppy wondered if—aside from the vet—a host of dentists, chiropractors, podiatrists, and other health professionals would soon be getting a visit from the lonely spinster...

The woman and her strange pet were soon forgotten, though, when Oren was called in for his turn. Poppy watched as the vet examined the ginger tom with expert hands.

"Hmm... looks like the diet is working well. He's in excellent condition. I think Oren can go back to his normal food, provided he has controlled portions and is not fed too many other treats," said the vet.

"Oh, Nick will be glad to hear that," said Poppy. Then, feeling that she needed to explain, she added, "I'm his neighbour. Nick couldn't come this morning; he's... er... busy."

"Yes, I saw the news. I believe Mr Forrest is helping the police with their enquiries?" said the vet tactfully.

"Yes, that's right." Poppy hesitated, then, on an impulse, began telling the vet the reason Nick was being detained at the police station. "...it's ridiculous for the police to think that Nick could be some kind of sexual predator," she concluded. "But I suppose it *is* a fact that there was a pile of bras found under his bed and he had no idea how they got there." She paused and looked at the vet earnestly. "Do you think Oren could be responsible?"

He raised his eyebrows. "I beg your pardon?"

"Well, Nick's father—Dr Noble—he thinks that it's actually Oren who's been going around the village and nicking the bras from people's washing lines. He says that it's common for cats to steal things and bring them home... is that true? He said it's called 'feline kleptomania'."

"Ah yes, Dr Noble is quite right," said the vet. "Feline kleptomania is a well-documented phenomenon. And in fact, thinking about it, it might not be surprising, given the recent changes to Oren's diet."

"What do you mean?"

"Well, no one really knows the cause of feline kleptomania, but it has been suggested that stresses like a change in the cat's environment or his diet could be a trigger for the behaviour. It's really a form of misplaced predatory instinct, you see." The vet looked thoughtful. "If you like, I can give the police a ring and tell them that I fully support the suggestion."

"Oh, that would be great!" said Poppy. "I'm sure that'll help Nick."

The vet turned back to Oren, who had wriggled free and leapt from the examination table onto the counter along the wall. He was busy poking his nose amongst the various tools and containers there, and paused now beside a large glass jar full of chicken jerky treats.

"*N-ow?*" said the ginger tom, pawing the lid of the jar and looking at them expectantly. "*N-OW?*"

The vet chuckled. "Is it just me or does Oren always sound like he's saying '*Now*'?"

"Oh, I always think so too!" cried Poppy, delighted to have found someone who shared her thoughts. "That was the first thing I noticed when I met him— I've never known another cat to sound like that."

"It *is* quite unusual," said the vet, smiling. He went over to the counter and addressed the cat. "Well, I suppose you're allowed a treat to celebrate the end of your diet, Oren. And let's hope being back on the old food will keep you out of trouble!"

He fed the ginger tom a piece of chicken jerky, then turned back to Poppy. "While Oren's here, I'd like to give his teeth a clean. He'll need to be lightly sedated, and it'll take a few hours. Would you be able to leave him for a bit and come back to pick him up later?"

"Okay, I'll just go and mooch around Oxford, then," said Poppy. "Actually, I know—I might go and visit the University Botanic Gardens! I've heard so much about it and haven't had a chance to visit yet."

"Oh, definitely worth a visit," agreed the vet. "It was the first botanic garden in the United Kingdom, you know, and even if you're not a keen gardener, it's a beautiful place to walk around."

"Well, I *am* a keen gardener," said Poppy, chuckling. "So it sounds perfect!"

CHAPTER SEVENTEEN

Half an hour later, Poppy walked through the majestic arched entrance of the Oxford University Botanic Gardens and sighed with delight at the beautiful grounds stretching out in front of her. She quickly realised, though, that the time she had was nowhere near enough to explore the Garden's many treasures. She peeked into the Rock Garden, created with sandstone from a local quarry and filled with Mediterranean species, then marvelled at the Gin Border, where plants used to flavour alcohol were grown, before glancing into the Glasshouses, filled with exotic species, and browsing the fascinating beds titled "Plants That Changed the World", which showcased botanical species that had played crucial roles in providing medicines, food, dyes, fibres, and more, in human civilisations across the globe...

The one place she lingered over was the

Herbaceous Border, which was designed to provide a classic example of the traditional English garden, and featured many of the plants found in her own gardens at Hollyhock Cottage. Like her own gardens, too, it wasn't yet at its best—the herbaceous perennials planted in the border really peaked in the summer months—but it was still a beautifully designed bed to admire. Besides, even without many of the plants being in bloom, there was colour everywhere from the swathes of spring bulbs scattered around the Garden: vibrant crocuses and delicate scilla, and cheerful daffodils mingled with fragrant hyacinths.

Finally, a rumbling tummy and thirsty throat forced Poppy to curb her explorations. She still hadn't seen the Walled Garden, the Water Garden, the Orchard, or the Herbarium, and she promised herself she would return soon for another visit. Leaving the Botanic Gardens, she wandered back up the High Street towards central Oxford in search of refreshment. This she found in a quaint little café in the Covered Market, a wonderful labyrinth of traditional shops and quirky boutiques, sandwiched alongside cake shops, cookie stalls, bakeries, and restaurants, right in the heart of the university city.

She had a simple but hearty lunch of home-made soup with crusty bread, followed by a pot of tea and a plate of warm, buttery scones. Then—mindful of the time—she hurried back towards the north of the city, where the veterinary clinic was located. She was just about to cross St Giles, one of the main roads leading out of Oxford, when she paused in her tracks. A sign above an office further down the street had caught her eye. It read: "Albrecht & Son | Chartered Accountants".

Poppy frowned. The name seemed somehow familiar... Then she remembered: Albrecht & Son was the accountancy firm that Martin the pub owner had recommended. *I'm here. I might as well pop in and see if I can make an appointment,* she thought, heading towards the sign. A few minutes later, she presented herself to the middle-aged woman sitting behind a desk in the dark, wood-panelled reception office.

"Hello," she said, smiling. "I'm interested in hiring an accountant and I was recommended Mr Albrecht."

"Well, the elder Mr Albrecht is not taking on any new clients, but you can see the younger Mr Albrecht if you like. He has taken over most of the management of the firm now." The woman glanced down at a desk diary. "He's away on business in Majorca next week, but I believe he's available the week after that—"

They were interrupted by a door to an inner office opening and a thin, middle-aged man stepped out. He was wearing a sombre grey suit, which seemed slightly at odds with his paisley-patterned waistcoat and goatee. Poppy recognised him as the man she had seen perched on the edge of Yvonne's desk when she had come out of the inner consulting room. Dr

Seymour had called him "Tim"—he was the Treasurer of the Oxfordshire Auricula Society, she recalled—and she had a vague memory of a dour, quiet man who hadn't made much of an impression.

He came towards the receptionist's desk saying: "Connie, can you see if the—" Then he broke off as he recognised Poppy.

"Hello," said Poppy. "We met at Dr Seymour's surgery."

"Yes, that's right." He offered a cool handshake. "I'm Tim Albrecht."

"I'm Poppy Lancaster. I own Hollyhock Gardens and Nursery, in the village. That's why I'm here, actually." She gave him a friendly smile. "I need an accountant to help me with my business and you were highly recommended."

Tim Albrecht didn't respond to her smile, only saying in a colourless voice: "I will look after you to the best of my abilities, Miss Lancaster. My secretary, Connie, will make an appointment for me to have a preliminary look at your business accounts."

"Er... thanks," said Poppy, slightly taken aback by his manner. She wasn't sure that she wanted such a cold, humourless man as her accountant!

Albrecht didn't say anything further, simply stood there looking at her, and—more to fill the awkward silence than anything else—Poppy blurted: "I'm sorry about what happened... With Yvonne, I mean. You must be very upset."

The accountant stiffened. He glanced at his receptionist, who was busy taking a call and not listening to their conversation. Nevertheless, he took Poppy's elbow and guided her to the other side of the room, so that they were out of earshot.

"It is certainly a tragic turn of events," he said with pompous gravity. "But as for personal distress—I would not say that I am greatly affected. After all, I only had a superficial acquaintance with Miss Nash."

"Really? I got the impression when I saw you two together in the surgery that day..."

"Yes?" said Albrecht quickly. "What impression did you get, Miss Lancaster?"

Poppy shrugged. "Just that you seemed to have a more... um, personal relationship."

Tim Albrecht drew himself to his full height. "I assure you that you were mistaken. My relationship with Miss Nash was purely business-related. Or club-related, I should say. As you are aware, I am the Treasurer of the Oxfordshire Auricula Club and Miss Nash was assisting us with some of the administrative duties. I... we were discussing the minutes from the last committee meeting."

"Oh. I suppose I must have got the wrong end of the stick. It's just that you were sitting on her desk and you seemed to be talking with a lot of... er... emotion. I thought you were closer than business acquaintances."

Albrecht's face took on an even more austere expression. "Both Miss Nash and I took our responsibilities within the club very seriously. You probably saw us in an earnest discussion about some point that was raised during the committee meeting."

Poppy wondered why the accountant was being so defensive. She thought back once again to the day she had seen him with Yvonne at the GP surgery. He had been leaning down towards the practice manager, talking in an urgent, passionate way, and had looked almost furtive when he jumped up and moved away from her desk when the inner door had opened. Poppy recalled the expression of frustrated embarrassment on his face and had a sudden thought: had Tim Albrecht been trying to convince Yvonne to go out with him?

She looked at him with new eyes as her imagination began running away with her. What if Albrecht had also been obsessed with Yvonne? What if he had been trying, time and time again, to get her to accept his advances? Maybe he'd got tired of being rejected by her... maybe he'd tricked her into meeting him at the surgery and then tried to force his attentions on her... And maybe when she had struggled and fought back, he had lashed out and killed her by mistake? It wouldn't be the first time that a frustrated, snubbed man had used aggression on a woman...

Something of her thoughts must have shone on her face because Albrecht said angrily:

"Whatever your sordid mind is thinking, Miss

Lancaster, I can assure you that you are wrong. There was nothing personal in the nature of my relationship with Miss Nash."

Poppy flushed, embarrassed to have been caught out, and stammered, "I'm sorry. I didn't mean... um... So do you have any idea who might have wished to harm Yvonne?"

Albrecht shrugged. "As I said, my dealings with Miss Nash were confined to OAC business. I have no idea nor any interest in what she did in her personal life."

"And you didn't see her that evening in the village pub? I was told that you live in Bunnington too."

"No, I did not go to the pub that evening. I spent the evening alone at home, with a good book and a glass of port." He glanced impatiently at his watch. "Now if you'll excuse me, Miss Lancaster, I'm extremely busy. I wish you good day."

Poppy watched him retreat into his inner office. How ever much Tim Albrecht might protest, she was sure that he wasn't telling the whole truth about his dealings with Yvonne. She hadn't imagined the tension in the waiting room that day at the GP surgery, nor the wariness in Albrecht's manner now.

He's hiding something, she thought as she stepped out of the accountant's office back onto the street. The question was... was his prickly reaction due to embarrassment over someone witnessing him being rejected? Or was it defensiveness to cover up something much more sinister?

CHAPTER EIGHTEEN

It was early afternoon when Poppy finally arrived back in Bunnington and she was surprised to see several uniformed policemen walking around the village green. In fact, half the village seemed to be out, with groups of people milling around excitedly, watching the policemen and gossiping amongst themselves.

What's going on? Poppy wondered, slowing down as she drove past the green and peering out the window. The policemen seemed to be fanning out into the lanes leading away from the green and making a stop at each house, where they spoke to each owner briefly before entering their gardens and poking around the beds. *What on earth are they doing?*

Poppy arrived back in her cul-de-sac, parked her

car, carried the cat carrier into Nick's house, and let a sleepy Oren out. She watched as the ginger tom sauntered into Nick's study and jumped up into the crime author's chair, where he curled into a large, furry, orange ball. It looked like Oren was settling down to sleep off the rest of his sedative.

Satisfied that the tomcat would be fine, Poppy left the house and hurried to Hollyhock Cottage. She was disappointed to find the nursery gardens empty of customers, although it was hardly surprising given the excitement on the village green. Nell was hovering over the rows of potted plants on display, moistening their compost with a watering can. She looked up as Poppy approached and said:

"My lordy Lord, Poppy, you've been gone ages! I got your text saying that the vet wanted to clean Oren's teeth, but I didn't think it would take so long. Was there a problem?"

"Sorry, Nell! No, everything was fine. I had to wait a few hours while they sedated Oren and did his teeth, so I took the chance to visit the University Botanic Gardens. Then I saw a sign for the accountant that Martin had recommended, so I thought I' pop in and make an appointment. But I'm sorry—I didn't mean to keep you waiting so long!"

Nell waved a hand. "That's all right. I wasn't planning to go anywhere. I was just getting a bit worried." She leaned forwards, her eyes gleaming. "You've been missing all the excitement, dear! The police are in Bunnington, searching for the murder weapon that was used to kill Yvonne."

"Oh! I wondered why there were so many policemen in the village." Poppy looked at her friend eagerly. "So they've worked out what the murder weapon is?"

Nell nodded excitedly. "I heard from Mrs Peabody this morning that they believe it could be a garden gnome."

"A *garden gnome*?" Poppy gave an incredulous laugh. "You're joking, aren't you?"

"Oh no, it fits what the forensic team have found. They know that Yvonne was hit on the head by a heavy, blunt object. Apparently, the autopsy found flakes of red paint in her head wound and they matched that to the kind of outdoor acrylic paint commonly used to paint garden gnome hats. The depression in her skull would match up to the end of a gnome too. So now the police are hunting through the entire village. They believe the murder weapon came from here and may still be hidden here."

"Wow..." Poppy digested this for a moment. "But surely they don't think the murderer would have been stupid enough to use a garden gnome from their own garden?"

"Oh no, he probably stole it from someone else's garden. Goodness knows, there are enough garden gnomes around." Nell waved a hand.

That's true, thought Poppy, recalling her walk to the GP surgery and all the houses she had looked at on the way. There had certainly been many garden beds sporting the little red-capped and bearded ceramic figures.

"I think the police are going house-to-house and asking people to check their gnomes and see if any are missing," said Nell.

"How's that going to help, though?" asked Poppy sceptically. "I mean, even if they find a garden with a missing gnome, they won't know who stole it."

"The property might have security cameras," Nell suggested. "Or maybe the owners can tell the police if anyone's temporarily removed one of their gnomes, such as for cleaning—"

"Cleaning!" Poppy whirled around to her startled friend. "You just reminded me! Last night when I took Dr Seymour back to his house, he was surprised to find that his wife wasn't home. She came back while I was still there and she said that she'd taken their garden gnomes to a restorer in town for cleaning, then decided to stay out for supper, which was why she was back late... Don't you think that's suspicious?"

"What do you mean?"

"Well, Emma Seymour just *happened* to need to remove their garden gnomes and take them for cleaning *right after* Yvonne was murdered... Don't you think that's all a bit too convenient?"

"It could just be a coincidence," said Nell.

"Aww, come on, Nell!" Poppy rolled her eyes. She pulled her phone out eagerly. "I must speak to Suzanne and tell her..."

The detective inspector's mobile number kept diverting to voicemail so, after several attempts, Poppy tried the CID department instead. Her heart sank as she was put through to Detective Sergeant Lee.

"Yes?" he said, his voice brusque.

"Um… I was hoping to speak to Suzanne—I mean, Inspector Whittaker," said Poppy.

"I've taken over as lead investigator on the case," said Lee importantly. "The DI's had to step aside. Conflict of interest and all that, you know. So if you have any information which can help the investigation, you can speak to me."

Poppy hesitated. She really wanted to speak to Suzanne. But if it was true that her friend had been taken off the case, then she really had no choice. She couldn't justify holding back relevant information just because of her personal dislike of the officer in charge. Poppy took a deep breath and recounted her suspicions about Emma's sudden removal of their garden gnomes for cleaning. But to her disappointment, Sergeant Lee didn't seem very impressed by the information.

"Don't you think it's suspicious?" pressed Poppy. "Emma could have removed the gnomes because one of them had been used to kill Yvonne, and now she's getting them cleaned to remove all traces of forensic evidence—"

"Miss Lancaster, may I suggest that you watch fewer Hollywood movies?" said Lee in a sneering voice. "These kinds of coincidences happen all the time in everyday life—as you would know if you were as experienced as I am. There's no need to apply a melodramatic interpretation."

Poppy ground her teeth. "I'm not being melodramatic! It's a perfectly possible scenario and Emma Seymour has the perfect motive."

"And what is that?"

"Jealousy, of course! Dr Seymour was having an affair with Yvonne—"

"How do you know that?"

"The whole village knows it! And Emma isn't the type to put up with another woman stealing her man. In fact, she has a reputation as a bad loser in the village: she got violent towards another woman just for having a better cake than her and winning the contest at the annual village fair... Can you imagine what she'd be like if she found out about her husband's mistress?"

"The DI questioned her and I've also interviewed Mrs Seymour myself," said Lee. "She has an alibi for the night of the murder. She was at home the whole evening."

"But how do you know that's true? She could be lying."

"Her husband vouches for her. He was with her. They were watching a film together."

Poppy rolled her eyes. *Bloody hell. He didn't fall for that?* She started to tell him that Ralph Seymour had lied about his alibi too and that the doctor had actually gone out walking in the woods after dinner, therefore he couldn't confirm that his wife had been home all evening. But then she realised that in order to do that, she would have to betray the GP to the police and expose his lie. She hesitated—she knew that she should just report him, but somehow she felt pity for Dr Seymour. It would have been cruel to bring the police down on him as well, on top of everything else. Besides, she just couldn't believe that he could be the murderer—he had seemed so distressed over Yvonne's death.

Then Poppy brightened as she suddenly recalled the conversation she'd had with Miss Payne at the veterinarian's. There was a way she could question Emma's alibi without involving her husband.

"I was speaking to one of the villagers this morning," she said. "Her name is Adeline Payne. She happens to live by the road leading out of the village and she told me that she saw Emma driving out of Bunnington on the night of the murder."

"Hmm... I remember interviewing Miss Payne— she lives alone, doesn't she?"

"I... yes, I think so."

"One of those typical busybody old women—"

"She's not that old," protested Poppy. "She's probably in her fifties? And yes, I suppose, she does keep an interest in what's going on around the village but—"

Sergeant Lee cut her off, his voice mocking: "You're telling me to rely on the testimony of some nosy, middle-aged spinster who spends her life twitching curtains and spying on people?"

"What does her lifestyle have to do with anything?" asked Poppy impatiently. "The point is, she saw Emma out driving that night, when Emma claimed that she was home all evening."

"Are you sure that your Miss Payne didn't imagine things? Just to liven up the tedious monotony of her life, maybe?"

"She didn't imagine it," Poppy snapped. "She told me that she saw Emma's car."

"It was dark. How could she be sure it was Emma's? Did she recognise the number plate?"

"I'm not sure; she didn't say," Poppy admitted. "She just said that she recognised the car."

"Unless she can identify the number plate, you simply have her word that she saw Emma's car. She could have been completely wrong."

"It sounded like she often looks out the window. I'm sure she's familiar with all the vehicles that come and go in the village and knows which is Emma's car, even if she can't recite the number plate."

"She could also be lying."

"Why on earth would Miss Payne lie?" asked Poppy in an exasperated voice. "Why can't you just accept that Emma Seymour is a strong suspect in Yvonne Nash's murder?"

"We have a strong suspect in custody already."

"Aww, come on! You're not seriously still thinking that Nick Forrest could be the murderer? That's just ridiculous!"

"I'll be the judge of that," growled Sergeant Lee. "There's a search being conducted for the murder weapon at the moment, and I'm pretty sure that when it's found, we'll find Forrest's prints or DNA on it." He sounded gleeful. "And then the case will be closed."

Poppy had to bite her tongue to stop herself from saying something she might regret. Instead, she counted to ten, then said: "Will you please at least just speak to Miss Payne about what she saw?"

"Fine, fine," said Sergeant Lee testily. "I'll send a constable to question her again. I did interview her, you know, in the initial round of questioning; we spoke to all the patients who were at the clinic that day. She didn't mention anything about Emma's car at the time."

"Well, she couldn't have known that it was important, could she? I mean, she didn't know about Emma's alleged alibi—" Poppy started to say, but the sergeant cut her short.

"Yes, well, if that's all, Miss Lancaster, I'd like to get on with my work. I do have a murder investigation to oversee. Good day."

CHAPTER NINETEEN

Poppy ended the call with Sergeant Lee, fuming as usual. It was infuriating to think that the investigation could be ignoring a key suspect, just because the detective sergeant wouldn't take her seriously.

"Nell—when does your first cleaning job start today? Would you be okay looking after things here for a bit longer?" she asked impulsively.

"Yes, of course. My first job's not until six this evening. I'm doing several offices in Oxford. But why? Are you off somewhere again?"

"I just need to pop over to the Seymours' for a bit. I'll be back soon!"

Poppy rushed out the front gate of Hollyhock Cottage and nearly collided with Bertie in the lane outside. He had Einstein with him and the little terrier was straining eagerly at the end of his leash, obviously excited about the prospect of a walk. For once, the old inventor seemed to be fairly normally dressed, with not a scuba flipper, antenna headpiece, or even lab goggles in sight. He was, however, carrying a goldfish bowl under one arm. Instead of being filled with water and a finned resident, though, the bowl seemed to be filled with coils of spiky green tentacles which protruded out the top like some kind of overgrown pet sea monster.

Bertie smiled with delight when he saw her, and Einstein gave an excited bark.

"Poppy, my dear! Where are you off to in such a hurry?"

Poppy gave the old inventor a distracted smile and bent to give Einstein a pat. "I'm just popping across the village to see the GP. What about you?"

"Oh, Einstein and I are taking my *Euphorbia caput-medusae* for a walk."

Poppy paused. "Your what?"

Bertie held up his goldfish bowl proudly. "My *Euphorbia caput-medusae*—otherwise known as Medusa's Head plant."

Poppy eyed the bowl askance. "*That's* a plant?"

"But of course, my dear. Succulents are an important branch of the plant kingdom! There are none so well adapted for drought and arid conditions." Bertie adjusted his spectacles and continued enthusiastically: "In fact, the word 'succulent' comes from the Latin word *sucus*, which means 'juice' or 'sap'—a reference to their wonderful fleshy leaves and stems that store water. The roots as well, in some cases, although there is active debate in botanical circles about whether one should include such structures as bulbs, corms, and tubers. Such a classification would mean losing the distinction between succulents and 'geophytes', which survive harsh seasons via a dormant organ underground. There's further confusion, of course, because while succulents are classed as xerophytes—that is, plants adapted to dry environments—not all xerophytes are succulents. After all, there are other ways of adapting to water shortage, like developing small, spiny, or leathery leaves." He looked at Poppy kindly. "I hope that makes it all clear, my dear?"

Clear as mud, thought Poppy, her head swimming with all the information and unfamiliar words.

"I can explain it again if you're not—"

"Oh no, no," said Poppy hastily. "It's all... um... fascinating, Bertie. But I still don't understand why you're taking your succulent for a walk."

"Ah, well, *Euphorbia caput-medusae* need quite a lot of sun to thrive. Six hours ideally. I think the spot I've chosen for her in the house just isn't adequate, so I was hoping that a brisk walk in the fresh air might cheer her up. She's looking remarkably depressed, don't you think?"

Bertie thrust the bowl of green tentacles at Poppy, who reeled back.

"Um... I suppose so. I mean, I'm not sure what a depressed succulent looks like," muttered Poppy.

"Well, she hasn't been growing any new arms at all recently, and you know, if they are happy, the medusoid Euphorbias can grow to the size of a human head or even larger! Hence their common name." Bertie stroked one reptilian tentacle lovingly. "Isn't she just marvellous?"

Poppy stared at the coiling succulent. Personally, she couldn't think of anything more repulsive than a weird mass of scaly, green growths the size of a human head. But Bertie had such a simple, childlike delight in everything that she never had the heart to burst his bubble.

"It's certainly different to most things you'd find in an English garden," she said brightly. "Well, I'll leave you to enjoy your stroll with Einstein and the... er... *Euphorbia whatsherface.*"

She waved and hurried on her way. Arriving at the Seymours' house ten minutes later, she paused in front of the property and hesitated. A part of her knew that she shouldn't really be getting involved and interfering in the investigation, but Sergeant Lee's attitude had infuriated her so much, she felt like she couldn't bear to just sit on the side-lines. *If I challenge Emma directly, she might admit that she lied about her alibi*, Poppy thought. *When people are taken by surprise, they often let things slip...*

Taking a deep breath, she walked up to the front door and rang the doorbell, mentally bracing herself to confront the GP's wife. It was Dr Seymour, though, who answered the door. He looked like he had barely slept the night before: his eyes were bloodshot, his jaw covered in dark stubble, and his clothes even more unkempt than when she'd last seen him.

"Hello." Poppy gave him an apologetic smile. "I'm sorry to disturb you, but I was wondering if it might be possible to speak to your wife?"

"Emma isn't here."

"Oh. Do you know when she'll be back?"

Dr Seymour shrugged helplessly. "I have no idea."

"Well... do you know where she might have gone?"

He shook his head. "She wasn't here when I woke up this morning. I just assumed that she'd gone out for an early morning power walk—she often likes to do that—so I got on with some calls I had to make. We've had to close the surgery and cancel clinics so suddenly that there are so many patients who need to be contacted. Some of them need to be referred to another practice. Yvonne would normally do all that but..." He trailed off, his voice wobbling slightly.

Oh God, he's not going to start crying again? thought Poppy in dismay. She felt sorry for the man, but she also couldn't help thinking that Ralph Seymour was a bit of a wet rag.

Quickly, she said in a brisk voice: "So you're saying that Emma hasn't come home from her walk yet?"

"Yes... that's right... I mean, no, she hasn't," said Dr Seymour. He looked vaguely around. "I had to make a house call late this morning so I was out for a couple of hours and I thought she'd be home when I got back, but she wasn't."

Poppy frowned. "So, you haven't seen her at all since last night?"

Dr Seymour shook his head. "I slept in the guest bedroom again. We... er... had another row after you left," he said, flushing.

"Do you know if Emma was planning to have lunch out somewhere today? Like, with a friend?"

"Not that I know of. Her car is still here."

"What about shopping?"

Again, Dr Seymour shrugged helplessly. His vague, feeble manner was beginning to get on Poppy's nerves.

"Look, are you worried about Emma?" she asked bluntly.

Dr Seymour shifted his weight, frowning. "It's not like her to go off without a word. Normally, she leaves lots of instructions for things I need to do... But I'm sure she's fine," he added weakly.

"Have you tried ringing her mobile?"

"She didn't take it with her. I found it in the kitchen. Her purse and other things were there too."

"Isn't it odd that she didn't take her phone?"

"No, not really. Emma isn't one of those people who's always glued to her phone. She often leaves her mobile at home when she goes for a walk. I mean, she doesn't normally go far, and anyway, the reception in the woods is terrible, so it's just an extra thing for her to carry, especially if she's wearing something without decent pockets."

Poppy chewed her lip, wondering what to do. It wasn't really her problem if Dr Seymour didn't know where his wife was. There could have been all sorts of reasons why Emma had chosen not to return home, none of which were her business. She had come to talk to Emma and, with the woman not being home, she should just leave.

And yet...

"Why don't you show me where Emma normally goes for her power walks and we'll have a look around?" Poppy said impulsively.

The GP looked surprised, but he obligingly took her outside the back of the house and showed her the track that led from their rear garden into the woods beyond. They spent the next half hour walking in the woods, looking for any signs of the doctor's wife and calling her name occasionally.

It was a beautiful spring day and, if it weren't for the nagging sense of unease, Poppy would have enjoyed the walk. She had been so busy with the garden nursery that she hadn't had much time to wander beyond the cottage garden walls and enjoy the Oxfordshire countryside. She'd forgotten how beautiful naturalised bulbs and wildflowers could be, from the sunny daffodils pushing up in clumps to the swathes of bluebells under the trees, and even the humble cowslip, with its dainty yellow flowers peeking through the undergrowth. A part of her wanted to sit down there, in the middle of the woods, and just enjoy the wonder and the beauty around her, but a glance at the man next to her reminded her why they were out there. Finally, after walking around various tracks in the woods, they headed back.

"Maybe you should call the police," Poppy said as they reached the house once more. "You don't have to wait twenty-four hours, you know, before reporting a missing person."

"Missing person?" Dr Seymour shifted uncomfortably. "But... I don't really like to bother the police. Surely you don't think that's necessary?"

"It might just be a false alarm, but I'd rather be safe than sorry, wouldn't you?" Poppy eyed the doctor curiously, surprised that he didn't seem more concerned about his wife's disappearance.

But she didn't have time to ponder it. A glance at her watch made her realise how much time had elapsed and she thought guiltily of Nell, still patiently waiting back at Hollyhock Cottage. "Look, I need to get back to the nursery. Just call the police and tell them everything that you've told me, okay?"

She left him still standing, looking uncertain, on the front doorstep, and hurried back across the village. Back home, she found the nursery still disappointingly empty. Nell was comfortably ensconced in an old garden chair next to the trestle table, happily engrossed in her latest romance novel, but she looked up with interest as Poppy joined her.

"She's run away, I expect," said Nell with relish after hearing about Poppy's search for the doctor's wife. "Everyone knows Emma murdered Yvonne out of jealousy, and now that the police are on the case and she knows she might be found out, she's decided to scarper."

Poppy frowned. "But if she was going to run away, surely she would have packed a case or something? She didn't even take her mobile phone, and Dr Seymour said her purse was still at home too. Wherever she goes, surely she would need money?"

"Maybe she's gone off with someone," Nell suggested. Her eyes gleamed. "Maybe *Emma's* been having an affair as well and her rich lover came to rescue her from the clutches of the police, and he's taken her away."

"Oh Nell! You can't have it both ways," said Poppy with an exasperated laugh. "If Emma was so jealous and possessive of her husband that she was willing to murder a rival for his attentions, how can she also be having an affair with another man at the same time?"

"People can be very dog-in-the-manger when it comes to affairs of the heart," said Nell loftily. "There was a case of a poor girl who fell in love with a handsome musician, who was stuck with the most horrible fiancée. Every time he tried to break things off, the fiancée would create a scene and threaten to hurt herself... but at the same time, she treated him horribly and was messing around with other men behind his back. She didn't want him, really, but she didn't want anyone else to have him either. She made their lives an absolute misery, until they finally decided that they'd had enough and ran away together."

"Is this a real story or did you read it in one of your books?" asked Poppy suspiciously, nodding at the lurid cover of the bodice-ripper in her friend's hands.

"Well, all right, it *was* in a book," Nell admitted. "But that doesn't mean that it can't be true! All the best stories are inspired by real life." She got up, placed a bookmark in the novel, and dusted her hands. "Anyway, I'm going to put the kettle on. Fancy a cuppa?"

"That would be great, thanks, Nell. And I'm sorry I was away so long—I hope I'm not going to make you late for work."

"Oh no, I told you, my first job doesn't start until after six. One of those big offices in the Oxford Science Park. So I've got plenty of time for tea now before I need to be off. By the way, I'm meeting some friends for some drinks at a pub afterwards, so I probably won't be back until late." Nell looked at her worriedly. "You'll be all right, won't you, dear? I've made a quiche—it's on the counter—so you can have that for dinner. There's a loaf of fresh bread too."

"Oh, that's really sweet of you, Nell. Thank you!" Poppy gave her friend an impromptu hug and once again reflected how lucky she was to have such a warm, motherly figure in her life. "You go and enjoy yourself this evening. Don't worry, I'll be fine."

CHAPTER TWENTY

Poppy found it hard to keep her mind on the nursery the rest of the afternoon. She kept wondering what was happening with the search for the murder weapon and even more if Emma Seymour had returned. By now, the village grapevine would surely have got hold of the news of the GP's wife's disappearance and Poppy knew the local gossips would probably know more than the police ever would. She would have loved to pop back to the village green, where the most busybody villagers were bound to be gathered, and pick their brains.

But the chance of a last-minute customer arriving meant that she had to remain at Hollyhock Cottage until the nursery officially closed. Poppy chafed at the delay and spent most of the time pacing impatiently up and down the garden path. It didn't help her mood that, by closing time, not a single customer had turned up, and she felt like she had waited around for nothing. Still, she was glad to be able to flip the sign on the front gate to "CLOSED" and hurry to join the action on the village green.

When she got there, she found the crowds even bigger and there seemed to be even more police officers milling about. Poppy spotted a young woman with a baby perched on her hip, standing at the edge of a crowd, and recognised her as the young mother she'd met at the GP surgery. Hurrying over, she gave the woman a friendly smile and said:

"Hello! We met at Dr Seymour's—"

"Hi! Yes, that's right." The young woman beamed at her and stuck out a hand. "We never got properly introduced that day, did we? I'm Tamsin Beckett... and you remember Oscar," she added with a grin, nodding at the baby who was gnawing on a Farley's *Rusk*.

"Hello, Oscar," said Poppy, bending down to smile at the baby. Oscar gurgled in delight and waved the soggy biscuit in her face.

"I'm glad I've run into you because I've got something to give you," said Tamsin, digging in her handbag. She rummaged around for a few moments, then pulled out her wallet and unclasped the coin pouch. "Here..." She lifted out a sparkling gold chain with a locket on the end.

"Oh! My mother's locket!" cried Poppy, delighted.

"Yes, I'm afraid Oscar must have pulled it off your

neck when you were playing with him that day," said Tamsin with a rueful smile. "I found it down the front of his playsuit when I was changing his nappy after I got home." She pointed at the locket. "He had been gnawing on the clasp too and had opened the locket. I hope he hasn't damaged the picture inside."

Poppy opened the locket to reveal a tiny photograph of a beautiful young woman smiling over her shoulder at the camera. The sunlight in the picture glinted off her honey-blonde hair and caught the mischievous twinkle in her blue eyes.

"Who's that?" asked Tamsin curiously. "She's gorgeous."

"That's my mum; she passed away a year ago," Poppy explained, smiling sadly as she looked down at the photograph.

"Oh! I'm sorry," cried Tamsin.

"That's okay." Poppy looked back up. "I'm just so happy to have the locket back. The police hadn't reported finding it at the crime scene, and I was beginning to think that it was lost."

"Oh dear, I didn't mean to worry you." Tamsin gave her a rueful smile. "It's a poor 'thank you' for looking after Oscar that day. I don't know how I would have managed without your help."

"Where's your other little one?" asked Poppy, looking around.

"Tommy? Oh, he's with Dr Noble..."

Tamsin pointed behind her and Poppy saw that the toddler was with Bertie and Einstein, who had obviously detoured to the green on their walk. The old inventor was crouching down beside the little boy, showing him the goldfish bowl filled with succulent tentacles, and Tommy was listening wide-eyed. Poppy wondered what on earth Bertie was telling the child, then decided that she'd probably rather not know!

Turning back to Tamsin, she asked: "What's going on? Have they found the murder weapon yet?"

"Oh, hadn't you heard? They've abandoned that search now, because they've got something more urgent. They're looking for a missing person: Dr Seymour's wife has disappeared!"

Poppy followed the other woman's gaze to see Ralph Seymour standing on the other side of the village green, talking to Sergeant Lee. The GP's shoulders were slumped, and he looked lost and helpless as he shook his head in answer to questions the detective sergeant was firing at him.

"Poor Dr Seymour," said Tamsin, watching him tenderly.

Poppy glanced at her, surprised by her tone. Far from seeing Ralph Seymour's lost-puppy-dog act as pathetic and annoying, the other woman seemed to find it appealing.

"He looks so tired and stressed. It must be horrible for him," said Tamsin, watching the GP with concern.

"What he needs is someone to look after him," said a woman nearby, who detached herself from the crowd and turned to join them.

"Yes, I would cook him a nice hot meal and then tuck him up in bed," Tamsin declared.

"The poor dear just hasn't had the right woman looking after him, has he?" said another woman coming to join them. She pulled a face. "That wife of his... all she ever does is boss him around, but she doesn't nurture him like he deserves."

"No," Tamsin agreed quickly. "Dr Seymour is the kind of man who needs a special woman to understand him."

"Yes, someone to *really* look after him and give him some proper TLC," said another woman, and several others nodded vehemently, looking like they wished they could be given the opportunity.

Poppy looked at them in surprise, but before she could think more about it, they were interrupted by a shout from the direction of the village church. Immediately, the crowd trooped across to see what the commotion was. Poppy joined the throng, walking next to Bertie and little Tommy, who was proudly holding Einstein's leash. They arrived outside the church to see Sergeant Lee conferring with a uniformed constable who was showing him an expensive cashmere scarf. The detective sergeant brought the item over to Dr Seymour and held it up.

"Does this belong to your wife?"

"I... er... yes, I think so," said the GP, peering at it. "Emma wears that sometimes in the mornings on her walks if it's chilly."

"This suggests that your wife came this way, instead of staying in the woods, like you said."

"Oh, she could have come this way as part of her walk," Dr Seymour said. He pointed to a stand of trees just behind the church. "That connects to the woods, you see, and the track near our house loops past here, so sometimes Emma will come out by the church and walk back home through the village, instead of retracing her steps on the track."

"And there's no other reason for her to come to the church?"

Dr Seymour looked doubtfully at the old Saxon structure next to them. "I don't think so. I mean, we attend services on Sunday morning occasionally, but Emma never shows much interest in the church at other times."

Sergeant Lee whirled dramatically and strode over to a group of officers. Poppy heard him shouting at the top of his voice: "Call the men out of the woods! I want them to concentrate on the area around the church. I want you to search every icehouse, henhouse, alehouse, and doghouse in the area! She can't have got far!"

I can't believe he had the bloody cheek to tell me I watch too many Hollywood movies! The plonker obviously thinks he's re-enacting The Fugitive *himself,* thought Poppy in annoyance. It also irked her that Lee was obviously now treating the doctor's wife as a suspect, despite mocking her own suspicions earlier.

Something bumping against her knee made her glance down, and she saw little Tommy struggling to control Einstein, who was straining on his leash. The terrier seemed incredibly excited about something, panting and whining as he lunged on his leash. Poppy started to tell Bertie that the little boy needed help but, before she could say anything, Einstein yanked the leash out of Tommy's hands and scampered across to the large yew shrub at the side of the church graveyard.

"Ansta!" cried little Tommy. "Ansta, come back!"

He toddled after the dog and disappeared behind some large boulders placed around the base of the shrub. Poppy watched worriedly, wondering what the boy and dog were doing. She was just thinking of going over herself to check when little Tommy reappeared and trotted back to his mother.

"Mummy... Mummy..." He grabbed a fold of her skirt in a grubby hand and tugged. "Mummy, Ansta—"

Tamsin Beckett paused in her conversation with one of the other village ladies and looked down distractedly. "Not now, Tommy... Mummy is talking..."

The little boy tugged her skirt again, but his mother had already turned back to her companion.

Poppy crouched down next to the little boy and asked: "What is it, Tommy?"

He looked at her shyly and stuck a finger in his mouth. Poppy gave him an encouraging smile.

"You can tell me, Tommy. Is it something about Einstein? Did he hurt you?"

The boy shook his head. Then he pointed back towards the yew shrub. "Ansta!"

"Einstein's over there? Behind the boulders? Here…" Poppy held her hand out to him. "Shall we go over together and see what he's doing?"

The little boy nodded happily and slipped his sticky fingers into hers. Poppy walked slowly over to the yew shrub with him. As they got closer, she caught sight of Einstein's bottom sticking out from behind one of the boulders. His tail was wagging furiously, and he seemed to be scrabbling at something at the base of the shrub.

"Einstein? What is it?" asked Poppy, climbing around the large, weathered boulders and bending down to see.

The terrier responded with an excited bark. Poppy caught her breath as she saw what he was nosing in the dirt.

It was a hand.

Her eyes fixed on the thin, expensive Cartier watch encircling the pale wrist. The last time she had seen that watch, it had been around Emma Seymour's wrist. Slowly, she leaned down further and lifted one of the heavy yew branches, then gave a gasp at the sight of the body revealed underneath. It had been shoved right under the shrub and the thick branches of the yew had draped over it, whilst the boulders placed around the base of the shrub had further hidden it from view.

Poppy stared at the crumpled figure. It was Emma Seymour and she was dead.

CHAPTER TWENTY-ONE

Poppy leaned back and read her statement again, then signed it and handed it to the young constable who was standing beside her, waiting. She rose wearily from the table in the interview room, grimacing as her stomach rumbled. Lunch was several hours ago, and she'd had nothing more than a biscuit with her cup of tea right before leaving Hollyhock Cottage to join the crowds on the village green. Since then—what with the discovery of Emma Seymour's body, the wait for the pathologist and forensic team to arrive, the trip to the police station, and the long delay before she was interviewed—she hadn't had a chance to even think of her supper. Now, though, Poppy realised that she was famished, and she thought longingly of the quiche that Nell had left her.

I'm going to have a huge slice of that... and a huge glass of red wine to go with it! she thought as she followed the officer back out to the station foyer. As they passed the desk sergeant, Poppy was surprised to see a familiar tall figure at the counter. It was Nick Forrest. The crime author turned away from the desk sergeant just as Poppy was passing and stopped as he saw her.

"Don't tell me they've had you banged up here as well," he remarked dryly.

"Oh no, I've just come in to answer some questions and give a statement. I found Emma Seymour's body, you see. She's been murdered."

Nick's eyebrows rose. "I see that a lot has been happening since I've been in custody." He gestured towards the station doors. "I've got my car here. Come on, I'll give you a lift home and you can tell me all about it."

A few minutes later, they were on the road. Although it should have been well past the rush hour, traffic was unusually heavy, and Nick cursed under his breath as he had to manoeuvre around aggressive cars and unpredictable drivers.

"Maybe you should slow down," suggested Poppy. "That car ahead is driving like an idiot. You won't have time to swerve if he suddenly decides to change lanes—"

"When I want your opinion of my driving, I'll ask you," snapped Nick.

Poppy drew an angry breath and started to retort,

then she caught herself as she glanced sideways at Nick's profile. He was unshaven, his clothes were rumpled, and he looked thoroughly tired and fed-up. Poppy reminded herself that Nick had spent the better part of the last two days in a police cell, and had probably had his patience tested to the limit by Sergeant Lee's supercilious attitude. Anyone would be more than a bit grouchy in this situation, never mind a moody writer with a notoriously short temper to begin with! *Perhaps I should cut him some slack...*

Even as she had the thought, Nick gave a great sigh and ran a hand over his face, rubbing it tiredly. Then he gave Poppy an apologetic look.

"Sorry. That was uncalled for. I've had a hell of a time and just want to get home and get into a hot shower and a change of clothes... but it's no reason to take it out on you."

Poppy gave him an understanding smile. "It's okay. I'd probably be really crabby too if I were you."

"Who said I'm crabby?" Nick growled.

Poppy shot him a look and Nick gave a reluctant grin. "All right, maybe a bit. Look, why don't you tell me what's been happening with the murder? It'll take my mind off the bloody traffic."

Poppy brought him up to date on the investigation and Nick whistled when he heard about Emma Seymour's disappearance and murder.

"I wondered why they suddenly decided to release me. I mean, I gathered from the change in tone yesterday that they were already struggling to justify holding me much longer, and then, earlier today, there was a call from the vet supporting Bertie's theory that Oren was behind the bra thefts—not to mention multiple calls from my father himself, offering to come down to the police station to help clear my name." Nick chuckled. "I think the DCC is still recovering from Bertie's last visit to the station, when the entire force ended up incapacitated by laughing gas. The threat of having my father 'help with the investigation' was probably more than enough to persuade them to release me. But this must have clinched it."

"What do you mean?" asked Poppy.

"Well, I know from my time in CID that, in cases like this, there are rarely two perpetrators. Nine times out of ten, the person who committed the first murder will be the same person who committed the second. Therefore, if I was safely locked up here last night and couldn't have murdered Emma, then chances are that I couldn't have been responsible for the first murder either."

"But that just makes it even more confusing," said Poppy, frowning. "I mean, who would want to kill both Yvonne and Emma?"

"Ralph Seymour?" suggested Nick. "He was the husband of one and the lover of the other. That would be enough to make him suspect number one in most situations."

Poppy wrinkled her nose. "Ralph Seymour is so wet, he probably couldn't kill a fly!"

"Appearances can be deceptive. He doesn't have an alibi," Nick pointed out. "If his wife really wasn't home on the night of the murder—as your Miss Payne said—then that means no one can vouch for when Seymour got back home. He could have been meeting Yvonne at the surgery, instead of out walking in the woods as he claimed. In fact, it could give him a motive for killing Emma too: to stop her from revealing that he didn't come home before midnight that night."

"No, I can't believe it," Poppy protested. "Ralph Seymour is so pathetic, he just doesn't have it in him to commit a cold-blooded murder."

"Who said it was cold-blooded? It could have been the desperate act of a man who cracked under pressure. You said Yvonne was pushing Seymour to leave his wife, but he was also totally under Emma's thumb and terrified of her finding out about the affair, terrified of losing his cushy lifestyle... Well, someone like that can feel backed into a corner and lash out in a panic. Perhaps he arranged to meet Yvonne at the surgery that night to try and reason with her, and when she refused to listen, he decided to cut his losses and get rid of his demanding mistress."

"But if Ralph Seymour was willing to murder his mistress in order to remain with his wife, why would he then murder his wife?"

Nick shrugged. "Once people start down the path of using murder to solve their problems, it becomes a slippery slope. Besides, what does he have to lose? It doesn't sound like he and Emma had a great relationship either, so by killing her, he gets rid of the domineering wife, while still keeping the trappings of his comfortable life." Nick gave a cynical smile. "I'll bet that Emma Seymour's will leaves everything to her husband."

"But... if he really did murder her, why didn't he dump her body further away? Why leave it in the village where it could be easily found?"

"Maybe Seymour decided that if he tried to dispose of the body further away, he would have risked being seen, so it was the lesser of two evils."

"You seem very sure that it's him."

Nick shrugged. "I'm not *sure*. Nothing is sure until the murderer is arrested. But it's certainly an assumption that has a lot of statistical support. Murder victims are usually killed by someone close to them, and a spouse or partner is often involved."

Nick's mention of a "partner" made Poppy remember something. "Yvonne had a boyfriend, you know," she said. "By your reasoning, he should be a prime suspect too."

Nick inclined his head. "He could be. But what's his connection to Emma? Why would he have wanted to kill her? Don't forget, this killer is someone who had a motive to kill *both* women. So far, Seymour is the only one with a connection to both."

Poppy was stumped and she sat for the rest of the drive in a thoughtful silence. She was so engrossed in her musings that she was surprised when they slid smoothly into the cul-de-sac where their houses were situated. To her relief, the paparazzi weren't about. It seemed that with the new developments in the case, the sex perversion angle was now "old news".

Nick guided his car into the garage, cut the engine, then turned to her and asked: "Fancy coming in for a drink and a bite to eat? I make a mean omelette." He grinned at her. "It would give me a chance to make up for snapping at you earlier."

Poppy hesitated. She had been planning to go straight home, but suddenly the prospect of sitting alone, eating Nell's quiche, seemed a lot less attractive. "Thanks, that sounds great."

She followed Nick into his house, looking around for Oren as they entered, but there was no sign of the ginger tomcat.

"Probably out nicking another bra," grumbled Nick. "I swear, when I see that cat, I'm going to wring his bloody neck."

Poppy laughed. "It's not really Oren's fault, you know. The vet said feline kleptomania is pretty common and it could have been triggered by the change in his diet. Maybe now that Oren's allowed to go back to his normal food, he might just stop doing it."

"Chance would be a fine thing," muttered Nick.

He gestured towards the kitchen. "Make yourself at home. Give me ten minutes to have a quick shower, then I'll be back to cook you the best omelette you've ever tasted!"

An hour later, Poppy popped the last mouthful of fluffy omelette into her mouth and leaned back in her chair, sighing with contentment. She had to admit that the meal had been every bit as good as Nick had promised. They'd started with crusty bread with an olive oil and balsamic vinegar dip, followed by an avocado, tuna, and sweetcorn salad, and then the beautifully cooked omelettes, bursting with mushrooms, tomatoes, and fragrant herbs. She had been impressed by Nick's ability to pull together such a great meal based on just a few items in his fridge and staples from his pantry, and even more surprised to discover that he was an adept cook. Somehow, the crime author hadn't fitted her idea of a man who would know his way around a kitchen. *Although he's certainly got the fiery temper of a stereotypical chef*, thought Poppy with an inward grin.

"What are you smirking about?" asked Nick.

Poppy looked up and quickly hid her grin. "Oh, nothing. That was really delicious. Thank you."

"There's some cheese and dried muscat grapes for dessert if you like. I'm afraid my culinary talents do *not* run to baking."

"No, no, I'm stuffed," said Poppy, laughing. "I couldn't eat another thing."

"Tea? Coffee? Hot chocolate?"

Poppy chose the last and, a few minutes later, she wandered into the sitting room and curled up in one of the huge armchairs beside the fireplace with a steaming mug in her hands. Nick followed her and, after lighting the fire, threw himself into the armchair opposite hers. His dark, curling hair was still damp from his recent shower, and he had changed into a ski-style, funnel-neck jumper in black Merino wool, paired with dark jeans. Poppy thought the whole ensemble, combined with his dark, brooding looks, gave him the lean, dangerous look of a trained assassin.

Your imagination is running away with you again, Poppy chided herself. She raised the mug to her lips and sipped the rich, milky hot chocolate while she gazed into the crackling flames. The whole room was bathed in the lovely orange glow of the fire and Poppy felt as if the strains and stresses of the day were melting away as she relaxed into the deep cushions of her chair.

She looked up, intending to ask Nick how his latest book was going, but the words died on her lips as she saw that his long legs were stretched out in front of him and his head had lolled back against the armchair. He had fallen asleep.

Poppy rose slowly and stepped closer to Nick's chair, looking down at him. His face was softened in sleep and, in spite of the silver streaks at his temples, he looked younger than his thirty-nine years. She had to resist a sudden urge to reach out and smooth back the tousled dark hair that fell across his brow. Instead, she turned away, preparing to let herself quietly out of the house.

Then she paused and looked back at Nick, hesitating. She hated to wake him—he looked exhausted and she was sure that he hadn't slept much while he was in custody—but on the other hand, if she just left him as he was, he might wake up in the morning with a terrible crick in his neck. Besides, if the fire went out, the room would get very cold...

Poppy took a step back towards him and gently reached down to touch his shoulder. "Nick? Nick...?"

Nick awoke with a jump. His hand shot out and grabbed her wrist in a punishing grip, twisting it painfully.

"Ow!" cried Poppy, trying to jerk her arm out of his grasp. Her efforts unbalanced her and, the next moment, she tumbled forwards, straight into Nick's arms.

For a long moment they stayed very still, staring at each other. There was no sound in the room except for the crackling fire and—what seemed to Poppy— the very loud thumping of her heart. She was sure it was just due to the surprise and surge of adrenalin, and nothing to do with suddenly finding herself on Nick's lap, her legs entangled with his and her arms around his neck.

The thought brought hot colour rushing to her cheeks and she started trying to extricate herself. Nick's arms tightened around her for a moment, then he released her. He rose from his chair and set her gently back on her feet, saying:

"Sorry. That was a reflex action. Too many years of dealing with violent criminals in the CID. You tend to react defensively if you're startled."

Before Poppy could reply, they were interrupted by a clatter in the hallway outside, followed by a familiar demanding cry:

"*Nnn-owrr? NNN-OWRR?*"

A minute later, Oren strutted into the room and Poppy realised why the ginger tom had sounded slightly muffled. He was carrying something in his mouth.

"*Nnn-owwwrrr!*" said Oren, marching proudly over to them and dropping something at Nick's feet.

"Bloody hell, not again," groaned Nick as he bent to pick the thing up.

Poppy peered at the item. "What is it?"

Nick made a face. "It's a sock. An ugly, smelly sock. Great... cheers, mate," he said, shooting a dirty look at Oren, who purred loudly and looked pleased with himself.

Poppy was relieved that Oren had interrupted their awkward moment and now she stifled a laugh as she looked at what Nick was holding fastidiously between a thumb and forefinger. It was a maroon sock, in a hideous paisley pattern, and had obviously been worn recently, judging by its stretched shape.

"Well, at least it's not a bra," said Poppy, grinning.

Nick tossed the sock onto a side table. "I suppose I'd better hand that over to the police first thing tomorrow morning, before it's discovered and I'm accused of being a foot pervert or something," he said, rolling his eyes. He turned back to Poppy. "Another drink?"

"No, thanks... I'd better go," said Poppy hurriedly. "Thank you for the lift and the lovely meal and hot chocolate and... and everything," she stammered, suddenly feeling shy.

Nick was silent for a moment, watching her, then he said: "It was a pleasure." A smile played at the corners of his lips. "I'll walk you back."

"Oh, there's no need," Poppy protested. "I'm literally next door!"

Nick ignored her and accompanied her back to Hollyhock Cottage. Nell wasn't back yet and the cottage was in darkness. Poppy unlocked the front door, then turned and said:

"Well... thanks again... um... Good night."

Nick leaned towards her and Poppy's heart began to pound again, but all he did was open the front door and throw a quick, cursory glance around inside. She felt a confusing mix of relief and disappointment when he drew back and said: "Make sure you lock the door."

Then, with a quiet "Good night", he turned and retraced his steps up the garden path, leaving Poppy staring after him as he went through the front gate and disappeared into the night.

CHAPTER TWENTY-TWO

Poppy eagerly checked the news the next morning for any developments on the case, but there was nothing about either woman's murder, other than a statement that the police investigation was still ongoing. With a sigh, she pulled on her gumboots and got ready for another day manning the garden nursery. She had barely set up the till and was just checking over her meagre supply of potted plants when she heard the front gate open and footsteps approaching.

Poppy turned around to find a young man coming down the path and blinked in surprise as she recognised him. It was Bryan Murray, Yvonne's boyfriend.

"Hello... can I help you?" she said, giving him a friendly smile.

He paused and looked around uncertainly. "Yeah. I wanted to get summin' for my gran," he said. "She loves flowers, 'specially the red ones."

"Oh, how nice. Is it a special occasion?"

Bryan shrugged, looking embarrassed. "No. I just go an' visit her each week. She's in a home, right, an' I like to take her summin' to make her happy."

Poppy shot him a covert look of surprise. Somehow, she hadn't thought that the belligerent young man she'd met at the pub would be the type to visit his grandmother regularly and take thoughtful presents. *Maybe that just shows how wrong first impressions and stereotypes can be*, she reflected. *Maybe Bryan isn't as much a "bad boy" as all the gossips make him out to be.*

"I'm afraid I don't have anything red," she said apologetically. "But I do have some lovely primroses in a beautiful bright pink. I think your gran would love those too."

"Yeah, okay," said Bryan, tilting his head and examining the pot that Poppy was holding out to him. "Can you, like, put a nice ribbon 'round it or summin'? And maybe I'll take a couple o' those? One looks a bit naff."

Poppy said impulsively: "I'll tell you what: I've got some old terracotta pots to spare. I'll make up an arrangement in that, if you like, with a couple of primroses and some violas—then you can give the whole thing to your gran as a ready-to-display gift. I won't charge you for the terracotta pot, just the flowers. What do you think?"

"Yeah, that sounds great!" said Bryan enthusiastically. "Cheers."

He watched as Poppy found an empty terracotta container and half-filled it with potting compost. Then she chose a couple of the biggest primrose plants she had and extracted them from their plastic pots. She positioned them in the terracotta container, turning and tilting until she was happy with the arrangement, then she tucked a few violas into the gaps at the sides, as well as a few ivy cuttings to spill over the edges. Finally, she filled in all the remaining space with more compost and gave the container a thorough watering.

"That looks wicked," said Bryan, eyeing the arrangement appreciatively. "The colours look brilliant together. My gran's going to love that. She can have it on the windowsill in her room. Thanks so much!"

He paid for the flowers, but when he should have taken the container and left, he surprised Poppy by turning back to her. Shifting his weight from foot to foot, he said in a gruff voice: "By the way... I'm sorry 'bout what happened that night at the pub. I hope you didn't get hurt... by me an' the doc fighting, I mean."

Poppy looked at him in surprise. She hadn't thought that Bryan had recognised her.

"That's okay," she said, giving him a sympathetic smile. "Yvonne's death must have been really upsetting for you. I'm sure emotions were running pretty high. Don't worry, I understand."

Bryan gave her a bitter look. "You'd be the first one. Everyone else just wants to pile on me."

"Oh... have people been unpleasant to you in the village?" asked Poppy in a neutral voice

"Yeah, everyone thinks I killed Yvonne... but it's not true!" Bryan burst out. "I loved Yvonne; I would never have hurt her! I was even going to ask her to marry me one day, you know? See, I've known Yvonne ever since we were at school together," he explained. "An' I always knew that she was the girl for me. But then last year, she started acting all different. Like all sour an' stuck-up, you know? An' sometimes we'd arrange to meet but then she wouldn't turn up, an' when I asked her 'bout it later, she wouldn't tell me where she went."

He hunched his shoulders, an expression of hurt crossing his face. "Then one day, I was out an' I saw her with that Seymour bloke. They were going into one o' them fancy restaurants in Oxford." His mouth twisted bitterly. "An' the next day, Yvonne was showing off this new designer handbag she got. How am I s'posed to compete with that?"

Poppy wasn't sure how to reply. Somehow, she seemed to have fallen into the role of therapist and confidante, much against her will. "Um... did you speak to Yvonne about it?" she asked lamely.

"Yeah, I told her I saw 'em together but she just laughed it off. Said she was just having a good time an' it didn't mean anything, an' Seymour gave her gifts just 'cos he's a nice boss." Bryan looked up, his eyes flashing. "Bollocks to that! I'm not blind! I could see that the wanker was just trying to get into her knickers!"

"Did you guys break up?"

"No," Bryan muttered, looking back down at his feet. "No, I didn't want to lose Yvonne. An' I thought she might go off him by herself, you know? Like, once she knew what Seymour was *really* like. I mean, all these rich bastards—they act all posh and stuff, but they're full o' crap! The doc is nothing more than a cheat and a thief."

"What do you mean?" said Poppy in surprise.

"You know Yvonne was doing work on the side, to earn some extra dough, right? She was helping out with that stupid flower club o' his, like some typing an' admin an' managing the club funds. Well, she told me she found all these inconsistencies."

Poppy frowned. "What do you mean, inconsistencies?"

"Someone's been skimming money off the account that had all the research grant money," said Bryan.

"Yvonne told you that?"

Bryan nodded. "That night at the pub, before she got killed."

"But how did she know that?"

"She saw it when she was going through all the records for last year. See, she was only s'posed to look at the club folders that the doc showed her, which were on the main computer in the reception. But she said everything was a real mess an' there were transactions that didn't make sense, so she decided to check out the doc's laptop too, in case he'd stashed some records there. 'Cos he took the laptop with him to the committee meetings, an' Yvonne said he was always forgetting where he's put stuff or getting things mixed up... He sounds like a right loser, if you ask me," said Bryan contemptuously. "Anyway, so last week when the doc had gone out to make a house call an' the afternoon clinic hadn't started yet, Yvonne decided to look in his laptop—"

"And she found evidence of him illegally withdrawing money from the research grant in the OAC account?" asked Poppy excitedly.

Bryan frowned. "No... not exactly. She said she found records showing money being transferred to Spain."

"To *Spain*?" said Poppy in surprise.

"Yeah."

"What for?"

Bryan shrugged. "Dunno. Yvonne said all she could see was that it was some company in Spain. But it was big money, though—it weren't just a couple o' quid. It sounded right dodgy. That's what I told Yvonne. I reckon the doc was skimming money off the grant an' sending it to Spain to put in a fake business or summin'." He clenched his fists in frustration. "But she wouldn't hear a bad word against him! She got all stroppy an' started yelling at

217

me. We had a big bust-up an' Yvonne stormed out." He stopped, then added in a low voice, "That was the last time I saw her alive."

Long after Bryan had left, Poppy stood lost in thought, pondering what the young man had told her. Could Ralph Seymour have been the murderer after all? Nick had certainly thought so, based purely on the man's connection to both victims and on statistical likelihood. Poppy had always rejected the idea simply because the GP seemed too weak and nice to be a murderer—and because, if she was honest, she felt sorry for him—but what if appearances were deceptive? What if her instincts had been completely wrong?

She thought back to the doctor's excessive grief over Yvonne's death: all the crying and public displays of emotion... was that genuine? Or was it a clever act to cover up his real intentions? After all, if everyone thought that he was devastated by Yvonne's death, they were unlikely to suspect him of being her murderer.

And what about his wife? Poppy thought of her visit yesterday and recalled Ralph Seymour's vague manner and lack of concern about Emma, despite not having seen her since the night before. He had seemed reluctant to involve the police, even when Poppy had urged him to report his wife as missing. Well, if he had been the one to murder her, he would have had good reason for wanting to delay reporting things to the police...

And now there's this new information from Bryan...
Poppy frowned. Nick had thought that Ralph
Seymour already had more than enough motive to
kill both his mistress and his wife, just based on the
sordid romantic triangle between them, but with
what Bryan had just told her, it would give the GP
even more reason to commit murder. If Yvonne really
had uncovered illegal activities with the OAC funds
and had evidence that Seymour was involved, that
would be strong incentive to kill her. No man would
have wanted such a stain on their professional
reputation, but as a doctor, Seymour had even more
to lose. A criminal conviction could have led to him
being struck off the register and unable to work as a
medical professional ever again...

On an impulse, Poppy rang Suzanne Whittaker.
She was delighted when the detective inspector
answered almost immediately and even more
delighted to find that—with Nick's release—Suzanne
was back in charge of the case. Quickly, Poppy
recounted her conversation with Yvonne's boyfriend
and added her own thoughts about Dr Seymour's
potential as a murder suspect.

"Hmm... Nick *is* right—statistically, husbands
and boyfriends are often found to be involved when a
woman is murdered," said Suzanne. "And I've
certainly had my eye on Seymour from the beginning.
If he *is* involved in these money withdrawals from the
OAC accounts, that would give him even more
motive."

"Did you know about them?" asked Poppy.

"Yes, Bryan mentioned the mystery transactions when I questioned him, and we got access to the club accounts so we could try to trace them." Suzanne sighed. "But so far, we haven't been able to ascertain who actually authorised the transactions. All we've found out is that the funds were transferred to an organisation in Spain—some kind of club."

"A club? You mean a Spanish auricula club?"

"A what?"

"The flower that Dr Seymour's club was interested in—it's called a *Primula auricula*," Poppy explained. "Maybe the withdrawals were transfers to a horticultural club in Spain that was helping Dr Seymour with his research into the plant's medicinal properties?"

"No... this didn't sound like a horticultural club. The name was Club Playa Las Cinco Palmas; it was in Marbella." Suzanne paused, then added: "'Playa' means beach in Spanish."

"A beach club?" said Poppy, puzzled.

"It seems to have been some kind of property development, probably on the beach. It's been difficult to get any more information because the company seems to have folded, and no one is answering any calls or emails. Don't worry, we'll track it down in the end," said Suzanne confidently. "The Spanish *Policía Nacional* is helping us. It just might take a bit of time."

"Do *you* think Ralph Seymour is the murderer?"

asked Poppy bluntly.

"I try not to form any opinions until I've gathered all the evidence," said Suzanne. "But Bryan certainly seems to think so. He was pushing the idea quite strongly during our interview. Of course, he's hardly a disinterested party," she added dryly.

"What do you mean?"

"Well, hadn't it occurred to you that Bryan might have committed the crimes himself and then framed Dr Seymour for them?"

"*Bryan?*" said Poppy. "But... but he loved Yvonne."

"Apparently so did Dr Seymour," said Suzanne in an even drier tone.

"But what would Bryan's motive be?" Poppy asked sceptically. "Jealous rage?"

"It *is* one of the oldest reasons in the book."

"Surely if Bryan *had* killed Yvonne in a jealous rage, he would have just lashed out when they were alone together?" argued Poppy. "Why would he have gone to the trouble of concocting an elaborate plan to lure her to the surgery late at night, and then kill her and leave her body there?"

"Like I said, to frame Ralph Seymour. Based on the way Bryan was talking during our interview, I gather that there's a lot of bitterness and resentment there. The 'jealous rage' might not only have been directed at Yvonne, you know. He could have wanted to get back at the doctor too, and what better way than to frame the man for murder?"

"What about Emma then? What would be Bryan's

reason for killing the doctor's wife? He hardly even knew her. Was it just to frame Seymour even more?" asked Poppy, still sceptical.

"Possibly. Or perhaps Emma had somehow found out about his role in Yvonne's murder and he had to silence her before she could expose him."

"No... I just don't believe it!" cried Poppy. "You're making Bryan sound like a cold-blooded killer! You didn't see him here in my nursery earlier today, choosing flowers for his gran... It was like another side of him. Okay, so he might be a bit hot-tempered and probably drinks more than he should, but Bryan Murray is a decent chap underneath all that bluster. He's not a murderer!"

"Well, perhaps you're right. One gets a bit cynical and jaded when one's been on the Force too long. We do tend to see the worst side of humanity. But remember—the statistics about spouses and lovers would apply to Bryan too. He *was* Yvonne's boyfriend and he did have a well-known jealous streak. He has a history of assault and reacting violently, especially where Yvonne is involved." Suzanne's voice was gentle. "Just because you like him, Poppy, doesn't mean that he's automatically innocent."

Poppy frowned, thinking back to her encounter with Yvonne's boyfriend. Was she just letting her own emotions and sympathies colour her judgement again, like she might have done with Dr Seymour? Bryan had seemed so genuinely distressed by the girl's death. She knew that, technically, the young man was a suspect too, but she couldn't help feeling sorry for him. She could see that not only was he grieving for a girl he seemed to have truly cared for, but that he seemed to be racked with guilt too.

The question is, though—is it just guilt at having parted from Yvonne in anger or is it guilt for something more sinister? she wondered uncomfortably.

Poppy sighed. "Yeah, you're right," she admitted to Suzanne. Then she gave a humourless laugh. "I suppose this is why I could never be a detective! I can't stop my emotions getting involved."

"Oh, I don't know—I think you've done a pretty good job so far, with all the cases you've helped to solve," said Suzanne with a smile in her voice. "And Nick was just like you when he was on the Force—he struggled to keep his emotions out of the equation. But he was a brilliant detective. Ask anyone in CID. His cases are still legendary."

CHAPTER TWENTY-THREE

Despite the lack of firm answers, Poppy felt strangely cheered after her phone call with Suzanne and she decided to put the mystery from her mind for the rest of the day. And while she was horrified by Emma's murder, she had to admit to herself that she also nurtured a shamefaced hope that the news might once again entice more visitors to Bunnington—and hence to the nursery. But business remained quiet, and Poppy found herself twiddling her thumbs as she waited hopefully for a customer to show up.

It didn't help that Nell was away. Most of her friend's cleaning jobs were normally in the evenings, for offices and commercial spaces in Oxford and nearby market towns, but today was one of the rare times when Nell had been called out to a daytime cleaning job by the agency she worked for. So Poppy found herself coping with the boredom alone. Even Oren didn't turn up. The talkative ginger tom made a surprisingly good conversational companion and Poppy had been hoping that he might come to keep her company, but the cat was not to be seen.

It was a long day, broken only by a handful of customers who looked disparagingly at the meagre selection of plants on offer and left again without buying anything. Poppy was in low spirits by the time she flipped the sign on the gate and officially closed the nursery. As she wandered back into the cottage, she caught sight of the trays of plug plants and seedlings laid out on the wooden table in the greenhouse. These were the rest of her stock and would provide more than ample plants for sale... if only they grew bigger faster!

Poppy sighed in frustration. She thought of the vial of growth serum that Bertie had given her, but resolutely pushed the idea from her mind. *No*, she told herself. *You know what happens when you mess around with Bertie's inventions. It never ends well. Still, there must be other ways to encourage faster growth...*

She pulled out her phone and began to do an internet search on stimulating plant growth. Within minutes, she came across several interesting articles online discussing the increased rates of growth in countries with more sunshine and warmer climates—countries such as Australia:

"Adelaide, in South Australia, for example, will receive over 4 hours of daily sunshine in the middle of winter, compared to only one hour and fifteen minutes in London. Over the course of a year, the Australian city receives 2,516 hours of sunshine per year compared to 1,460 in London—almost double the total amount of sunlight and UV exposure.

It has been observed that many plant specimens grow significantly faster and reach a larger size when exposed to the increased sunlight and UV levels Down Under. The higher ambient temperatures also contribute to increased growth. A shrub rose, which is originally quoted as reaching a modest height of 3 to 4ft back in Europe, can easily produce 20ft-long canes in these conditions and be grown as a climbing rose instead, especially if grafted onto a vigorous rootstock..."

Poppy looked up from her phone and stared thoughtfully through the glass panes of her greenhouse. She could see the afternoon sun slanting across the garden outside. Although temperatures were still on the chilly side at night, the forecast for the next few days was for sunny, clear skies and warm days.

Well, I might not be able to transport my baby plants to Australia... but I can move them outside! Surely if they're out in the garden, they'll get more UV exposure than here in the greenhouse... which means they'll grow faster?

Poppy turned excitedly back to her array of plug plants and seedlings, picked up two of the trays, and hurried outside. She found a spot at the base of a sloping lawn in the back garden, which was exposed on all sides and would have the best chance of catching the most sunlight throughout the day. She made a few more trips to transport the rest of the trays outside, then stood back and smiled with pleasure as she saw the warm rays of the afternoon sun playing across the tender young shoots and stems.

"There... soak up all that lovely sunshine and grow big and strong, my little babies," she cooed.

"*N-ow?*"

Poppy turned to see Oren a few feet away, watching her with his big yellow eyes. He was sitting with his tail curled neatly around him and one front paw raised, as if halfway through washing his face.

"There you are!" she exclaimed. "Where have you been all day?" She grinned at the expression on the cat's face. "Yes, Oren. I am actually talking to the plants."

"*Nooo-ow!*" said Oren, putting his paw over his face.

"Oh, shut up," said Poppy, giggling. "Even Prince Charles does it, you know. So it's got the royal seal of approval!"

She turned to head back into the cottage and Oren followed at her heels. As the big tomcat watched, Poppy changed out of her gardening clothes, washed

227

her hands thoroughly at the kitchen sink, then—humming a happy tune—put the kettle on. A short while later, she settled into the sagging old armchair in the living room with a contented sigh. She had a mug of sweet tea in her hands, Oren purring on her lap, and a renewed sense of hope in her chest. She had no idea if putting the plants outside would work, but just doing something—even a little thing—made her feel less helpless and despondent.

Poppy went to bed that night still feeling upbeat, and when she awoke early the next morning, the first thing she thought of was her baby plants. She knew that it was silly to expect any change already (especially given that they were hardly going to benefit from any extra sunshine overnight!)—nevertheless, she was excited to check on the trays. She jumped out of bed and dressed quickly—the morning was much colder than she'd expected, and she shivered as she pulled an extra jumper over her head—then she let herself out of her room.

Tiptoeing so as not to wake Nell, who had come home late and seemed to be having a lie-in, Poppy made her way through the cottage and hurried out the back door, through the greenhouse extension, and into the rear garden. She crossed the grassy slope to where she'd left the trays—then stopped short.

"Oh my God!" gasped Poppy, staring in horror.

Instead of the little plugs of healthy green shoots and leaves she'd left behind the night before, there were now rows of wilted plants with blackened shoots and limp, browned leaves.

"*Noooo...*" wailed Poppy, rushing forwards and dropping to her knees next to the trays.

As she did so, she noticed that the grass she was kneeling on was covered in a coat of soft furry grey, which sparkled in the morning light. Her heart gave an uncomfortable lurch as she realised what it was: *frost*. At the same time, she suddenly remembered reading somewhere about "late spring frosts"... oh, why hadn't she paid more attention?

Poppy turned back to the trays of plug plants and examined them with shaking hands. She had never seen plants look so dreadful: the leaves and shoot tips looked like they had been scorched, and some of the stems looked mushy and almost translucent. When she touched them, everything disintegrated under her fingers.

What am I going to do? wondered Poppy in despair. She felt tears welling up and clogging her throat. These were the last of her seedlings and plug plants. If she lost them, she would have nothing to sell. She had used up all her remaining savings on buying the last batch of plug plants from the wholesalers—she couldn't afford to put in another order until she started to at least earn some profits from the nursery. She did still have some seeds which she could sow for quick-growing annuals, but even if she did those today, they would still take weeks to grow big enough for sale.

Poppy looked back down at the frost-damaged plants and wished fervently that Joe Fabbri was around. Aside from helping with repairs and heavier work around the cottage, the village handyman had also taught her a wealth of gardening skills and knowledge. It had given Poppy reassurance to know that she could always turn to him in times of plant trouble. But Joe had recently accepted a temporary contract to work on a large estate in the Cotswolds. It had meant him leaving Bunnington for a few months, but the pay had been too good for him to turn it down. While Poppy had been glad for Joe, she had missed her unofficial mentor terribly—and now she bemoaned his absence once again.

Joe would have known what to do, she thought as she looked at the damaged plants again. For a moment, she was tempted to call the handyman... then she pushed the thought away. Aside from the fact that it was barely past daybreak and much too early to be calling anyone, she didn't like to bother Joe. *I can't go running to him all the time*, she reminded herself. *I need to learn to deal with garden problems on my own.*

Then Poppy brightened as she suddenly remembered another avuncular figure in her life who was also a fount of knowledge and wisdom. *Bertie! Yes, if anyone might know how to save these plants, it would be him.* Snatching up one of the frost-damaged plug plants, she sprang to her feet and hurried next door to find the old inventor.

CHAPTER TWENTY-FOUR

Poppy let herself through the gate of Bertie's property and walked up to the front door, watching warily for explosions, billowing smoke, strange laser beams, or any of the other things that usually came out of the old inventor's house. Everything seemed to be quiet for once and, in fact, she wasn't even sure if anyone was at home after knocking several times and getting no answer. She was just about to give up when her ears picked up the sound of excitable barking on the other side of the door, faint at first but growing louder. A few minutes later, the front door swung open and Poppy found herself facing the old man and his little terrier.

"Poppy, my dear!" Bertie beamed. "How nice to see you! Forgive me for not answering the door earlier. I was at the back of the house and wouldn't have known you were here if Einstein hadn't alerted me."

Poppy stared at him. "Er... Bertie, do you realise that your hair is on fire?"

"Is it?" said Bertie, reaching up to pat his scalp. He jerked his hand away as his fingers encountered the flames. "Ah, yes... excuse me while I douse the flames."

Slightly bewildered, Poppy followed the old man back into the house and watched as he pointed a miniature fire extinguisher at the top of his head. Soon a cone of white foam replaced the crackling flames, making Bertie look like a Regency gentleman wearing an old-fashioned night cap. Poppy was relieved to see, though, that when the old inventor finally wiped the foam off his head, his scalp didn't seem to be badly burnt. In fact, to her amazement, his hair didn't even seem to be slightly singed.

"Wow, you were really lucky," she commented, standing on tiptoe to examine the top of his head.

"Oh, luck had nothing to do with it," declared Bertie. "It's the new fire-retardant hair gel I'm developing. Using the latest anti-burn technology, it protects the hair shaft and coats the scalp, so that even if your hair goes up in flames, your skin will remain untouched!"

"Er... that sounds very reassuring," said Poppy, wondering who on earth would need such a hair gel.

"Now, my dear, what can I do for you?" asked Bertie, smiling at her.

In answer, Poppy held up the plug plant she had brought with her. "Oh Bertie—I put all my young plants outside last night so they could get more sunshine, and look what's happened to them!"

"Dearie me," said Bertie, taking the plant from her and examining it closely. "Hmm... yes... yes... classic signs of frost damage."

"But I checked the weather forecast and it didn't say that temperatures would drop below freezing," protested Poppy.

"Oh, you can get frost even if the official temperature is above zero," said Bertie. "You see, the temperature measurements reported on the news are normally measured in specialised shelters several feet above ground level, so they can be significantly higher than the actual ground temperature. Especially on clear, calm nights with no cloud cover—like we've been having recently—the coldest air sinks to the ground while the warmer air rises above it. So it could be freezing right at the surface of the ground, even if the official air temperature is above zero. Furthermore, you might have inadvertently placed them in a frost pocket," he added.

"A frost pocket?" said Poppy, frowning. "What's that?"

"Well, as cold air is much denser than warm air and tends to sink, you can get little pools of cold air in certain areas of the garden. Usually where there's a depression or—"

"Oh!" Poppy gasped. "I just remembered! I put all the trays in a spot at the base of a grassy slope."

"Ah…" Bertie shook his head. "Slopes can be particularly dangerous. The cold air, which forms from cooling objects higher up the slope, sinks to the ground and literally flows downhill to pool at the base."

Poppy sighed. "Well, I'll know for next time."

"Yes, and if you do leave tender plants outside, it's best to cover them with mulch or straw or perhaps even horticultural fleece," said Bertie. "But probably best to just wait until the risk of frost is over before putting young plants out. Their tender new growth is particularly susceptible."

"I'll remember all that," said Poppy fervently. "But in the meantime… Bertie, is there anything you can do to save the plants that have been damaged? It's my last batch of stock and if I lose them, I won't have anything to sell!"

Bertie examined the plug plant again and shook his head sadly. "I'm sorry, my dear. This is beyond even my capabilities. You could have a look and see if any of your other remaining plants have unaffected parts close to their crowns." Bertie pointed to the centre of the plant, where the leaves and stems had sprouted from. "Sometimes, if you cut away the frozen sections above, you might be lucky and have some undamaged buds or growth points below the damage, which could re-sprout."

"Thanks, Bertie, I'll try that," said Poppy, taking the dead plant back from him.

"You could also give them a bit of my growth

serum to help them along. And be sure to keep them in the greenhouse, in a nice, warm, sheltered environment, until they've recovered and are growing well again," added Bertie. He patted Poppy's hand. "Don't lose heart, my dear. Nature is more powerful than anything man can invent, and plants have wonderful powers of regeneration."

Poppy gave him a wan smile, then she bent down to cuddle Einstein, who had been dancing excitedly on his hind legs around her, waving his front paws in the air and whining for attention.

"I'm so pleased you popped by, my dear, for I have something exciting to show you," said Bertie, beckoning her to follow him.

Curious, Poppy accompanied him to the rear of the house, where Bertie seemed to have converted one of the bedrooms into a kind of studio with cameras, monitors, and digital equipment everywhere. He had obviously been watching something, as evidenced by the monitor in the corner showing a frozen picture: a video on pause. Poppy tilted her head, trying to figure out what she was seeing on the screen, then realised why she was struggling to orient herself. The footage had obviously been filmed from a very low vantage point, almost a "worm's-eye view", and simple everyday items like doors and street signs loomed gigantically at the edges of the screen.

As Bertie pushed "Play", the screen stirred to life and things began moving. Poppy noticed two furry orange paws appearing and disappearing at the bottom of the screen, pacing along the lane which extended forwards.

"Is that...? Are those Oren's paws?" she asked in surprise.

Bertie paused the video and beamed at her, as if she were a pupil at one of his tutorials back in Oxford and she had come up with a clever answer.

"Yes, my dear. This is footage from the micro-camera I'd attached to Oren's collar. It's only a primitive prototype, of course—nothing as sophisticated as what you can get on the market these days—but it was the best I could rig up with what equipment I had at short notice. You see, I thought it could be an insurance policy of sorts: if I couldn't follow the cat and catch him in the act, I might at least gain some footage which could provide proof of his thieving ways." He looked at her eagerly. "I'm hoping that will convince the police to release Nick."

"Oh, Bertie, didn't you know?" cried Poppy. "They've released Nick already."

"Eh?"

"Yes, he was let out the night before last—we came home from the police station together, actually." Poppy looked at the bewildered old man and added gently, "Maybe he hasn't had time yet to call you and let you know."

But Poppy knew that she was probably just making excuses for Nick. When she had first arrived at Hollyhock Cottage, she had been shocked to discover that the old inventor and the crime writer were father and son. Although they lived within waving distance of each other, on either side of her property, they barely spoke to each other. Nick, in particular, had refused to even acknowledge his father's existence and, despite all Poppy's efforts to probe, the reason for the estrangement between them had remained a mystery.

In recent months, though, Poppy had been heartened to see that Nick's manner towards his father seemed to have thawed—at least he was responding to Bertie's friendly overtures and calling him "Dad", and had more than once stepped in to look after or defend the old man. So she was disappointed now to find that Nick still wasn't making much effort to keep his father in the loop.

He knew that Bertie would be worried about him— he should have let his father know as soon as he got home! thought Poppy with a flash of irritation. As someone who had desperately longed for a father figure all her life, she couldn't understand Nick's lack of appreciation for his parent and his unwillingness to involve Bertie in his life.

Still, she was grateful that Bertie's sunny, childlike disposition meant that the old man rarely held grudges or dwelt on negative assumptions. Now, he brightened at Poppy's words and said:

"Oh yes, I'm sure you're right, my dear. Nick must have been exhausted after his ordeal and probably forgot to call me before he went to bed... and no doubt he's been busy ever since catching up on his writing. Well, never mind. The effort wasn't wasted—as you'll see!"

"What do you mean, Bertie?" asked Poppy, puzzled.

"Ahh...!" The old inventor looked like someone bursting to tell a juicy secret. He leaned towards Poppy, his eyes bright, and said: "During my quest to obtain ample evidence supporting my feline kleptomania theory, I found something unexpected..."

He turned back to a computer next to him and fiddled with some buttons. Poppy saw the screen blur for a few moments before the footage settled once more into a clear picture. This time, she saw that the view was no longer of one of the back lanes of Bunnington but a more open part of the village. The screen was dark, as most of the village was poorly lit at night, and the colours were so washed out that the picture seemed almost monochromatic. Still, Poppy could make out a thick frame of bushes and greenery surrounding the screen, which suggested that Oren must have been sitting underneath a shrub of some kind. Like many cats, the ginger tom enjoyed finding a secluded spot and watching the world from his hiding place.

Poppy frowned, tilting her head from one side to the other, as she tried to look at the screen from different angles. The whole setting seemed somehow familiar, although it was hard to match it up to any of the pictures in her own memory, since the angle and perspective were so different. She could see the side of an old stone building through the branches on the right, as well as several tall flat stone slabs in the near distance, and beyond them, she thought she could catch a glimpse of a large expanse of grass...

The village green, she realised. *Which means that Oren must have been sitting underneath a shrub near... the church! Yes, that's right—those "stone slabs" are gravestones.*

She turned to Bertie to make a comment, then froze as two feet stepped into the frame. They were visible only up to the knees, the rest of the body being beyond the edge of the screen, and they were clad in nondescript trousers and unisex loafers. The only thing that was noticeable about them was that they were wearing mismatched socks: one in an argyle check, the other in a paisley pattern. Poppy was just trying to decide if they were men's or women's when a second pair of feet joined the first in the frame.

These definitely belonged to a woman: Poppy could see the bottom of shapely calves in thick Lycra tapering into a pair of fashionable women's trainers. They stopped in front of the first pair of feet and it was obvious that the two people were talking.

"Can you turn the volume up, Bertie?" asked Poppy urgently.

"There's no sound," said Bertie apologetically. "That would have required me to take even longer to design the micro-camera, and I didn't think it was necessary for my purposes when I only wanted visual evidence of Oren stealing bras from a clothesline."

Poppy turned back to the screen in frustration. It was maddening being unable to hear what was being said, especially as she could see from the body language, and the way the feet shifted, that the two people were having a confrontation of some sort. Even as she watched, the feet in the trainers spun on their heels and turned to walk away. But the legs had barely disappeared off the screen when the other pair of feet lunged in their direction. The next moment, there was a blur of movement and then something slumped down on the ground in front of the camera.

Poppy gasped and jerked backwards, staring at the screen. It was now almost completely filled up by a woman's head, twisted sideways as she lay on the ground. She had obviously fallen down just in front of where Oren was hiding. She was staring straight at the ginger tom—straight into the camera attached to Oren's collar—but her eyes were wide and empty. Poppy felt slightly sick as she recognised the high arched brows, thin lips, and patrician nose.

"Oh my God," Poppy said in a faint voice. She turned to Bertie. "I think we just watched Emma Seymour being murdered!"

CHAPTER TWENTY-FIVE

"Is there anything else from the video which strikes you? Anything which might have a bearing on the case?" Suzanne asked.

Poppy frowned as she stared at the screen in front of her for what seemed like the hundredth time. When she had woken up that morning, she certainly hadn't planned on spending several hours at Bertie's house, watching and re-watching the video footage of Emma Seymour being murdered. Still, at least Suzanne Whittaker was back on the case and she didn't have to deal with Sergeant Lee's contemptuous attitude anymore. The detective inspector had come as soon as she was called, and had spent the better part of the morning going over the footage with them.

Poppy hesitated. "No... not really... except..."

"Yes?" Suzanne looked at her sharply.

"Well..." Poppy pointed at the screen. "The murderer—did you notice that he was wearing mismatched socks? And one of them has a paisley pattern? I just remembered that when I saw Tim Albrecht in his office the other day, he was wearing a paisley-patterned tie."

"Tim Albrecht?" said Suzanne, frowning.

"Yes, you know—he's a friend of Dr Seymour's and he's also Treasurer of the OAC."

"Yes, I do know the name, although I didn't interview him myself. Sergeant Lee did that. I was aware that Albrecht had visited the surgery on the day of the murder, but I didn't think that he'd had any specific interaction with Yvonne. I was under the impression that he'd only popped in to talk to Dr Seymour about Oxfordshire Auricula Club business."

"Well, that might be true, but I also saw him talking to Yvonne at her desk and it didn't look like a casual conversation to me. Um... I did mention it to Sergeant Lee," Poppy added, trying to keep her voice neutral. She didn't want to sound like she was criticising Suzanne's second officer, although at the same time, she felt annoyed that Lee's own prejudices might have caused the police to ignore a potentially important lead.

Suzanne compressed her lips. "Yes, well... for some reason, Amos didn't mention it in his report. I will speak to him about that." She looked back at Poppy. "But just because Albrecht was chatting to

Yvonne that day may not mean very much—"

"It wasn't just 'chatting'," insisted Poppy. "It wasn't random small talk about the weather or something like that. Albrecht seemed to be speaking to her really earnestly about something."

"But what motive would he have?" asked Suzanne. "What reason could Albrecht have for wanting to kill Yvonne?"

"Maybe... maybe he was secretly in love with her! Maybe he'd been trying to get her to go out with him and she kept rejecting him..." Poppy trailed off as she saw Suzanne's scornful expression. "You *did* say 'jealous rage' is the oldest reason in the book," Poppy reminded her.

"Yes, but there's been nothing to suggest a romantic relationship between Albrecht and Yvonne," Suzanne pointed out. "The whole thing could be circumstantial."

"I still think it's too much of a coincidence," said Poppy stubbornly.

"Too much of a coincidence for what? All we've got is that a man seen talking to Yvonne also owns a paisley-patterned tie... and the killer owns some paisley-patterned socks."

"But paisley is an unusual choice for a man, isn't it?" Poppy argued. "At least for a sombre accountant type like Tim Albrecht."

"It's certainly something to note, but I'd be careful drawing too many conclusions from that. Paisley is a popular pattern in general—although I agree, perhaps not for a conservative gentleman's wardrobe," Suzanne conceded. "However, don't forget: we don't know for sure that the murderer is a man. It's hard to tell with the limited view in the video. Those feet could just as well belong to a woman. Until we have more information or evidence, I'm afraid we can't jump to any conclusions. That's what happens with police work in real life—as opposed to in Nick's novels." Suzanne smiled at Poppy. "But I do appreciate your theories and insights. I know that officially I'm not supposed to sanction any involvement in the investigation by the public, but unofficially, I really value your input, Poppy."

Poppy glowed at the words. She often felt like Suzanne was the big sister she'd never had, and she was filled with pride at the other woman's praise. She watched as Suzanne collected a copy of the video, then accompanied her out of Bertie's studio. They found the old inventor outside showing a bemused young constable his Medusa's Head plant.

"...know the prickly bracts look a bit threatening, but she is very friendly, really. Here, you can stroke one of her arms, if you like—" Bertie offered, lifting the plant towards the young constable.

"Uh... no, thank you, sir," he said, hurriedly stepping back.

"Oh, do not be alarmed by the name," said Bertie earnestly. "The association with a Greek monster who can turn people to stone is purely superficial, I assure you. If you take a closer look at her, you will see that she is really the most marvellous plant. Look... look at the halo of elongated stems that radiate out from the central caudex—the symmetry is almost hypnotising, isn't it?"

He thrust the bowl of bristling tentacles into the face of the hapless young constable, who reeled back and instinctively threw up his hands. The action brought one of his palms hard against the side of the bowl, smacking it out of Bertie's grip and sending it flying. It smashed on the floor, spilling compost, broken glass, and green tentacles everywhere.

"My *Euphorbia caput-medusae*!" cried Bertie in horror, rushing over to the prostrate plant.

"I'm... I'm terribly sorry, sir," stammered the young constable. "I didn't mean to..."

He hurried over and attempted to help Bertie scoop as much of the compost and plant back into the broken bowl as possible. Luckily, most of the Medusa's Head seemed to have survived the impact intact—all except for one coiled tentacle which had broken off the main stem.

"Um..." The constable picked this up and handed it to Bertie, shamefaced. "I'm sorry, sir, but it looks like one of the... er... arms has come off."

"Oh, not to worry," said Bertie cheerfully. "That's the wonderful thing about succulents. They are so easy to propagate from broken pieces. In fact..." He whirled to face Suzanne. "...this would be perfect for you, Inspector Whittaker!"

"For me?" said Suzanne, startled.

"Yes, yes," said Bertie, holding the tentacle up to show her. "You just have to wait a few days for the end to callous over, then stick it in a pot of well-draining compost and it will grow into an entirely new plant!"

"Er... thank you, Dr Noble. That's very kind of you, but really, with my workload and lifestyle at the moment, I just don't have the time to look after any plant—"

"Aha, but that's why this would make the perfect housemate for you!" cried Bertie "You see, being a succulent—which are the most forgiving of plants—she would practically thrive on neglect. All she needs is a warm spot with bright light, a bit of water once a week, and hardly any other maintenance! And you can grow her in anything you like: a pot, a glass container, a teacup..." He glanced down at Suzanne's immaculate black boots. "...or even a shoe!"

The young constable chortled, then hastily wiped the smirk off his face as Suzanne gave him a steely look. She turned back to Bertie, who held the long section of coiled succulent out to her.

"Here you go—your perfect partner for 'domestic bliss'," he said, beaming.

It was obvious that sharing her home with a huge green tentacle was not Suzanne's idea of "domestic bliss". Still, like many before her, she found it difficult to resist Bertie's simple goodwill and childlike enthusiasm. She reached out and took the tentacle gingerly between thumb and forefinger, saying weakly, "Well... er... thank you, Dr Noble."

"Would you like one too?" asked Bertie, rounding on the constable. "I can easily break off another piece—"

"Ah... no, no..." said the young officer, stepping back in alarm. He shot Suzanne a panicked look. "I... um... I'd better go and check on the car, ma'am!" Then he turned and fled from the house.

***

When she finally got back to Hollyhock Cottage after the morning's excitement, Poppy followed Bertie's advice and went through her frost-damaged plants, discarding most of them as they were obviously dead, but managing to salvage a tray's worth of plug plants that looked like they might still have living tissue at their bases. Carefully, she trimmed away the damaged leaves and stems, and then placed the survivors back in the greenhouse. Now all she could do was wait and hope...

In the meantime, she occupied herself mulling over the mystery. It helped to take her mind off her worries about her plants and the future of the nursery. Business was quiet all day, so Poppy spent a lot of time going over her conversation with Suzanne that morning and pondering Tim Albrecht's involvement. When Nell arrived home from her cleaning jobs late that evening, Poppy couldn't wait to pounce on her friend to have someone to discuss the case with. She told Nell about the new evidence found on Oren's micro-camera footage and went over the interview with Suzanne.

"...I just can't shake the feeling that Albrecht is guilty in some way!" said Poppy as she concluded.

Nell looked up placidly from where she was making a mug of late-night cocoa and said: "But Suzanne is right, dear—what motive could he have? Why should he want to murder Yvonne—and Emma Seymour too?"

"I'm surprised you don't like my idea that Albrecht was secretly in love with Yvonne and murdered her for rejecting him," said Poppy, giving her friend a teasing look.

Nell sniffed. "One love triangle in this case is more than enough. Besides, that wouldn't explain why Albrecht killed Emma as well."

Poppy sighed. Her friend was right. She was grasping at straws. She knew that unless Albrecht could be shown to have a good motive for both murders, the chances of convicting him were slim. She closed her eyes for a moment as she thought back to the day she had gone to the village GP: she saw herself coming out of the inner consulting office and seeing a middle-aged man with a goatee leaning over Yvonne's desk in the waiting room. Tim Albrecht. The accountant had jumped up—almost furtively—as she and Dr Seymour had come out of the inner office.

"Tim!" Dr Seymour had exclaimed. "What are you doing here, old chap?"

"I... uh... I had some club business to discuss with Yvonne..."

The scene in Poppy's mind flashed forward to Dr Seymour smiling and saying: *"It'll be great to have someone with more organisational ability manage things... Tim's the official Treasurer, but he's been hopeless! We seem to have got ourselves into a complete muddle with the club funds."*

Poppy opened her eyes again, her pulse quickening with excitement. "Nell! I just thought of something which could give Tim Albrecht the perfect motive!" she cried, grabbing her startled friend by the arm. "Listen, you know Bryan was convinced that Ralph Seymour was the one secretly withdrawing funds from the research grant. But what if it wasn't him? What if it had been *another* member of the OAC? Albrecht is the club treasurer... well, who better to have access to the funds in the OAC account?"

"You think he's the one who made those withdrawals?" said Nell.

Poppy nodded eagerly. "Yes, and that would give him a very good reason to kill Yvonne: to stop her from exposing his guilt! Maybe that was why he was speaking to her on the day I saw them at the surgery. Maybe he was trying to convince her to help him cover things up and, when she refused, he decided that he had to kill her."

"But what about Emma?" asked Nell.

"He could have killed her for a similar reason," said Poppy. "Remember I told you she kept insisting on helping with the Oxfordshire Auricula Club affairs that day—in fact, she specifically mentioned wanting to take over the club accounts."

"I thought that was nothing more than a 'tit-for-tat' to get back at Yvonne," commented Nell.

"Yes, it probably was, but whatever the reason, it would have meant Emma examining the club accounts in more detail—and Tim Albrecht couldn't afford that." Poppy paused and thought for a moment, then added excitedly, "Oh Nell! I just thought of something else! You know that night when you were out and I went down to the Lucky Ladybird for dinner, I was asking Martin for an accountant recommendation and he told me about Albrecht. Well, he mentioned that Albrecht had offered them 'investment advice' as well—in particular, trying to convince them to invest in an overseas scheme where they could 'buy a share in a foreign holiday home' which would give them 'guaranteed time in the sun each year'—"

"That sounds just like a timeshare scheme," said Nell, pursing her lips. "I've heard some horror stories about those, I can tell you. Especially in places like Portugal and Spain—"

"Yes, exactly, Spain!" Poppy cried. "Suzanne said that the withdrawals from the OAC account went to a company in Spain; it was some kind of property development on the beach. I'd have to check with Martin again to confirm, but I'll bet that the scheme that Albrecht had been promoting to him was located in Spain too!"

"Are you suggesting that Albrecht was involved in some kind of timeshare scam?" asked Nell.

"Well, maybe not a scam outright. After all, he's part of a respectable local accountancy firm. But maybe it was a business venture on the side that got into trouble. You know, Suzanne mentioned that they were having trouble finding a contact for the company in Spain because it had folded," said Poppy thoughtfully. "So maybe Albrecht had been secretly skimming money off the research grant in the OAC accounts in order to support his failing business. And then when Yvonne had found out..." She trailed off ominously.

"It's a pretty good theory," Nell agreed.

"Yes, it all fits! Oh, I can't wait to tell Suzanne!"

Poppy whirled around, looking for her phone.

"Oh, leave the poor woman be," said Nell. "She seems to work all the hours that God gives as it is. Give Suzanne the evening off. You can call her first thing in the morning. It's not as if Tim Albrecht is going to go anywhere."

Reluctantly, Poppy put her phone back down. Nell was right. It wasn't as if she had hard evidence which would enable the police to arrest Tim Albrecht on the spot. All she was doing was relaying a hunch to Suzanne and that could easily wait until the morning.

Still, Poppy found it hard to go to sleep that night and she tossed and turned, her mind buzzing with speculation about the case. And when she awoke the next morning, her first thought was of something that made her sit upright in bed: when Oren had returned to Nick's house the other night and had interrupted the "awkward" moment between them, the ginger tom had been carrying a sock... *A paisley-patterned sock!* thought Poppy excitedly. Could Oren have stolen it from Tim Albrecht's house? She recalled Martin telling her that the accountant lived in the village. It could also explain why the murderer had been wearing mismatched socks in the video— because he couldn't find the other one!

If only cats could talk! thought Poppy ruefully. *If Oren could just tell us whose house he'd stolen the paisley sock from, we might have our killer!*

She pushed back the covers and glanced at the windows. From the pale light seeping through the curtains, she guessed that it was barely after sunrise. Still too early to call Suzanne.

I'll go for a walk, she decided impulsively, jumping out of bed. She always loved that feeling of being out and about first thing in the morning, when the day was fresh, and the world was just awakening. A morning walk would be the perfect way to start the day.

CHAPTER TWENTY-SIX

A short while later, after a hasty wash and getting dressed in warm clothes, Poppy let herself out the front gate of Hollyhock Cottage and started up the lane towards the centre of the village. As she walked along the narrow streets meandering through Bunnington, she couldn't help recalling a similar stroll she'd taken only a few days ago. That had been the morning she had returned to the GP surgery to retrieve her locket. It was strange to think that she had been walking this same route, past these same houses and gardens, with no idea of the dead body she was about to find and the can of worms she was about to open.

She had almost reached the Seymours' property when she saw a familiar orange shape come out of the gate of a house further up the lane. It was Oren, and Poppy's eyes widened as she saw what the ginger tom was carrying in his mouth.

"Aha! Caught you in the act!" she cried, rushing up to intercept the cat. "I can't believe you're still stealing bras, you wretch!"

"*Nnn-oowrr?*" said Oren, muffled, as he looked up at her innocently.

"Give me that," said Poppy, reaching down to tug the bra out of Oren's mouth.

The ginger tom released it, but then lunged and grabbed at the straps with his paws.

"Oy! Let go, Oren... let go!" said Poppy, jerking and twisting the bra in frustration as she tried to pull it out of the cat's grasp.

The ginger tom gave a chirrup of delight and rolled over onto his back, grabbing the straps with his teeth and kicking furiously with his hind legs, obviously thinking it was a wonderful new game. Poppy wrestled with him for a few minutes and got several scratches for her pains, but finally emerged triumphant, clutching the freed bra. "You're a terror!" she said, scowling down at the cat. "The vet said you should be stopping all this behaviour now that you're back on your normal diet."

Oren lolled on his back and tilted his head to give her a cheeky look. "*N-ow?*"

"You stay here while I go and return this to its rightful owner," said Poppy sternly.

Of course, Oren took no notice and trotted after her as Poppy took the bra and walked up to the front gate of the property that she had seen him slinking out from. He jumped over the gate before she had a chance to open it and sauntered beside her, totally without shame, as she went up to the front door. Clearing her throat, Poppy rang the bell, hoping fervently that the owner wouldn't be another village resident like Mrs Busselton. She was surprised when the door opened to reveal Adeline Payne. The other woman was obviously an early riser as well—in fact, from the orange stains on the apron she was wearing, it looked like she was already busy in the kitchen.

"Oh hello!" The woman smiled shyly at her. Then her gaze dropped to the bra that Poppy was holding in her hands and her eyes rounded in surprise.

"Hello, Miss Payne. I think this is yours," said Poppy with a rueful grin, holding up the brassiere.

The other woman gave a squeak of embarrassment. "Oh... oh, it is! But how—?"

Poppy gestured to Oren, who was sitting by her feet, nonchalantly washing a paw. "Meet Bunnington's resident feline thief."

"Feline thief?" Miss Payne looked bewildered. "But I thought... didn't Mrs Busselton say that it was a sexual pervert and the crime author who lives—"

"That was all a misunderstanding," said Poppy quickly. "In fact, the culprit responsible for stealing all those bras is right here. This is Oren. He belongs to Nick Forrest, the crime author, and he's the one who's been nicking all the lingerie in the village and taking it back to Nick's house."

"Really?" Miss Payne looked at Oren in disbelief. "But why on earth would he have done that?"

"Who knows why cats do anything?" said Poppy, rolling her eyes. She held out the bra. "Anyway, here you go, Miss Payne... I caught Oren coming out of your house with this just now and I thought I'd better return it."

"Coming out of my house? But all the windows and doors are shut," protested Miss Payne.

"Well, maybe not literally coming out of your house. I meant: coming out of your front gate. I'm guessing that Oren probably stole it from your washing line. That's what he usually does, I think."

"But I don't use the washing line," Miss Payne said, frowning. "At least, I only use it once it really warms up in the summer. At this time of year, I usually dry my things in the dryer, or I hang them up indoors." She looked worriedly at the cat. "So how on earth did he get hold of my bra?"

As if in reply, Oren suddenly stopped washing his paw and got up. He walked across the threshold into the house, strolling past a bemused Miss Payne and ignoring Poppy's indignant calls to come back. Both women watched as he sauntered down the hallway and disappeared around the corner.

"Sorry," said Poppy with an apologetic smile. "He's terrible sometimes! Do you mind if I come in to fetch him?"

"Of course... come in, come in," said Miss Payne, gesturing Poppy into the house. "And please... do call me Adeline."

They hurried together after Oren and found him in the cramped laundry room at the rear of the house. He had climbed onto the top of the washing machine and was eyeing an octopus-shaped clothes hanger with interest. Several items of underwear, socks, and lingerie were hanging from the pegs of the circular plastic device, and Poppy could see one empty peg where the bra that had been stolen had obviously been attached.

"Oren! Leave those alone!" she said, giving the tomcat a stern look.

Oren ignored her and reached out insolently with a paw to pat a dangling sock.

"He's quite a naughty character, isn't he?" observed Miss Payne with a laugh.

Poppy heaved a sigh. "You have no idea." Then she paused as she spied something: a small dog door embedded in the door connecting the laundry room to the back garden. "Have you got a dog?" she asked.

Miss Payne shook her head. "No, but the previous owners must have done. I found that dog door already installed when I moved in here."

"Ah, well, there's your answer to how Oren managed to steal your bra," said Poppy with a smile. "He obviously found the dog door and thought it was a personal invitation. Maybe you should lock it, if you can."

"Ohhh... you're right. Yes, I'll make sure to do that. I suppose I ought to anyway, for security reasons. Mrs Busselton was just warning me the other day that even if burglars can't get in through a cat flap, for example, they can reach in and hook things with a tool." The other woman shuddered. "It makes me scared to live alone sometimes."

"I'm sure it'll be fine if you can just lock the flap or wedge it shut," said Poppy, feeling bad for frightening her. "Bunnington is really quite safe, you know. I used to live in London—in one of the dodgy parts—and I can tell you, this is nothing like a big city!"

"Oh. Well, it's just... Mrs Busselton has been telling everyone in the village..." Miss Payne paused uncertainly. "She says that Yvonne was killed by some sex maniac, and at first everyone thought it was the crime author, but then when I heard that he was released by the police... I thought..."

"You thought what?" Poppy asked.

"I thought about that bearded chap."

Poppy frowned. "What bearded chap?"

"You know, the man who came to talk to Yvonne at the surgery that day."

Tim Albrecht? Poppy looked at Miss Payne in surprise. "I didn't realise you'd seen him with Yvonne. I thought he arrived after you'd left."

"Well, I *was* just leaving," admitted Miss Payne. "He came in just as I was on my way out. There was no one else in the waiting room by then, of course, as you'd gone in with Dr Seymour."

"And Tim Albrecht?"

"Pardon?"

"Oh, that's the 'bearded chap's' name," Poppy explained. "What did he do?"

"He went straight over to Yvonne's desk to talk to her and, since I had to stop by the door to adjust my scarf, I couldn't help overhearing a bit of what they were saying," said Miss Payne.

Yeah, I'll bet, thought Poppy in amusement. *You probably dragged out the scarf-arranging so that you could have an excuse to linger and eavesdrop on their conversation!* Aloud, she said: "So you heard what they were talking about?"

"Well, not exactly. I mean, he was bending over her desk and talking in a low voice, so I only got snatches here and there. He seemed quite agitated, though." She paused, furrowing her brow in thought, then added, "I think he was trying to persuade her to do something—I heard him say 'Please, Yvonne' a few times. Perhaps he wanted her to go out with him on a date and she didn't want to."

"Why d'you say that?"

"Well, I heard him say 'meet me' and 'tonight'—"

"You heard Albrecht asking Yvonne to meet him that night?" Poppy cut in. "You know, the murderer lured Yvonne to the surgery with a note inviting her to an assignation there... Do you realise what this means? Your testimony could help prove that Tim Albrecht could be the murderer!" she said excitedly. "You must ring the police and tell them your story! Or... or maybe even go down to the station in person," she added, thinking that if Miss Payne had to speak to Sergeant Lee instead of Suzanne, he might be forced to take her more seriously if she were standing in front of him, whereas he might fob her off on the phone.

"Oh... all right. But I have to change," said Miss Payne, looking flustered as she fussed with her clothes. "I've been cooking and I'm such a mess."

"I'm sure the police won't mind," Poppy reassured her. She gestured to the other woman's apron. "If you just take your apron off, you'll be fine. Most of the stains seem to be on that."

"Oh yes, that's a good idea. Thank goodness I put on this apron this morning," said Miss Payne, untying the apron and tossing it into a heaped laundry basket next to the washing machine.

"Looks like it didn't catch everything, though," said Poppy, pointing regretfully to an orange stain on the front of the woman's white blouse.

Miss Payne glanced down. "Oh, that's an old stain. It's from that day at the surgery—those dreadful lilies and their pollen."

"Yeah, I'm not that keen on lilies either," said Poppy, making a face. "And they're poisonous to cats so—" She broke off suddenly, staring at the woman in front of her. "Wait... when did you say you got that stain on your blouse?"

"A couple of days ago, at Dr Seymour's surgery. There was a vase of lilies on Yvonne's desk. I must have brushed against one of the flowers when I was bending over and didn't notice. In fact, I only saw the stain when I got home." Miss Payne made a face. "I did try to get it out—I tried rinsing with soda water and dusting with baking soda—but nothing seems to have worked. I have a bad feeling it's permanent now. Why?" She looked at Poppy quizzically.

"Oh... nothing... I just thought that maybe if it was still fresh... um... you might have a better chance of getting it out," mumbled Poppy. "Er... I'll just grab Oren, shall I? And then we can leave..."

She turned to where the ginger tom was still sitting atop the washing machine. She was trying to act nonchalant, but her mind was racing. She could vividly remember Emma Seymour bringing the bunch of lilies into the surgery that day and ordering Yvonne to put them in a vase on the reception desk. But that had been *after* Poppy had come out from her consultation with Dr Seymour—*after* Miss Payne had already left the surgery.

So how had the other woman got lily pollen on her blouse? The only way she could have come into contact with the lilies was if she had gone back to the surgery later that night.

Poppy flashed back suddenly to the morning she had discovered Yvonne's body. The vase had been lying shattered on the floor next to the dead girl, with the lilies scattered everywhere, as if they had been knocked over in a struggle. Poppy felt a chill run up her spine as an incredulous thought struck her. *No, it couldn't be...*

Then she heard the sound of the laundry door clicking shut and she whirled around to find herself staring into the eyes of a murderer.

CHAPTER TWENTY-SEVEN

"That was silly of me, wasn't it?" said Miss Payne pleasantly. "A slip of the tongue. After I said it, I realised what you must have just worked out: that I couldn't have got the stain on my blouse at the surgery that day. At least, not when I was officially there."

"You killed Yvonne? *You* are the murderer?" said Poppy, staring at the other woman. "And you killed Emma too, didn't you? But... why?"

"Why? Because they were both silly, selfish cows who didn't deserve Ralph!" snapped Miss Payne, scowling. "Yvonne was dragging him into a sordid affair, and Emma treated him like a pet dog. They were both witches who were making him miserable!" Then her face changed, softened, and she added in a pensive voice: "Ralph needs a woman who loves him and understands him, and who is willing to sacrifice everything for him..."

"This is all just because you're in love with Ralph Seymour?" said Poppy in disbelief.

Miss Payne gave Poppy a coy, girlish look. "Oh, he's in love with me too. He just doesn't realise it yet. But I can be patient. I've been watching and waiting for months now... biding my time... waiting for the right moment... And in the meantime, I had my regular visits to the GP surgery to look forward to, when I would have ten minutes or so alone with my Ralph while he listened to all my problems..." She sighed blissfully.

"So Emma was right. You *were* making up excuses to see him, just like some creepy stalker," said Poppy in disgust.

"I'm not a stalker!" cried Miss Payne. "I didn't follow Ralph around or break into his house and steal his things. Well, other than a few notes that I filched from his desk at the surgery when he wasn't looking. But that was only because I needed a sample of his handwriting so I could copy it for that note to Yvonne." She giggled suddenly. "Oh... and I did pinch a gnome from their garden. But I meant to return it, you know. I was just going to give it a bit of a clean. It was so dirty."

"Is that what you used to kill Yvonne?"

"Yes. Well, I didn't intend to kill her. Not really," said Miss Payne earnestly. "I just thought she was being so unreasonable. I told her she had to leave

Ralph alone but she just wouldn't listen! She actually laughed at me. It made me so cross, you know. So I gave her a little knock on the head with the gnome. How lucky that I happened to have it with me! I'd been intending to put it back in Ralph's garden, you see, and so I was carrying it around in my satchel with me, waiting for an opportune moment."

Poppy couldn't believe the surreal conversation she was having. Miss Payne was talking about a murder she'd committed as calmly as if she were describing an afternoon's gardening she'd done.

"What about Emma?" asked Poppy. "How did you lure her to the churchyard?"

"Oh, I didn't arrange that—that was a happy accident," said Miss Payne, beaming. "I happened to see her walking past my kitchen windows that morning, and I decided to follow her. I wanted to speak to her, you see, and explain that she really needed to divorce Ralph so that he could be free to marry me. He's much too noble to leave her, so she had to be the one to let him go." Her face darkened. "But Emma was just like Yvonne! Only thinking about herself! And she called me all sorts of dreadful names, too, just because I told her that I'd fibbed to the police about seeing her car on the night of Yvonne's murder—"

"You mean you didn't?" said Poppy, aghast to find that she had been duped as well. "So Emma really was home that night?"

Miss Payne shrugged. "I suppose so. Well, I

thought if I could get her in trouble with the police, they would take her away. Then Ralph would be free! But unfortunately, it didn't quite work. So I decided that I'd have to kill her after all. So inconvenient." She brightened. "Still, like I said, it was lucky that I happened to spot her walking past that morning. And even more lucky that I hadn't returned Ralph's gnome to his garden yet. It was in my hallway, amongst my shoes, you see. I grabbed it on my way out and it was so useful for hitting Emma on the head."

She reached into the laundry basket next to the washing machine and rummaged around, then extracted something from beneath the pile of clothes. Poppy felt slightly sick as she saw that it was a garden gnome, stained and dirty, with one end smeared with blood.

Miss Payne turned the ceramic figure over, examining it thoughtfully. "I haven't had a chance to clean it yet since killing Emma. But not to worry— the paint on the ceramic is still very waterproof and the stains should wash off easily." She looked back up at Poppy and said with a smile, "I'm really beginning to think that this is my lucky gnome, and I ought to keep it. Do you think Ralph would mind if I don't give it back?"

She's completely barking, thought Poppy wildly. *Absolutely stark raving mad. I have to get out of here!*

But even as she had the thought, she saw Miss Payne's eyes narrow and the other woman said, "It's such a pain. I'll have to kill you too now. After all, I can't have you telling the police what you know."

"Er... let's not rush into anything," said Poppy hastily, taking a step back and looking nervously around the laundry room.

It was a narrow, cramped space, connected to the house by a door at one end and another door leading out into the garden at the other. Miss Payne had shut the adjoining door to the house and was standing in front of it, so that route of escape was blocked. But the other door which led into the garden was right behind where Poppy was standing. If she could somehow open it and get out before Miss Payne got hold of her...

"So... um... are you planning to marry Ralph immediately?" she asked, trying to distract Miss Payne as she backed up another few steps, until she felt the solid surface of the back door against her shoulder blades.

"Well, I suppose we'd have to wait a short amount of time before announcing our engagement, otherwise it wouldn't look very decent, would it? I'd like some time to find my wedding dress too," said Miss Payne, her eyes becoming dreamy. "I want something with lots of lace... and ribbons... and a veil that reaches to the ground..."

Slowly, Poppy slid her hands behind her back and groped around for the door handle. Her fingers found it and she twisted it urgently, but nothing happened.

Bugger! she thought. The door was obviously

locked.

Then her spirits lifted as her fingers slid downwards and encountered the shape of an old-fashioned brass key, protruding from a keyhole. She glanced at Miss Payne. The woman was still gazing into space, dreamily reciting the details of the wedding reception she was going to have. Slowly, trying to be subtle, Poppy shifted her position until her fingers caught hold of the head of the key. She turned it with a slow, deliberate motion, hoping that the unlocking mechanism wouldn't make a loud sound...

"What are you doing?"

Poppy froze and looked up to see that Miss Payne had broken off from her daydreaming and was watching her now with hard, suspicious eyes. The other woman's fingers clenched around the garden gnome and she took a menacing step forwards.

Oh, to hell with subtlety! thought Poppy, whirling, and throwing herself at the door. Her fingers fumbled frantically, trying to turn the key in the keyhole.

She heard a satisfying loud *CLICK,* but before she could turn the handle and yank the door open, something came down on her like a pouncing cougar.

Poppy screamed. She crumpled to her knees, with Miss Payne on top of her.

"*NOOOOOO-OWWWW!*" yowled Oren from the top of the washing machine, hissing and puffing up to twice his size as he watched them.

Squirming and struggling like mad, Poppy

managed to wriggle her top half free of the other woman's grasp.

"Let me go! LET ME GO!" screamed Poppy.

She flailed around, trying to find something to grab on to and pull herself upright, but the tiled floor of the laundry was slippery and there was nothing around her except the wall on one side, the corner of the washing machine on the other, and, right in front of her, the solid face of the door leading out to the garden...

Then there was a flash of orange next to her and Poppy felt a furry tail brush her face as Oren shot past her and seemed to disappear straight through the door.

No, wait, he hasn't disappeared—he's gone through the door and out into the garden on the other side, Poppy realised. She saw, as if for the first time, the square opening with a flap embedded in the bottom of the door.

Lunging forwards with all her strength, she shoved her head through the dog door and tried to wriggle through. But it was too small. Her shoulders were wedged in the opening and she could still feel Miss Payne's vise-like grip around her legs.

"HELP!" she screamed. "HELP ME!"

There was no reply and Poppy wondered despairingly if anyone would hear her. There wouldn't be many people about this early in the morning, and Miss Payne's cottage was at the edge of the village. Who was going to save her?

Then, to her shock and disbelief, she heard a familiar booming voice shouting in reply: "KEEP CALM AND HOLD ON! The Bunnington Brigade is on the way!"

CHAPTER TWENTY-EIGHT

"I never thought I'd say this, but I was so happy to see Mrs Busselton when she came charging around the corner of that garden, I could have kissed her!" said Poppy with a laugh. "Thank goodness for her Neighbourhood Watch obsession and her paranoia about crime in the village. If she hadn't been doing the Bunnington Brigade's 'early morning patrol' or whatever she calls it, I might not be sitting here."

"My lordy Lord, Poppy, you still had a narrow escape. Miss Payne sounds absolutely off her rocker! She could have killed you yesterday and no one would have been the wiser," said Nell, tutting and shaking her head. "The next time you go haring off to confront a murderer, make sure you let someone know where you're going. You won't always have Mrs

Busselton there to save you, you know."

"Aww, come on, Nell—how could I have known that Miss Payne would turn out to be the killer? Nobody suspected her!" protested Poppy. "Even Suzanne never considered her a suspect. She seemed so docile, so pitiful, so unthreatening—just the stereotypical sad, lonely spinster—"

"That just goes to show: you shouldn't rush to label people with stereotypes," said Nell.

"Although, thinking about it, it wasn't totally unrelated," Poppy said thoughtfully. "I mean, in this case, Miss Payne's personal circumstances did play a part in the murders. If she hadn't led such a socially isolated life, maybe she wouldn't have developed this obsessive romantic fixation with Dr Seymour and built this fantasy that they were destined to be together."

"Yes, I heard that her mental state will be taken into account at her trial," said Nell. "I do feel sorry for the poor woman, in a way."

"Oh God, so did I and so did everyone!" said Poppy. "That was why she was so successful at deflecting suspicion from herself and framing others. Everyone just saw this shy, middle-aged lady who might be a bit eccentric but who wouldn't hurt a fly... and everyone believed whatever she said." Poppy paused. "Actually, no, wait—not everyone. Sergeant Lee didn't."

"Sergeant Lee?"

Poppy made a face. "Yeah, much as I hate to admit

it, Sergeant Lee was right for once. I told him that Miss Payne said she saw Emma Seymour driving out of the village on the night of the murder, but he was really sceptical. He said Miss Payne might be lying. Well, he turned out to be right! Although it wasn't for the reason he thought. He thought she was just a busybody with an overactive imagination, whereas she was actually doing it on purpose to make Emma look suspicious. It was the same with Tim Albrecht: Suzanne told me last night that she questioned him and he admitted to talking with Yvonne at her desk that day. He did actually have a bit of a soft spot for her and had been trying to flirt with her, but he never asked her to meet him or any of the other things that Miss Payne had told me she overheard him saying. She just made that all up to make him look guilty."

"Well, now, that sounds quite manipulative and calculating," said Nell, looking surprised. "Maybe she doesn't deserve much sympathy after all!" She rose briskly from the kitchen table. "Anyway, you'd better hurry up and finish your breakfast, dear, or you'll be late opening the nursery."

Poppy sighed as she thought of the day ahead. It might be satisfying to know that the mystery of Yvonne and Emma's murders had been solved, but her bigger problems still remained. How was she going to earn an income and keep the nursery going with no plants for sale?

Nell looked at her with sympathy. "How were the plants this morning?"

Poppy shrugged. "They look much the same." She had checked on her frost-damaged seedlings first thing that morning, hoping in vain that they might have already started showing signs of regrowth. But although they weren't dead, they didn't seem to be doing much better either.

"It'll take time, dear," said Nell soothingly. "I'm sure, given a chance, they'll recover and grow into healthy, beautiful plants you can sell. You just need to be a bit patient."

"Yes, but what do I do in the meantime?" asked Poppy.

"Are you completely out of stock?"

"I have a few pots left," Poppy said. "They're the last of the batch that were on display. I'm totally out of cyclamens now, but I've got a couple of primroses left, and a few pots of violas. Oh, and a small batch of hollyhock seedlings which I was going to plant, but now I think I might as well offer for sale. But even if I sell all of those things, it's not going to bring much in..."

"Well, I've been wanting to talk to you about this for some time," said Nell, coming over to stand in front of Poppy. "I know when you invited me to come and live at Hollyhock Cottage with you, you said you wouldn't take any rent. That was really sweet of you, dear, but I'd like to give you some of my income. It won't be much, unfortunately, as my cleaning jobs don't pay that much, but at least—"

"No, Nell!" cried Poppy, jumping up from her

chair. "No, I'm not taking any money from you. You already pay for a lot of the food and groceries we share, and besides, it's important that you keep the rest for yourself."

"What am I going to keep it for?" asked Nell.

"Well, you might want to go on holiday... or... or just build up a nest egg for retirement. I mean, you won't be able to keep doing cleaning jobs for ever," said Poppy.

"I'm only in my sixties. I'm hardly decrepit!" said Nell, bristling slightly. She rolled her sleeves up to her elbows. "And I shall be cleaning until I'm lying in my grave!"

Yes, and probably have the cleanest, shiniest coffin too, thought Poppy with amusement. Aloud she said, "I'm not taking money from you, Nell. So you can forget the whole idea."

Nell compressed her lips. "Well... fine... we'll leave it *for now*," she said, stressing the last two words.

"Maybe the damaged plants will recover better and grow faster than I expect," said Poppy with false brightness. "I just need to get through the next few weeks, that's all!"

She found it hard to keep up the façade of cheerful optimism, though, when she arrived at the trestle table an hour later and was reminded once again of how meagre her offerings were. It was particularly frustrating because the media attention from Miss Payne's arrest had put Bunnington in the news again. Just like before, the notoriety brought a rush of curious tourists from afar, as well as nosy residents from the surrounding area, and many of them came to the nursery when they heard the role its owner had played in the solving of the two murders.

Poppy watched the customers arrive with a mixture of elation and frustration. It seemed like such a wasted opportunity to have so many people finally come and visit Hollyhock Cottage, only to have them disappointed! Instead of proudly displaying a variety of vigorous plants for sale, Poppy found herself once again fielding the same embarrassing questions and disparaging comments about the poor quality of her stock. By lunchtime, after most customers had left empty-handed, she was feeling more dispirited than ever. But she plastered a smile on her face as she went up to the latest arrivals: a smartly dressed couple who looked disgruntled as they examined the spindly specimens lined up on the trestle table.

"So... is this all you've got?" asked the wife. "Haven't you got more advanced plants?"

Poppy dredged up a breezy smile. "Um... not at the moment. But they are... er... in production and I'll have more advanced stock soon. Maybe if you could pop back in a couple of weeks...?"

"I need something now," the wife said impatiently. "I'm putting my house on the market and I need the garden to look its best. I was hoping to find some ready-to-plant potted colour and annuals, to spruce up the beds."

"Oh... I'll have plenty of those," said Poppy quickly. "Just... um... next week."

The husband rolled his eyes and heaved an irritable sigh. "We haven't got time to muck around," he growled to his wife. "I *told* you we should have gone to one of the big garden centres. I don't know why you insisted on coming to this poky little place—"

"Well, everyone says you should support local businesses," his wife protested. "I was just trying to do my bit for the community."

The husband cast a contemptuous look around. "Yeah, well, I doubt this place will be around much longer, so why bother trying to support it?"

Poppy flushed and clenched her hands, shoving them into her pockets. Her right hand encountered something small, hard, and cylindrical. Surprised, she pulled it out: it was a tiny glass vial filled with a clear amber liquid.

It's Bertie's growth serum, she realised. She had almost completely forgotten about it. Now, she rolled the tiny vial between her fingers as she watched the husband and wife move to hover over a row of seedlings set apart from the rest.

"What are these?" asked the wife.

"Those are hollyhocks," Poppy replied.

The wife leaned over to peer at the row of small pots, her mouth turning downwards. "Hollyhocks? I thought they'd be much bigger. If you're going to buy seedlings, you want them a decent size—otherwise you might as well sow the seeds yourself!"

"The... um... the weather hasn't been very cooperative," said Poppy weakly. "But they'll grow very fast once you get them into the ground."

The husband sneered: "I thought a nursery called Hollyhock Cottage would at least have decent hollyhocks, if nothing else."

Poppy felt a surge of anger and her fingers tightened around the vial of growth serum. When the couple turned away, she leaned impulsively over the pots, uncorked the vial, and sprinkled a few drops of the serum onto the hollyhock seedlings. Then she watched them with bated breath.

Nothing happened.

Poppy sighed. Well, it seemed that, for once, Bertie's invention wasn't working. She shoved the vial back into her pocket and turned away, disappointed.

Maybe I can try what I did with Bryan, she thought, approaching the couple, who looked like they were getting ready to leave.

"Um... how about a ready-planted container for a pop of colour?" she offered brightly. "I've got some lovely terracotta pots and I can make an arrangement with several plants in each. You won't notice their smaller size so much when they're grouped together." Poppy smiled persuasively. "I won't charge you for the terracotta pots. You could place them by your front door, for example—they'll look lovely and provide an attractive welcome to any potential buyers coming to view your house."

"Hmm... I suppose," said the wife, obviously tempted by the offer of free pots. She wandered back along the trestle table. "Can I choose from any of the plants here? I suppose the—" She broke off and stared. "Were these here before?"

"What?" asked Poppy, surprised. She followed the direction of the woman's gaze. "Oh... yes, those are the hollyhock seedlings you looked at, remember?"

"I could have sworn they were smaller," said the woman, frowning. "They seem to have doubled in size. I'm sure they didn't have so many leaves."

Her husband lifted one of the small pots off the trestle table and peered at the seedling quizzically. A leaf bud poked suddenly out from the crown and elongated. It unfurled rapidly into the distinctive palmate shape of a hollyhock leaf and smacked the husband in the face.

"Uuugghh!" he said, reeling back. "What the—!"

"Well! These actually look quite vigorous," said the wife, smiling. "I suppose I didn't get a good look at them the first time. I think I'll take all six of these."

Poppy was delighted. She hurried to get a cardboard box to place the seedlings into. But when she returned to the trestle table, she was taken aback to find that the seedlings seemed to have doubled in size again! And by the time she managed to cram them into the box, they were already developing sturdy flower stalks shooting up from the centre of the rosettes of leaves.

The husband staggered slightly as Poppy handed the box to him and his face was soon hidden by the large hairy leaves sprouting from the stalks coming out of the box.

"Uunnghh... I'd better get these.... uuhh... into the car first," came the husband's muffled voice.

Clutching the box to his chest, he walked bowlegged as he staggered down the path to the front gate. The hollyhock stalks were now nearly three feet above his head and swayed in the breeze, making him struggle to keep his balance. The wife hastily paid, then hurried after her husband, who was now trying to manoeuvre the box into the back seat of their car parked in the lane outside.

Poppy followed them and watched as the husband pushed and shoved, his head barely visible amidst the tangle of leaves, stems, and flower stalks. He looked like he was wrestling a plant monster with multiple stalk arms and Poppy had to fight the urge to burst out laughing. She stood watching until the car had disappeared down the end of the lane, the hollyhock stalks jutting out the open windows on either side of the rear seats, already full of fat flower buds ready to burst open.

Wow, Bertie's serum really does work, Poppy thought, stifling a laugh as she had a sudden vision of the couple arriving home and being eaten alive by rampaging hollyhocks.

Then she was seized by an idea. Whirling, she

rushed back to the greenhouse and hurried up to the trays of frost-damaged plug plants and seedlings. She stared at them, then she stared at the tiny glass vial of growth serum in her hand. *What do I have to lose? And if it* does *work... I'll be able to raise my prices*, she thought excitedly. *And with the extra profits, I'll be able to save up enough to buy another batch of plug plants from the wholesalers sooner than I expected...*

Quickly, Poppy found a watering can and filled it with fresh water; then, taking a deep breath, she uncorked the vial. She hesitated. She'd just had a dramatic demonstration of the power of Bertie's serum and she definitely didn't want that kind of crazy, uncontrolled growth! But if she *diluted* the serum, then she should be able to get the growth-boosting effect without overdoing things. The question was: what was the Goldilocks number of drops to add to the water?

Poppy agonised for several minutes, then finally decided on three drops. Carefully, she poured them into the can, then stirred the contents vigorously until it was almost frothing. Heaving the can up, she leaned over the trays of damaged plants and carefully watered them with the solution of diluted serum. Then she stepped back and surveyed the trays, her heart pounding.

For several long minutes, nothing happened, and Poppy was just beginning to wonder if she should make up another can of solution and try once more, when a movement caught her eye. She leaned closer to the tray, then a wide smile spread across her face.

Tiny new buds had swelled and miniature leaflets had begun to unfurl from the growth nodes at the bases of the plants. They were growing! Not crazily fast, but steadily, and in a few days she should have a trestle table bursting with pots of large, vigorous specimens for sale.

Poppy leaned back and sighed, feeling the tension melt from her neck and shoulders. The tiny spark of hope which she had nurtured in her heart now grew into an exuberant flame. *It's going to be okay*, she thought, relief and happiness making her almost giddy. *It's going to be okay!*

CHAPTER TWENTY-NINE

Poppy found that—now that she knew there was a solution to her troubles on the horizon—she was able to cope with awkward situations and disappointed customers at the nursery much better. In fact, as the afternoon wore on, she even found herself enjoying the occasional gossip with the various village residents who popped in. While most people were shocked to learn that the shy, mousy Miss Payne had turned out to be the murderer, several were also quick to insist that they had always suspected her.

"I always thought there was something odd about that woman," said Mrs Peabody with a sniff. "*I* certainly never trusted her."

"Nor me!" "No, me neither!" "Me too!"—came a chorus of voices as several women around Mrs

Peabody nodded vigorously.

One of them leaned forwards and said, making a face: "Did you know that she keeps a *pet slug*?"

"Eeuww!"

"Really? How bizarre!"

"I always wondered why I saw her at the GP's so much," another woman spoke up.

"Me too!" said her friend. "I put it down to coincidence, you know, but thinking about it now, it was obvious that she was stalking poor Dr Seymour."

"Yes, poor Dr Seymour!"

"How dreadful for him!"

"And now with Emma dead, he has no one to look after him..."

All the women in the group sighed wistfully.

"Well, I'm sure he would be grateful for any help that he can receive from the ladies of this village," Mrs Peabody said briskly. "It is our duty to support our village doctor during his time of crisis."

"Chicken soup, that's what he needs," another woman spoke up. "I have a wonderful recipe; works better than medicine." She paused, then added casually, "I might take some over to him tonight. Can't have the doctor going without dinner."

"What he really needs is some home baking," declared another woman. "How lucky that I've just made a batch of my famous jam doughnuts. They won First Prize at the last village fair, you know. I'll put some in a basket for him."

"Well, I've got several bottles of homemade

elderflower cordial. I'm sure he'd like some of that..."

"Nothing like a Scotch egg. Best sort of snack to cheer a man up. I'll take him some..."

"I make a wonderfully nourishing shepherd's pie. I'm sure Dr Seymour would like that. He looks like he needs a good feeding-up ..."

"The poor dear probably needs someone to give him a hand tidying the house. I'm sure I could spare a few hours..."

Poppy stared at the group of women next to her in astonishment. Ralph Seymour's vague, emotional manner had simply irritated her and made her lose respect for him, but obviously for a lot of other females, the handsome GP stirred an ardent protective instinct instead. Half the women in the village seemed to be falling over themselves to mother him!

Just as the group was starting a passionate discussion of the best way to wash Dr Seymour's socks, the man himself suddenly arrived. His appearance through the front gate caused quite a stir and, as the handsome GP walked up to the trestle table where Poppy was standing with the other ladies, several women became quite pink and giggly.

"Hello, Miss Lancaster—I've brought something for you," Dr Seymour said with a smile, lifting up the large wooden structure he was carrying.

"Thank you. Er... what is it?" asked Poppy, eyeing the gift with curiosity.

It looked like a wall-mounted bookshelf or

ornament case, with a slanted roof at the top and multiple levels and compartments within the frame. It reminded Poppy of a doll's house—a very shallow one, with very many rooms. Except that each "room" was filled not with miniature furniture or dolls, but with a little potted plant bearing a rosette of furry green leaves.

"It's an auricula theatre!" said Dr Seymour, his face glowing with pride. "I made it especially for you, so you can display these auriculas that I have selected for you. Hopefully, this way, your customers will have a chance to learn about these marvellous plants, and they might even be encouraged to plant a few of their own. In fact, I've got several pots of young auricula plants which I'll bring over to you when they're ready, so you can sell them here in the nursery."

"Oh! That's really kind of you. But... er..." Poppy threw an embarrassed look over her shoulder at the other women, who were all avidly listening, then stepped aside with the GP so that they were out of earshot. She lowered her voice and said: "I'm not sure if I've got the funds at the moment to pay for more stock—"

"Oh, I wouldn't take any money for them!" Dr Seymour declared, waving a hand. "These are just plantlets that I've propagated by division of my existing stock. I have far too many to know what to do with them all. I shall be delighted to donate them so that others can be introduced to the wonderful world of auriculas and enjoy their beauty."

"Wow... thank you very much," said Poppy, surprised and touched. "That's really generous of you. Thank you!"

She looked over at the auricula theatre, which had been propped up alongside the trestle table. It was now surrounded by the crowd of village ladies, loudly admiring the wooden structure. Several of them threw envious looks at Poppy for being lucky enough to receive a personal gift from the GP.

"Um... where should I put it?" she asked.

"Oh, ideally somewhere where it gets bright light, but no direct sunlight. By that wall would be perfect," said Dr Seymour, indicating the side of the cottage. "That way, your customers will be able to see it as they come up the path. The flower stalks are just coming up... you should get some lovely flowers in a week or two, although several of them probably won't hit their peak until mid-April."

"And how often should I water them?" asked Poppy nervously.

"Just when the compost feels dry. I've got them in gritty compost, with lots of perlite and sharp sand, so it should be very free-draining. But you'll still need to be careful not to over-water. Don't forget, auriculas are alpine plants, so they're adapted to low water needs. They're very prone to root rot, so it's better to keep them on the dry side."

"Okay." Poppy swallowed, thinking that "over-watering" tended to be her biggest shortcoming. "I'll do my best."

Ralph Seymour smiled at her. "Don't worry, you'll be fine. Perhaps you might like to consider joining the Oxfordshire Auricula Club at some point, to get more tips."

"Yes, I'll think about it." Poppy paused, then added awkwardly, "Um... I'm really sorry about Emma. This must have been a devastating week for you."

The GP sighed. "Yes, it all feels slightly surreal, to tell you the truth. Almost like a nightmare that I'm going to wake up from any minute... at least, that's what I keep hoping. I suppose things will sink in more once I've had to attend the official inquest into Emma's death, and then her funeral..." He trailed off, his expression sober, although Poppy was interested to note that Ralph Seymour wasn't showing the same violent burst of emotion in reaction to the death of his wife as he had to that of his practice manager. She wondered just how much love had really been lost between the handsome doctor and his controlling wife.

"I suppose the surgery may have to close for some time now?" she asked.

He brightened and said, glancing over at the group around the auricula theatre, "Well, actually, several ladies in the village have offered to help out at the surgery until I can hire a new practice manager. So I will be able to resume clinics faster than I anticipated. It is very kind of them—I have been quite overwhelmed by the offers and goodwill."

Poppy glanced at the group as well, and wondered with amusement if many of them were not only hoping to help in his search for a new practice manager, but also in the search for a new wife!

CHAPTER THIRTY

As Poppy was tidying up after closing the nursery that evening, she had a surprise visitor in the form of Suzanne Whittaker. The detective inspector was holding a small plastic takeaway container rather gingerly, and looked relieved as she set it down on the trestle table.

"Hello!" said Poppy, smiling warmly. "This is a nice surprise."

Suzanne returned her smile. "I'm afraid this isn't a purely social call."

"Oh, do you need to ask me more questions? Are there more loose ends to tie up on the case?" asked Poppy.

"No, no, that's pretty much all in hand. Payne has made a full confession and I've also spent a very productive afternoon with Tim Albrecht."

"Albrecht?" Poppy's ears perked up. "You know, I'd been convinced that he was the murderer, but then when I realised that it was actually Miss Payne, I thought I must have been totally wrong about him. Don't tell me that he *is* involved after all?"

"Not in the murders, no, but he *was* guilty of stealing money from the Oxfordshire Auricula Club account." Suzanne nodded at Poppy's jubilant exclamation. "Yes, you got that part right. When I confronted him with records of the illegal withdrawals and told him that we'd traced them to a company in Spain, Albrecht caved in and confessed everything."

"So it was a timeshare scam, like I thought?" asked Poppy eagerly.

"Well, not a scam exactly. Albrecht had intended for it to be a legitimate property venture. Unfortunately, I don't think he's much good as a businessman, however good he might be as an accountant. It seems that he ran into trouble pretty quickly and needed money to bail the company out. He tried diverting funds from his own accountancy firm, but it wasn't that easy to do. Even though his father is preparing for retirement, Albrecht Senior still keeps a sharp eye on everything in the family business and he would have noticed the missing money immediately."

"So Albrecht decided to take money from the research grant instead!" said Poppy.

Suzanne inclined her head. "Yes, the OAC club

accounting was a mess, no one seemed to be keeping track of things, and that huge amount of money was just sitting there, unused... it was all just too tempting." She gave a cynical smile. "Of course, Albrecht told me that he never intended to 'steal' the money as such—he was simply 'borrowing' and planning to put it back later, when the timeshare company started becoming profitable."

They heard a sarcastic laugh and a deep male voice say: "Yeah, right. Where have I heard that one before?"

They both turned to see Nick Forrest coming up the garden path to join them. He was dressed to go out and looked very debonair in a classic navy blazer paired with a crisp shirt and jeans, with his dark hair slicked back and still damp from a recent shower.

"You know, if I wrote something like that in one of my books, I would get slammed in reviews for having cardboard characters and 'unrealistic' dialogue—and yet people do ridiculous things like that in real life all the time," said Nick, shaking his head.

"Don't they say 'life is stranger than fiction'?" asked Poppy.

"Actually, the original quote is: 'truth is stranger than fiction'. But the sentiment is the same," Nick said. Then he added with a chuckle: "And it's bang-on in your case! I'm beginning to think that I should just follow you around, Miss Lancaster, the next time I'm stuck on plot ideas for a book."

Poppy blushed slightly. "I don't go around looking

for trouble on purpose" she protested.

"No, you're just like Oren. Trouble seems to follow the two of you naturally," said Nick with amusement.

"Speaking of pets... that reminds me why I came: I have a message for you, Poppy, from Adeline Payne," said Suzanne.

"For me?" said Poppy in surprise.

"Yes, I wouldn't normally accept such requests but, well, I thought I'd make an exception this time on... er... compassionate grounds, as she *did* seem very distressed." Suzanne reached for the plastic takeaway box that she'd placed on the trestle table and cleared her throat. "Payne has asked if you could... er... adopt her slug Solly."

Poppy gaped at her. "*What?*"

"Well, now that she's been arrested and is remanded in custody, she's worried that no one will look after her pet." Suzanne's lips twitched. "She says she remembered how interested you were in Solly when she encountered you at the vet and she was hoping that you might find it in your heart to give Solly a home."

"The woman tries to kill me... and now she wants me to adopt her slug?" spluttered Poppy.

Next to her, Nick guffawed, then hastily turned it into a cough. Poppy shot him a dirty look. Then she stared at the takeaway container that Suzanne was holding out to her. She took it and opened it. On a bed of lettuce leaves lay Solly the slug: limp, brown, and slimy.

Nick peered over her shoulder and said with a wicked grin: "He's quite handsome... for a mollusc."

"Oh, shut up," said Poppy.

Suzanne looked like she was fighting to keep a straight face as well. "You can refuse, of course. All I did was promise Payne that I'd pass on the request." She reached out a hand to take the container back.

Poppy hesitated, moving the container out of Suzanne's reach. "What will you do with Solly?"

Suzanne shrugged. "Chuck him in the bin, I suppose. Or flush him down the toilet."

"No, wait..." Poppy stared down at the slug, which seemed to have come to life slightly. It was now leaving a slime trail as it crawled over a lettuce leaf, the dainty feelers on its head waving around curiously. Poppy knew she should just hand it back to Suzanne and wash her hands of the whole thing. After all, people killed thousands of slugs all over the country every year. And yet...

"All right. I'll keep him," she said.

Suzanne raised her eyebrows. "Are you sure?"

I must be bonkers, thought Poppy as she nodded.

Nick burst out laughing. "You'll be the only gardener in the whole of England with a pet slug!"

Suzanne chuckled, then she glanced at Nick. "Are we off? I thought I was coming in for a drink first."

"Well, I thought we might as well get there early and have the drink at the restaurant bar," said Nick.

Suzanne turned back to Poppy. "Nick's insisted that I leave the station early tonight so he can take me out to dinner. It's my birthday, you see."

"Oh! Happy birthday!" cried Poppy.

"Thanks," said Suzanne, wrinkling her nose. "I have to say, I wouldn't be going if Nick hadn't insisted. Honestly, when you're only three years from the big Four-O, birthdays aren't something you're that keen to celebrate!"

"If I don't drag you out, you'll never take a break," growled Nick. "You've been working flat out for weeks now—you can do with an evening off. You're the worst workaholic I've ever met."

"Says the person who stays up writing all night when he's in the throes of a first draft," retorted Suzanne, giving him a playful dig in the ribs.

"That's different," said Nick, retaliating with a fake tackle of his own which had Suzanne squealing and giggling.

Poppy watched them teasing and laughing together. Nick and Suzanne looked so relaxed and comfortable in each other's company... she often thought it was a mystery why they had broken up. There was an easy intimacy between them which could only come from genuine closeness and affection. Poppy wondered suddenly if they might get back together and was conscious of an uncomfortable prickly sensation.

Surely I'm not feeling jealous? she thought in surprise. Hastily, she pushed the thought away and said, more to distract herself than anything else:

"Um, Nick—have you spoken to Bertie since you

were released from police custody?"

He looked up, surprised. "No, not really. I waved to him when I saw him passing the house yesterday with Einstein for a walk. Why?"

"You really should have called him as soon as you came home. He was worried about you, you know," said Poppy.

"Why should he be worried? He knows I can take care of myself. I've been doing it for years."

"Because he's your father!" Poppy burst out. "It's only natural that he should be concerned, and it would have been kind to keep him updated."

Nick frowned and, for a moment, Poppy thought he was going to bite her head off and tell her to mind her own business. But to her surprise, he gave a great sigh instead and ran a hand over his face.

"You're right," he said. "I should have let Bertie know. I suppose I've got so used to just looking after myself all these years... I'm not used to having to think about someone else."

"Why don't we pop over to Bertie's now, before we leave for the restaurant?" Suzanne suggested. She winked at Poppy. "I've got to give him a progress report on how his tentacle is doing on my windowsill."

"What tentacle?" asked Nick.

Suzanne linked her arm through his. "It's a long story. I'll tell you on the way..."

She threw a parting smile over her shoulder at Poppy, who waved them goodbye as they walked up the path and out the front gate.

CHAPTER THIRTY-ONE

Poppy took herself into the cottage after Nick and Suzanne had left and went around drawing the curtains and turning on the lights. Nell was once again at a bingo night with friends, and—thinking of everyone out enjoying themselves that evening whilst she remained in the cottage alone—Poppy felt a sudden pang of loneliness. Then she gave herself a mental shake and told herself to stop being silly. *I'll have a nice hot bath, then rustle up some dinner and spend a cosy evening in front of the TV*, she decided.

As she was undressing, a glint of gold in the bathroom mirror caught Poppy's eye and she paused to study her reflection. Her mother's locket shifted against her throat and the gold chain caught the light again, glittering in the mirror. Poppy leaned closer to the glass and frowned, noticing for the first time that one side of the heart-shaped locket was covered by a thin brown crust. Unclasping the chain from around her neck, she held the locket up to the light and peered at the dried coating, trying to figure out what it was. Parts of the crust crumbled and fell away as she scraped at it gently with a nail, revealing the engraved surface of the locket underneath.

Is it food? Poppy wondered. She held the locket closer and sniffed it cautiously. It had a sweet, milky smell that was vaguely familiar. *Oh! Farley's Rusk!* she thought suddenly. She smiled as she remembered seeing Baby Oscar gnawing on a Farley's Rusk the last time she'd seen him, and she realised what must have happened. When the baby had played with her locket that day at the GP's, he must have put it into his mouth and bits of soggy biscuit, which had probably been left in his gums, must have transferred onto the locket and got stuck.

Poppy had been so busy since the locket had been returned to her that she hadn't paid close attention to its condition. She had simply clasped it back around her neck and gone about her day, preoccupied with the challenges at the nursery and the mystery of the murders. Now, however, she was determined to get it clean again. She rinsed the locket under the tap and rubbed its surface with a towel, trying to remove the dried biscuit.

Some of it came off easily, but several bits had got embedded in the grooves of the engraved surface and were stubbornly resisting all efforts to dislodge them.

Poppy paused and blew a breath of frustration. Then she had an idea. Quickly, she rummaged in the bathroom cupboard until she found what she was looking for: a safety pin. Using the sharp end of the opened pin, she prodded and scraped the grooves of the engraving and was delighted as crumbs of dried biscuit fell out. She was just jiggling the pin alongside the hinge to dislodge a particularly stubborn piece when she heard a faint *CLICK*. To her surprise, the back of the locket suddenly eased away.

Poppy had always assumed that the locket simply opened the usual way, to show the photo of her mother, but now she realised that a second compartment had been hidden underneath the first. Slowly, she swung this away to reveal another photograph: a handsome young man with soulful dark eyes, a sensitive mouth, and hair exactly the same shade of brown as her own, gazed moodily out of the frame.

Poppy's heart began thumping as she stared down at the tiny, faded photograph. *Could this be my father? Could I have finally found a clue to the greatest mystery of my life, at last?*

A loud knocking at the cottage door yanked her out of her thoughts. Hastily setting the locket down by the side of the sink, she hurried out of the bathroom. She opened the front door to find a familiar large lady in a headscarf, mackintosh, and dark green wellington boots standing on the doorstep.

"Ah! Miss Lancaster! Glad I caught you at home."

"Hello, Mrs Busselton," said Poppy, giving the woman a wary smile. "Won't you come in?"

"No, no, I'm halfway through my evening patrol," said the other woman, waving a hand. "But I wanted to pop by and tell you that the next Bunnington Brigade meeting is this Sunday." She eyeballed Poppy. "You *are* joining us, aren't you? After your own brush with a murderer, you know how important it is that we citizens come together and use our individual abilities to protect the community."

"Er..." Poppy hesitated. The last thing she wanted to do was join Mrs Busselton's own "barmy army", but at the same time, she felt like she owed the woman a debt of gratitude for saving her life. "Well... um... I'll try my best... although you know the nursery is open on Sundays so—"

"No excuses!" Mrs Busselton bellowed. "We need more young members like you to stop the wave of crime sweeping through this village!"

"Aww, surely it's not that bad?" protested Poppy. "Bunnington is hardly Harlem or Johannesburg. And now that these murders have been solved, there aren't any real dangers—"

"Don't you believe it!" cried Mrs Busselton, wagging a finger in Poppy's face. "Just this evening, I learnt of a new and alarming crime: Colonel Bradley has had his new dentures stolen! Can you believe that?"

"Are you sure they were stolen?" asked Poppy. "I

mean, who would want a set of false teeth? Maybe he mislaid them or—"

"Oh no! They were definitely stolen. The poor man removed them to give them a good clean and left them on his bedside table while he went to fetch the brush, but when he returned, they were gone!" Mrs Busselton's chest swelled. "But fear not! The Bunnington Brigade is ready and we will begin the hunt for this wicked criminal. We shall discuss our plans and strategy at the meeting this Sunday. I'll see you there!"

She turned and marched away up the garden path, leaving Poppy to sag against the door frame. Wearily, she closed the door and returned to the bathroom. She stopped short as she walked in. Oren was sitting beside the sink, playfully batting at something on the vanity unit with one paw. Poppy's heart lurched as she saw that it was her locket.

"No! Oren, stop that!" she cried, hurrying to grab the piece of jewellery and untangle the chain from the cat's claws.

"*Nooo-ow!*" said Oren sulkily, surrendering the locket with bad grace. He jumped down and disappeared from the bathroom.

Poppy picked up the locket and wiped it clean with a towel, then carefully opened the hidden compartment again. She was almost afraid that the photo would be gone—that it had been nothing more than a figment of her imagination—but it was there. She stared longingly at the tiny picture and was just wondering how to find the man's identity when she heard Oren's demanding voice again.

"*Nnn-oowrr? Nnn-oowrr?*

Poppy glanced up at the muffled cries and, from the corner of her eye, saw the ginger tom's furry shape slink back into the bathroom.

"What is it now, Oren?" she asked distractedly, her eyes still on the photo. "What do you—" She broke off as something cold and wet suddenly dropped onto her bare feet. She looked down and saw a set of yellowed teeth surrounded by glistening pink gums.

"*AAAAAAAAAHHHH!*" Poppy shrieked, hopping around.

Oren, who had dropped his gift proudly on her foot, hissed and jerked out of the way, just as Poppy inadvertently kicked the teeth and sent them flying. They hit the wall and bounced back into the sink, swirling around a few times before finally coming to a stop next to the drain.

Poppy caught her breath, then she glared at the ginger tom. "Oren! You have to stop doing things like that!"

"*N-ow?*" said Oren cheekily, cocking his head.

Poppy approached the sink cautiously and peered at the set of glistening teeth encased in the bright pink gums. Gingerly, she lifted them out by a thumb and forefinger, and examined them closer. *They're dentures*, she realised with a sigh of relief. Not real teeth.

Then she recalled what Mrs Busselton had said about Colonel Bradley and she groaned out loud. Turning, Poppy put her hands on her hips and looked sternly at the ginger tomcat.

"Where did you get these, Oren?" she asked. "What mischief have you got up to this time?"

Oren twitched his whiskers and gave her an innocent look. *"N-ooow?"*

Poppy heaved a sigh of exasperation. Maybe she had better attend that meeting on Sunday, after all. With Oren obviously deciding that he enjoyed a life of crime, it looked like peace wasn't returning to Bunnington any time soon!

THE END

ABOUT THE AUTHOR

USA Today bestselling author H.Y. Hanna writes fun cozy mysteries filled with clever twists, lots of humor, quirky characters - and cats with big personalities! She is known for bringing wonderful settings to life, whether it's the historic city of Oxford, the beautiful English Cotswolds or the sunny beaches of coastal Florida.

After graduating from Oxford University, Hsin-Yi tried her hand at a variety of jobs, including advertising, modelling, teaching English, dog training and marketing... before returning to her first love: writing. She worked as a freelance writer for several years and has won awards for her novels, poetry, short stories and journalism.

Hsin-Yi was born in Taiwan and has been a globe-trotter all her life—living in a variety of cultures, from Dubai to Auckland, London to New Jersey—but is now happily settled in Perth, Western Australia, with her husband and a rescue kitty named Muesli. You can learn more about her and her books at: **www.hyhanna.com**

Sign up to her newsletter to be notified of new releases, exclusive giveaways and other book news! Go to: **www.hyhanna.com/newsletter**

ACKNOWLEDGMENTS

As always, I am indebted to my beta reading team Kathleen Costa, Connie Leap, Basma Alwesh and Charles Winthrop, for their unwavering enthusiasm and for making so much effort to fit me into their busy lives, even in the middle of a pandemic. Similarly, my editor and proofreader, for always finding time in their schedule for me and adapting to my constant changes. And of course, to my amazing husband who is more wonderful than all the words can ever say.

Made in the USA
Coppell, TX
10 April 2021

53458979R00184